Dear Readers,

Writing "the end" when I finished Knox's story was a little sad. When some of you readers asked me to write about what happened to those seven little girls in the original Paradise story, *Trouble in Paradise*, I had no idea the series would grow like it has. But even as I leave Spanish Fort, I can see the next generation of the Paradise family and wonder if maybe someday they will come knocking on my door, asking me to write their stories.

My name is on the cover of each book in this series, but it takes a village to produce a finished book. Thanks to everyone who lives in that village, with a special thanks to all my fans who asked me to write about the sisters who grew up in the old Paradise. Also to Deb Werksman and Sourcebooks and everyone on the team who worked so hard to polish my stories. To my agency, Folio Management, and my agent, Erin Niumata. To all those folks behind the scenes who made the gorgeous covers. To my readers—bless your hearts for all the support. And to my family, who continues to love me even though I spend hours and hours in the writing cave.

Raising my cup of coffee this morning to a great series and to Aunt Bernie for all her input. She sat on my shoulder the whole time I was writing.

Until next time,

Carolyn Brown

Also by Carolyn Brown

What Happens in Texas
A Heap of Texas Trouble
Christmas at Home
Holidays on the Ranch
The Honeymoon Inn
The Shop on Main Street
The Sisters Café
Secrets in the Sand
Red River Deep
Bride for a Day
A Chance Inheritance
The Wedding Gift
On the Way to Us
Chasing Dreams

Sisters in Paradise

Paradise for Christmas
Sisters in Paradise
Coming Home to Paradise

The Paradise

Meet Me in the Orchard
A Little Christmas Matchmaking

Lucky Cowboys

Lucky in Love
One Lucky Cowboy
Getting Lucky
Talk Cowboy to Me

Honky Tonk

I Love This Bar
Hell, Yeah
My Give a Damn's Busted
Honky Tonk Christmas

Spikes & Spurs

Love Drunk Cowboy
Red's Hot Cowboy
Darn Good Cowboy Christmas
One Hot Cowboy Wedding
Mistletoe Cowboy
Just a Cowboy and His Baby
Cowboy Seeks Bride

Cowboys & Brides

Billion Dollar Cowboy
The Cowboy's Christmas Baby
The Cowboy's Mail Order Bride
How to Marry a Cowboy

Burnt Boot, Texas

Cowboy Boots for Christmas
The Trouble with Texas Cowboys
One Texas Cowboy Too Many
A Cowboy Christmas Miracle

Until It Gets Real

CAROLYN BROWN

Published by Sourcebooks Casablanca, an imprint of Sourcebooks
1935 Brookdale RD, Naperville, IL 60563-2773
(630) 961-3900
sourcebooks.com

Cataloging-in-Publication Data is on file with the Library of Congress.

Printed and bound in the United States of America.
KP 10 9 8 7 6 5 4 3 2 1

This one is for my three grandsons,
Brenton Brown, Kurtis Morgan, and Seth Brown

Chapter 1

"I need a boyfriend," Lottie whispered seductively as she threw a long leg over the bench beside the picnic table and sat down close to Knox. "Are you game?"

What was wrong with this woman? She *had* appeared to be kind of sweet at his brother's wedding when she introduced herself as Charlotte Johnston.

Maybe he heard her wrong.

"Would you repeat that, please?" he asked.

"Do you need to get your hearing tested?" Her voice went from silky smooth to as rough as forty-grit sandpaper.

"I hear just fine—most of the time," he answered and then realized what day it was. "April Fools."

"I'm serious as a…" she started.

He held up a palm and butted in before she could finish. "You are a pretty good actor, but I'm not falling for her joke."

His thoughts went back to Spanish Fort, where Aunt Bernie, the matchmaking queen of north Texas, was already hard at work attempting to set him up with blind dates every weekend. The Universe might have just plopped a good situation down into his lap, but then again, this was most likely the workings of Bernie. She could be very manipulative, and she and Lottie *had* spent time together at his brother Tripp's wedding.

Lottie flipped her straw-colored braids over her shoulders, nudged him, and crossed her heart with her finger. "This is no one's idea but mine, and it's not an April Fool's joke. I promise."

"Yeah, right," Knox said.

"No one put me up to it."

Knox shook his head. "Not happening, and I still don't believe this is anything but another attempt to fool me."

"I just need a boyfriend for six weeks, and then we'll go our separate ways."

"Are you talking about a *fake* boyfriend?" Knox asked.

"Of course. What did you think I meant?"

"You need to be clear when you sit down beside a man and whisper sweet nothings in his ear that sound desperate and more than a little bit scary."

She threw up her palms. "You should have known what I was asking without me having to say it. It's a simple yes or no answer. Bernie told me that you weren't seeing anyone, so I figured you would be a good guy to ask."

So, Bernie was at the core of the whole thing after all.

"Good God!" she hissed in a whisper. "Did you really think I was asking for real?"

"Yep, I did," Knox answered. "Why do you want a fake boyfriend? Why not a real one?"

She dropped her hands back to her lap. "I'm damn sure not interested in all the bells and whistles of falling in love and getting married, even if I did catch the bride's bouquet. I just need a boyfriend, and not a real one."

"Again, why?" He felt a little spark at her touch, but then she was an attractive woman with all those curves and big brown eyes.

"You aren't stupid, are you?" she barked.

"Last time I checked, I could still add two and two without using my fingers to count," he shot back. "And I still smell a really stinky April Fool's joke."

Was Aunt Bernie trying to play matchmaker on the sly?

"I'm the only woman carpenter here," Lottie answered with a long sigh. "Like I said, no one put me up to this. Are you going to answer me or not? And for your information, I haven't even talked to Bernie since the wedding. But she did tell me all about her matchmaking business and website, and said she would fix me up for free. I told her I wasn't interested, and we went on to another subject."

"So, why do you need a boyfriend so badly that you'd ask an almost complete stranger to pretend?" Knox asked.

"I'm here to work, and when the rest of the crew begins to arrive in a few days, all the single guys will begin to hit on me. I'm tired of it, and them. They're all good workers or Uncle Jack wouldn't have hired them, but…" She let the sentence hang without finishing it.

"But what?"

"On the last job, they had a betting pool going as to who would spend the night in my trailer first. I have two rules on the job. I don't date coworkers, and not even Uncle Jack gets to call me Charlie," she said. "Do I need to explain any further?"

"Yep, you do," Knox said. "If I'm going to commit to a long-term fake relationship, I should know your whole dirty past."

"I'm not asking you to marry me," she snapped. "Would you please answer me and stop beating around the bush?"

Knox chuckled. "Are we having our first fight before I even get a good-night kiss?"

"What makes you think…"

Knox leaned over and whispered softly, "All of the guys will need to believe that we are together. They can spot a fake a mile away. Are you ready to do a good job of pretending, or do you want to call it off right now?"

Lottie cupped his face in her hands and brushed a kiss across his lips. "Is that good enough?"

"It's a start," he said with half a shrug, even though he could feel and practically see the sparks shooting all around them. "Now, say the words."

"I do not tell a boyfriend, fake or real, that I love him unless I mean it." Lottie's eyes flashed with aggravation.

He nodded toward the three framers standing down by the lake. "They probably think we are fighting. Does this mean that we'll have to make up before morning?" Knox teased.

"It does not!" she growled.

"Well, I'm disappointed. Seems like setting my trailer to rocking a little bit is what we really need to do if we're making up after this argument."

She cupped his cheeks in her hands and looked deeply into his eyes. "That kiss is us making up, and it was for the guys standing out there. They are all married, but before long, five more guys will be here to put the cabins in the dry. Then roofers and siders will be here right along with them, and then the Wednesday evening after that, the drywall fellows and painters will start coming in to get things ready for the finish carpenters. Not all of them have a partner, and they all give me hell."

"Why do you stay with it?" Knox got lost in her brown eyes.

"I love what I do. Uncle Jack has this business organized so that the six cabins will be up and ready for the people who've already purchased them to move in by our deadline. Then we all go to a project out around El Paso where we will be building minimansions in a gated community. If I have a boyfriend, it makes things easier for me."

"Log cabins to crystal chandeliers, but I probably won't be headed out west for that job. I wouldn't even be here if Walter hadn't fallen and broken his wrist. He should be back for those minimansions."

"Yep," she answered and dropped her hands.

"That means this is going to be a short relationship, right?" he asked.

She nodded.

Knox rubbed his chin. "Do I have to defend your honor? I'd hate to mess up my hands and lose my job. Or worse yet, get my pretty face all torn to shreds."

"I can take care of myself," she answered. "What makes you think you are pretty?"

A wide grin spread across his face. "A woman as gorgeous as you wouldn't ask an ugly man to be her boyfriend."

She air-slapped him on the arm. "Any more questions?"

"Just one. What if I want to have a long-distance fake relationship even when this job is done?" Knox's mind raced ahead past the six weeks. He could keep Aunt Bernie from her matchmaking indefinitely that way.

"Fine by me, and if we decide to go our separate ways, then we'll have a very public breakup," Lottie answered.

"Okay, then." Knox's blue eyes twinkled. "I will be your fake boyfriend. Do I sign a contract?"

"Since you are kin to Bernie, your word is good enough." She stood up with the grace of a ballerina, dropped a kiss on the top of his head, and headed back to her trailer.

"Whew!" Knox uttered under his breath. "What have I done?"

He had told his brother, "I will have to get a fake girl-friend," when Tripp teased him about being next in line for Bernie's matchmaking business. The old gal had already found mates for all seven of the Paradise sisters and both of his brothers, Brodie and Tripp, and she had half the population within a thirty-mile radius dating one another. But Knox was determined that when he got ready to settle down, he would pick his own woman with no help from the meddling queen of Spanish Fort, Texas.

Aunt Bernie wasn't really related to him or his brothers

at all. Explaining the social dynamics of everyone at the Paradise back in Spanish Fort would take a book the size of one of the romance novels that his stepmother, Mary Jane, was famous for writing. There were seven sisters, a half brother, an adopted sister, and then Tripp and Knox, who were shirt-tail kin. Aunt Bernie was related by blood to the sisters, but from the beginning, she had declared that the adopted sister, Ivy, and three Callahan brothers were also kinfolks. It didn't take Brodie, Tripp, or Knox long to figure out that what she said was the law.

One of the other guys that arrived on-site at the same time as Knox eased down onto the bench across the table. "Hey, I'm Thomas Lopez. Looks like you and Lottie were having a disagreement. Did y'all get it figured out?"

"I hope so, but I hear that you are all three married, so you know how that goes," Knox said with a chuckle. "Lottie said that she's worked with y'all before. Just how good is she?"

"Jack's crews all work together like a well-oiled machine," Thomas said, "And believe me, Lottie is one of the best framers you will ever work with. I'd have to say the only one who is better is Walter, and that's because he's been doing this so long that he can step in and help with anything from foundation to finish carpentry. We're sure going to miss him this time around, but he's supposed to be back with us when we go to El Paso. Next week, we'll have the first cabin ready for the next group coming in from a site down south, and most of them aren't married, so the whole feel of the place changes. You ever worked with a woman before?"

"No, and especially not a girlfriend, but I have worked with Jack. We put up some minimansions down in central Texas around Austin several years ago. I trust his judgment." Knox couldn't remember the last time he had introduced a woman as his girlfriend and was surprised at how easy the word fell out of his mouth.

"We've worked with her, but not you, so try to keep up. Like Jack said at the pizza party tonight, anyone who falls behind on the schedule don't last long," Thomas said.

"I'll do my best. Do you live around these parts?" Knox asked.

Thomas ran his fingers through his curly black beard. "No, just through the workweek. My trailer is at the end of the line out there. My brother will be arriving next Wednesday with the crew that puts the houses in the dry," Thomas answered. "We go home to Randlett, Oklahoma, on weekends. That's about an hour drive. We can leave on Friday after work, and if we want to get up early, we can stay over until Monday. My wife likes me to do that so I can spend more time with her and the kids. But when we go out to El Paso, school will be out for the summer, so we'll take our RV and spend the time out there as a family."

Knox nodded toward the other two framers who were standing at the edge of the lake. "What's going on in the bullpen over here?"

"They're talking about you and trying to figure out what y'all were arguing about." Thomas whistled and waved the other men toward the pavilion. "Hey, you two, come on over here and get it out in the open."

Gabe brought a six-pack of beer over and set it in the middle of the table. "All of us, plus Lottie, have worked together on other projects. You are the newcomer, and we're wondering if Jack hired you because you are dating his niece."

"I can promise you that he did not!" Knox answered. That put a whole new spotlight on the matter.

"So, how long have you been in this kind of business?" An air force tat on Gabe's upper arm peeked out from under the stretched fabric of his T-shirt.

"For more than a decade. Pull up a piece of concrete and sit down," Knox said.

Gabe and Eddie sat down on the other side of the table, one on either side of Thomas.

"I just want you to know that I'm glad Lottie is your girlfriend," Gabe said. "My wife is the jealous type, and even though Lottie is just a coworker, Hayley will rest easier knowing that Lottie has a man in her life."

Eddie nodded. "So will Jeannie."

Thomas raised his hand. "And Angie makes three."

"So, you are all married and live up in Oklahoma, right?" Knox asked.

"Yep," Thomas answered. "But the drywall guys, the painters…"

"The finish carpenters and those who'll put up the log-cabin-type siding don't all have wives, and they can be pretty wild after we finish each day," Gabe finished for him. "Don't get me wrong. They're really good at what they do, but they like to party, and they will all try to steal Lottie right out from under your nose."

"And Micah will lead the pack," Eddie added.

"Then I reckon I'd better hang on to her real tight," Knox said.

"Where are you from?" Gabe asked.

"Spanish Fort. A little more than two hours from here," Knox answered.

"That's just over the Red River from Ratliff City, right?" Thomas asked.

"A little more than an hour south of that place," Knox answered.

"I remember seeing a sign for Spanish Fort when we started home from a project east of Nocona," Gabe said.

"You must've crossed the Red River on the Taovayas Bridge. Spanish Fort is a little west of there, but still right on the river. My sister and her husband own a little convenience store slash fishing shop there. We all tell her it's a beer, bait, and bologna place."

Eddie pulled a can of beer free from the plastic ring and handed it to Knox. "I like those kinds of stores. Yep, we crossed the river on that bridge. Not much on either side of it, and a strange name for a bridge. Is Spanish Fort really named after an old fort?"

"Nope, and it almost became a ghost town. But, it's growing, and now has about two hundred people living there."

"I guess if things get serious between you and Lottie, you'll be an FJ couple," Eddie said.

Knox took a long drink, wiped his mouth with the sleeve of his knit shirt, and asked, "What is that?"

"Our wives call us 'framing junkies.' We just shortened it to FJ's," Thomas answered with a chuckle. "We've been working for Jack putting up these kinds of gated communities for about five years. Lottie's been part of the crew even longer than we have. He hired her during the summers between her high school and college years. Looked like y'all were having a disagreement. Did you work things out?"

"We did," Knox said. "Sometimes, new relationships are tough."

"And older ones are too." Gabe chuckled.

"Hey, have you ever been up to Ratliff City?" Eddie asked.

"No, but I know where it is," Knox answered. "And I've heard that it's just a wide spot in the road, a lot like Spanish Fort."

"Yep," Gabe answered. "We went through that place on the way home a few times."

"And stopped at a little bar for a beer," Eddie added. "We loved that bar, but it burned down, or maybe it was a tornado that got it, but no matter what, it's gone. I wonder what ever happened to Bernie. She was this spicy old gal who owned and ran the place. Had a yippy little Chihuahua that hated Micah. The rest of us could pet him, but not my brother."

"She retired from bartending and moved to Spanish Fort. She's my step-aunt," Knox replied.

Eddie slapped his leg and laughed. "It really is a small world. Spicy as she is, I bet she keeps you on your toes. Does she still have that dog?"

Knox grinned. "She does, and he's still just as yappy as ever."

"Lucky you," Gabe said. "She would be a hoot at parties. What's she doing now?"

"Matchmaking," Knox answered.

"I bet she's good at it." Thomas chuckled.

Knox finished off his beer. "Yes, she is."

"Did she fix you up with Lottie?" Eddie asked.

"No, but she'll probably take credit for it," Knox answered.

═══════════

Lottie paced the floor of her trailer—from the living room to the far end, where her bed was located—back and forth several times, and talked to her black-and-white cat, Prissy.

"What have I done, Prissy? It seemed like a good idea at the time, but now I'm wondering if I opened a can of worms or, worse yet, of spiders." She shivered at the visual that popped into her head of a long-legged bug with big eyes that seemed to stare at her.

The cat hopped onto the bed and curled up on one of the pillows.

"Well?" Lottie asked.

Prissy meowed once and closed her eyes.

"You are no help at all."

The cat opened one eye and meowed again.

"I wish Knox wasn't so sexy, but then beggars can't be choosers, can they? If this doesn't work, I'm seriously considering trying my hand at banking or the oil business. Or maybe I'll get a job digging ditches."

Prissy tucked her paw over her nose.

"Don't ignore me, or you'll have to eat that cheap cat food that you don't like." Lottie groaned and went back to the other end of the small trailer. She plopped down on the sofa and let her thoughts wander back to when she finished college. She'd had a degree in business and three job opportunities waiting for her. Her oldest brother, Steven, wanted her to move to Austin and work at his bank. Her youngest one, Ryan, begged her to come to Houston and work as his assistant at an oil company. The middle one, Paul, offered her a very good job at his bank in El Paso. But the idea of working in an office, even if it was a corner one with a view, practically gave her hives.

She couldn't wait to strap her well-worn tool belt around her hips and get started on framing houses for her uncle. After years of trying to carve out a place in a man's world, she couldn't throw in the towel now. Or could she?

"I can't," she muttered as she picked up her cell phone, scrolled down to her mother's name, and tapped the screen.

"Hello, are you settled in?" Darlene asked.

"I took your advice," Lottie blurted out.

"Praise the Lord!" her mother shouted. "Which of your brothers are you going to work for? Of course, I'd rather it was Ryan since he lives closest to us, but I won't fuss if it's Paul or Steven."

"None of the above," Lottie said.

"Then what?" Darlene sighed.

"Remember when I was griping about all the guys hitting on me?"

"Yes, I do, and I told you if you had a boyfriend, that wouldn't happen," Darlene answered.

"Do you remember Bernie from the Chicken Coop bar over in Ratliff City, Oklahoma, that burned down?" she asked. "It wasn't far from Duncan, where y'all lived while I was in college. I drank my first legal shot there when I turned twenty-one."

The mention of Duncan and the Chicken Coop brought memories of her school years—elementary, high school, and college—to Lottie's mind. The bullying in elementary school because she was taller than everyone else. The ugly remarks in high school and college when no one wanted someone like her in their little clique—boring, they called her.

"Lottie! Are you there?" Darlene yelled into the phone.

"I'm here. Sorry, I was woolgathering."

"I was saying that my mind is fine," Darlene snapped. "Of course, I remember Bernie and the Chicken Coop and you drinking there long before you were legal. I've kept in touch with Bernie through the years, but for the life of me, I can't figure out what one has to do with the other."

"On my way here, the route took me to within a few miles of where Bernie lives now. A little place near the Red River called Spanish Fort. I called her to say hello and invite her to have lunch with me. She insisted that I not only come to see her, but that I spend a night so we could catch up."

"You don't have to start with 'and God created dirt' to tell me what's going on," Darlene said.

"I didn't… I don't…" Lottie stammered.

"Yes, you do, but go on," Darlene argued.

Lottie sucked in a lungful of air and let it out so fast she snorted. "Okay, then, on the sixth day God made dirt and…"

Darlene butted in before she could say another word. "You should have listened better in Sunday school, girl. It was the second day that He separated the water from land, so officially, that was when He made dirt."

"Do you want to hear this or not?" Lottie snapped.

"Don't you talk to your mother in that tone. You might be a grown woman, but I can still make you stand in the corner," Darlene told her.

"Yes, ma'am," Lottie said in a softer tone. "To get back to what I was saying, Bernie's place is only about fifteen miles out of the way."

"And you found a boyfriend at Bernie's? Did she rebuild her bar, and what have I told you about men you meet in bars?" Darlene asked.

"The bar burned, and she moved to Texas to be near her kinfolks. While I was visiting Bernie, she took me to a wedding, and I met this guy. She is kind of an aunt to the groom, and she introduced me to his twin brother, Knox. Imagine my surprise when I learned that he is working with me on this project. So, anyway, I just asked him to be my fake boyfriend a few minutes ago, and he agreed. So, I took your advice and am now in a relationship that's not real, but no one knows but me, Knox, and now you."

"Charlotte Diane, you could go to hell for a stunt like that. That is right next door to a lie, and you know how God feels about liars." Darlene gasped.

"Mama, it's not a lie," Lottie protested.

"I'm not going to tell your dad about this new thing you've done. He would put you in a convent. You don't know a thing about this man. He could be a good-for-nothing bum."

Lottie inhaled deeply and butted in before her mother could catch a breath and go on another rant. "Bernie says all three of the Callahans are good people. His brothers, Tripp and Brodie, are married and living in Spanish Fort."

"I don't need to know their histories since the day they were born," Darlene said. "Just promise me you'll be careful."

"I will…" Lottie said.

"Whoa! Wait a minute!" Darlene said. "Callahan rings a bell. Your brother, Ryan, was all up in the air over near Austin a year or so ago about his company merging with another one called Callahan Oil Company—or maybe they were outright buying it. When it comes to business stuff, I listen with one ear. It can't be *those* Callahan brothers that were selling out, could it? Is this Knox fellow one of those guys? No, that's not possible. One of those rich guys wouldn't be framing houses."

"I have no idea," Lottie said, "but I have to go. Someone is knocking on my door. Uncle Jack may be bringing in more blueprints for me to go over before we show up for work tomorrow. See y'all soon."

"Are you coming home for Easter? We're having a pot-luck at the church, and the new preacher is single. I've been telling him all about you." Darlene kept talking.

Lottie shivered as she took a step toward the door. She hadn't planned on making the long drive from one end of Texas to the other, but if she had, she would've changed her mind. She definitely did not want her mother's Sunday school class to try to play matchmaker between her and the new preacher.

"Mama, I have to go. Love you," she said.

"Brother Wyatt might not be as tall as you, but he's a sweet man," Darlene said.

"I'm not coming home for the holiday. I really have to go." She ended the call before her mother could get started again. She rolled her eyes toward the ceiling as she slung the door open.

"Sweet Jesus!" she gasped.

"I'm Knox Callahan, not Jesus, by any stretch of the word, but I can be sweet every now and then unless my fake girlfriend argues with me," he said with a wide grin.

A soft breeze blew his blond hair to one side. His beard had been trimmed, and he smelled like expensive cologne—something woodsy with a hint of leather. "Are you going to invite me in, or are we fighting tonight? I'm new at this game, but I figured if we were really in a relationship, we wouldn't be holed up in our separate trailers every night. I brought leftover pizza from the party this evening and…" He handed the box to her and pulled two root beers from the pockets of his cargo pants. "And these. It always tastes better out of a bottle than a can."

"Come on in," she said. "I suppose we do need to figure out our story."

"Yep," he said. "That's why I'm here, and why I got all cleaned up. Can't have the guys think I'm not serious about dating the boss's niece."

She motioned across the space to the booth-type table. "Have a seat."

He slid into the back and set the bottles on the table. Like the one in his trailer, the table could be lowered and cushions arranged to make a second bed. It would be nearly as hard as sleeping on the floor for softness, but it was an option.

She opened the box, put it in the middle of the table, and sat down across from him. She twisted the cap off the bottle and took a sip. "This has ice crystals in it."

He opened the box and snagged one of the two pieces of black olive and mushroom. "I just took it out of the freezer in my fridge. I had a beer with the guys, but one or a shot is usually my limit."

She picked up the remaining slice with black olives and mushrooms buried down in the cheese. "Uncle Jack knows this is my favorite, so he always gets at least one when we have our meet and greet. Now, to get on to our story. Let's keep it as simple as possible. We met at a wedding, which we did."

"It would be smart to keep it as close to the truth as possible," Knox agreed with a nod. "It wasn't love at first sight, but there was an attraction, especially when they took a picture of us after you caught the bouquet, and the garter flew into my hands. We were surprised to find that we would be working on the same project for Jack, right?"

She got a jittery feeling every time she thought about the effect he'd had on her when he draped an arm around her shoulders for the photograph. Did Bernie have some kind of magical power that threw attraction dust over a couple?

"And we decided to see if the chemistry was true or just a case of wedding fever," she said after a moment. "This is pretty new, so we're still finding our way, but we could be headed down the serious trail."

"Why?"

"Because if it was a casual fling, then the guys who are showing up next week wouldn't blink twice about being jackasses," she said. "So, does that about do it...*darlin'*?"

"Yes, *sweetheart*, it does." He grinned. "Now we just have to spend a while in your trailer to seal the deal."

A big, fluffy calico cat came out from under the bed at the far end of the trailer and jumped up in his lap. Knox finished off his slice of pizza except for one bite and offered it to him. The cat gobbled it down.

"Hey, feller, you don't have to inhale it." Knox chuckled. "There's four more leftover pieces in the box."

"She is not a 'feller,' and her name is Prissy," Lottie said. "She loves pizza, but one bite is all she gets. Human food isn't good for her."

"Rule number one: Don't feed the cat." He nodded toward the television mounted on the wall. "What kind of reception do you get? If we have to spend time together, we might as well watch something, right?"

"Not very good if you are wanting a ball game or to watch regular TV, but I travel with entertainment." She stood up and dragged a cardboard box of movies out from behind a closet door. "DVD player is hooked up and ready."

"When we run out of things to watch here, I've got a box about twice that size over in my trailer we can work our way through. I also have a few books. What do you like to read?"

"Anything that has women empowering other women," she said, "and romance books."

"I can't help you out there, but speaking of romance, have you told Jack that we are a couple?" Knox asked.

"I haven't, but I will," she answered and dreaded having to lie to her favorite uncle.

"Should we do it together to make it real?" he asked.

"That would be great. Maybe we could go to the rec center a little early for breakfast tomorrow morning and tell him then, before the others arrive," she suggested.

"Okay. Do we tell him that we're a fake couple?"

"Oh, no! Me, you, and my mama are the only ones who

need to know the truth. We want to keep this as close to the vest as possible."

"What if there's a rule against dating the niece of the boss?"

She shrugged. "If there is, I'll kiss you goodbye."

"You'll quit this job over a rule like that?" Knox teased.

"No, you will be the one leaving, but we can still have that long-distance thing if you want," she answered.

"You are a hard woman, Charlotte."

"Yes, I am, and don't forget it."

Knox reached for a second slice of pizza. "I need to know a little more about my girlfriend. At this point, I know your name, and how we met, which was only a few days ago. But if we want people to think we've been dating for a while, you should have let me in on a few of your secrets. How old are you?"

"Didn't your mama teach you not to ask a woman about her age or weight?"

"She did, but I don't date underage women," Knox answered.

"Thank you for even thinking that I might be underage," she said.

"I'm looking at thirty in the rearview mirror," Knox offered.

"Twenty-eight," she said. "My hair is naturally this color. I don't have the time or patience to keep it dyed. I don't wear contacts or glasses. I'm five feet, nine inches tall, but don't ask about my weight. Only God and me and the nurse at the doctor's office know that, and she will never say the number out loud for fear that she will disappear and never be found."

"Six feet, one ninety-five. I don't dye my hair, either, and my eyes are really blue. Have you ever been married?" Knox asked.

"No, not even close. You?"

Knox shook his head. "No, ma'am, and I'm not interested in doing so. Do you have children?"

"Nope."

"Me neither," Knox said. "You pretty much know about my family. You met them at my twin brother's wedding."

"Tripp is your twin?" Lottie gasped.

"Yep, but not identical," he answered. "My family is complicated. Brodie, my older brother, and I have the same mother. But his father is Joe Clay Carter, but they were never married. Joe Clay didn't even know that Brodie existed until a little over a year ago. Brodie owns an organic farm, and Tripp has a leather shop, both in Spanish Fort. They are both married, and Tripp has an adopted son, Nicky."

"Three brothers, Steven, Paul, and Ryan. They were sixteen, fourteen, and twelve when I was born," she said. "I reckon that's enough for the first few dates, don't you?"

Knox reached for another slice of pizza. "Just a couple more. Why are you a framer?"

"I love my job. Fresh air and the smell of sawdust are like perfume to me. I would hate to sit behind a desk all day," she answered. As bad as she didn't like being inside and wearing anything other than work boots, she might consider a change if she wasn't happy after the El Paso gig.

"Same here. Brodie enlisted in the military. Tripp worked as a CEO. My parents wanted me to go to college, but I'd been working in construction in the summers. I fell in love with it," he answered. "Just one more question. What's your favorite food?"

She pointed at the pizza box. "Black olives and mushrooms are at the top of the list, but I'll eat about any kind. I also like Italian food of any shape, with lasagna heading that list. What's yours?"

"My brother's step-mama, Mary Jane—you met her at the wedding—makes a mean pot of chili, but I also like fried chicken and all the trimmings that we get pretty often on Sunday after church. Do you cook?"

"Yes, sir. I make a mean sandwich and am a pro at heating up canned soup."

"What kind of sandwich?" Knox flashed a brilliant grin.

"You name it, I can build it, and I don't even need a how-to book. What about you?"

"My mother insisted all three of us guys learn to cook," he answered. "I can teach you if we get serious."

"Ain't damn likely," she said. "Enough of the learning about each other. Let's watch a movie, and then you can go back to your own trailer."

Chapter 2

ON THURSDAY MORNING, THE first rays of sun created an orange reflection in the lake's still waters and turned the black blobs around the edges into willow trees. But Lottie couldn't appreciate the beauty, not when butterflies the size of buzzards fluttered in her stomach as she walked beside Knox on the way to the rec hall for breakfast. Jack always had pizza delivered on the night they arrived, and pastry, juice, and coffee the next morning. After that, everyone was on their own unless someone cooked up enough to feed the whole crew as a treat.

To get her mind off talking to her uncle, she let her thoughts race ahead for six weeks. Either she would be breaking up with Knox at that time, or Jack would talk him into traveling with them to El Paso. If they split up, then she would be too distraught for another boyfriend for several months. On the other hand, if they decided to have a long-distance pretend relationship, that might help for a few more months. As long as Jack was good with the situation, she didn't really care which way it went.

Knox pushed open the door into the rec room and held it for her.

"You are a good imitation boyfriend," she whispered.

"I do my best," he told her.

Jack waved from the back of the room. "The early bird gets the choice of the pastries. There's half a dozen maple doughnuts, and I hid one in the kitchen just in case you were late."

"We need to talk to you," Lottie blurted out.

Jack eyed them both carefully, laid down the chocolate doughnut in his hand, and took a couple of steps forward. "That sounds ominous. Do we have another harassment issue?"

"No," Lottie said, "nothing like that, and I'm hoping to avoid any future problems. But…"

Knox took a blueberry-filled doughnut from the box. "Lottie and I are dating. If there's a company rule against that kind of thing, I'll go on back home."

"Well, hot damn!" Jack raced across the room and hugged Lottie. "This is the best news I've had in forever." When he released her, he stuck out a hand toward Knox. "I thought Gabe was yanking me around last night when he told me that y'all were a couple. Figured it was an April Fool's joke."

"You're not mad?" Lottie asked. "We've kept things under wraps for a little while, but now that we're working together, we wanted to get it out in the open."

"Hell, no!" Jack said. "This solves all kinds of problems. The single guys might flirt a little, but they'll back off if they know you are dating Knox. You might get some flak about being a gold digger but dust any remarks about that off your shoulder and do your work."

"Gold digger?" Lottie asked.

"I'll leave that explanation to Knox." Jack chuckled. "I see the others coming this way, so you better hurry up and grab whatever you want from the pastries. It amazes me how much Eddie can eat and still look like a beanpole."

Gabe waved as he came inside. "Good mornin'. Y'all ready to go to work?"

Lottie removed two maple doughnuts from the box and put them on a paper plate. "Y'all think you can keep up with me?"

"Girl, you want to back up that brag?" Steven asked.

She poured two cups of coffee and handed one to Knox. "It's not a brag. It's a fact. We *will* have the first house framed and be ready to start on number two when the next crew arrives."

"Without Walter?" Gabe asked.

"Hey, now, I'm not chopped liver. I can measure sixteen inches for the studs without even taking off my shoes," Knox protested. "You'd better scarf down a dozen doughnuts each if you plan to keep up with me and Lottie. We'll have all the sill plates down before y'all get the first wall ready to put up."

"So, y'all are working as a team?" Eddie asked, already on his second bear-claw pastry.

"We *are* a team!" Lottie declared, but she wished the other three would have stayed away long enough for her to ask Knox what Jack meant when he said *a gold digger*. Could her mother be right about the Callahan brothers having a lot of money?

"I have a question," Knox said. "Why are we starting this in the middle of the week rather than Monday? Especially since this coming weekend is Easter."

Jack laid the doughnut he had been eating on a disposable plate and set it to the side. "I was going to wait to make this announcement until the end of the project, but since you asked…" He paused and sat down. "Any of y'all want to guess what the finishing touch will be?"

"You mean when you hang the sign on the front gate just before we leave for El Paso in May?" Lottie asked. "My guess is 'Lakeside Estates.'"

"That's too common," Gabe argued. "It will be something like 'Sunny Side Estates.'"

"You are both wrong. This is my personal project, and the name is 'Swan Song Estates.' My wife, Mandy, and I plan to retire when we are all done here. The others have been bought by some of our family who're ready to throw in towels for the nine-to-five jobs too."

Thomas refilled his coffee cup and picked up another doughnut. "Why did you name it that?"

"Have you ever heard the story of the swan song?" Jack asked. "It comes from the ancient Greek mythology. Swans aren't musical, but they sing a beautiful song just before their death. So, this is my personal retirement swan song, as well as Mandy's and her three sisters', and my brother and sister's. We all threw names around, and this one came out as the winner. And yes, Lottie, your mom and dad are moving up here with us."

"You've got to be kidding me!" Lottie gasped. "They are moving again!"

"This time, Darlene says it's for good. She's already packing," Jack said. "That means you are building your mama's new house, and after this year, we will have family holidays right here in this rec room, starting with Independence Day."

"We haven't had family gatherings in years," she said.

"None of us are getting any younger," Jack reminded her.

"I get the feeling you don't really like your family," Knox whispered.

"Love every one of 'em," she answered. "But my mama meddles worse than Bernie."

"Not possible," Knox said.

Jack cleared his throat and stared at Knox and Lottie. "If our two new lovebirds will listen up, I'll go on."

"Sorry," Knox said with a nod. "We're all ears."

"Every one of y'all will still have a job," Jack went on to say. "Walter is taking over as boss in the business. He's fair, and you know him, so the transition will be a smooth one. As far as starting in the middle of the week… You've got six weeks until the El Paso job is ready for you to begin. I slipped my own project in between that one and what y'all just finished. I wanted to give you more time to rest up and see your families, but it wasn't possible."

"I can't believe you are retiring." Eddie sighed. "Walter is great, but things won't be the same without you."

"I'm seventy years old, and Mandy gave me an ultimatum. Retire or she would throw my things out on the front lawn," Jack said with a grin. "She didn't have to push me too hard, though. I'm ready to spend more time with her and my family."

"Then we'll make this the best project ever," Lottie said with a hitch in her voice as she crossed the room and hugged Jack. "I understand, but I don't like it."

Knox followed her and patted Jack on the back. "Congratulations. At the end of this whole thing, the celebration dinner is on me."

"Thank you," Jack said. "That's very generous, but do you realize how many people might be here?"

"I reckon around somewhere between fifty and seventy-five, right?" Knox answered. "I can handle it, unless you expect surf and turf."

Lottie looped her arm into his. "Since you can cook, I thought maybe we'd have smoked brisket and all the trimmings."

He kissed her on the cheek. "Your wish is my command."

"Bullshit!" Thomas said. "By then, y'all will be broken up. No couple can work together all day and expect a relationship to last. I'll be happy with bologna sandwiches and barbecue potato chips. But like Eddie said, we're damn sure going to miss you, Jack. Walter will be a good boss, but he ain't you."

"Thanks for that," Jack said with a nod.

"Whether Lottie and I are together or not, I'll take care

of the retirement dinner." Knox took Lottie's hand in his and headed for the door.

Eddie grabbed another doughnut and followed behind them. "If you think y'all are getting a jump start on us, you are wrong."

———

At the end of the day, Knox stepped into the shower at the rec hall and let the hot water pound against his sore back muscles. "That bet broke me from sucking eggs, even if we did win bragging rights," he muttered when he finally turned off the water and stepped out. The doorknob turned, and he quickly wrapped a towel around his waist.

"What… I didn't…" Lottie stammered and dropped her tote bag beside his army-green duffel.

"This is a community bathroom, isn't it?" he asked.

"Yes, but…" She glared at him. "Learn to lock the door!"

"Why, darlin'," he teased. "We *are* dating, and that means we can take a shower together, doesn't it?"

She picked up her bag. "I'll leave and come back."

"And let everyone who's out there waiting on us think that we are pulling a fast one on them?" Knox asked. "Turn around and face the wall while I get dressed. Then I'll do the same until you finish. We'll go out together, and the guys will *think* that we still had the energy for some hot shower sex."

"*You* turn around until I get in the shower, and then you can get dressed."

Knox whipped around and waited until he heard the shower curtain closing. He picked up his grooming kit, set it on the narrow edge beside the sink, and shaved while he waited. By the time she finished her shower, he was dressed and had his back to her again.

"You are a gentleman," she muttered.

"But not an officer," he said.

"What does that mean?"

"Have you never seen *An Officer and a Gentleman?*" he asked.

"Nope," she answered. "I'm dressed, so you can stop looking at the wall."

"I've got it in my box of movies. We should watch it sometime." His voice sounded a little hollow to him when he turned around. Her damp hair hung down her back, and what little makeup she wore had washed away. She looked like she belonged on a beach scene in a modeling session in her denim shorts and oversized chambray shirt.

For a split second, he wished that their relationship wasn't fake.

Chapter 3

EDDIE RUBBED HIS EYES in a dramatic gesture when Lottie and Knox walked out of the rec room bathroom together. "I don't believe it, not even after I've seen it for myself."

Lottie set her bag of dirty clothes and the one with her toiletries on a chair and took two bottles of sweet tea from the refrigerator. "Believe what? That Knox and I shower or that we're about to do our laundry?"

"That y'all are really together," he answered. "If you are taking showers together, then I guess it's for real."

"You didn't believe us? Have I ever lied to you?" Lottie asked in a hurt tone.

Knox had to swallow fast to keep from spewing tea all over his clean shirt. The jeans, shirt, and underwear he had worn all day were folded neatly on top of his duffel bag. He shrugged when he realized that Eddie was staring at him. "Dating has its benefits. We don't waste water, and we can share a washing machine."

"Don't forget your towels," Eddie said. "You know the rules. Jack provides them, but we have to keep them clean and folded."

"I'll get them." Knox slid a sly wink toward Lottie on

his way to the bathroom. "In all our excitement, we forgot about them."

"I bet you did." Eddie chuckled, picked up his olive-green tote bag, and headed toward the bathroom.

Knox hurried in ahead of him, gathered up the wet towels and washcloths, and stood to the side to let Eddie enter the bathroom. "We left a little hot water for y'all."

Eddie wiggled his thick eyebrows. "From the looks of that foggy mirror, that's not all the heat you left behind."

"A gentleman does not kiss and tell." Knox grinned.

"But a nosy coworker can see it in the glow on y'all's faces." Eddie grinned and closed the door.

"Did you bring laundry soap?" Lottie asked on her way down the short hallway.

"No," Knox answered. "I didn't even know we had a laundry on-site. I'd planned to take all my stuff home on the weekends and do it at the Paradise or at my brother's house."

"I've got enough for tonight, but you better pick up some on your way back down here this weekend. We'll take turns buying it."

"Yes, ma'am. Do you have a particular brand that you like?"

She shook her head. "Anything that doesn't have fabric softener in it. That stuff makes me break out in hives."

Knox nodded and piled the towels into one of the two stacked washers and dryers that sat side by side. "Not a bad setup, but aren't the new cabins plumbed for washing machines?"

"Yes, but in most of Jack's estates, he has a setup like this installed. If there's a party or some kind of event, they can do the laundry here instead of taking it back to one of the houses," she answered. "Putting our things in together seems pretty personal for a fake relationship."

"Got to keep up appearances," Knox said.

"Who knew that"—she lowered her voice—"this could be so much trouble?"

Knox kissed her on the forehead and whispered softly, "Be careful what you say. The walls could have ears."

She nodded and sighed. "You are right. We've got thirty minutes. Want to go whip up some supper for me, or wait around long enough to put our things in the dryer?"

"It's your night to cook," he teased.

"How do you figure that?"

"I brought leftover pizza last night," he said with a wide smile.

"Then it's either bologna or grilled cheese sandwiches and a can of vegetable soup," she said.

He took her hand in his and led her out of the laundry. "You can have that if you want, but I'm having shrimp scampi over linguine noodles and steamed vegetables. I have a small turtle cheesecake thawing for dessert. I can set a place for you if you want to stay here and finish up the laundry."

"Is it one of those frozen things that you heat up in the oven or made from scratch?" she asked.

"My mama would come down from heaven and beat me with a wooden spoon if I ever served my girlfriend a premade meal," he answered. "She didn't allow those things in our house."

Lottie pulled out a chair, sat down at one of the tables, and removed a book from her toiletries bag. "I'll be at your trailer in an hour, then."

He started toward the door. "White wine, beer, or…"

"Sweet tea for me," she answered.

Knox opened the door just as Eddie came out of the bathroom, and Thomas and Gabe entered the rec hall. He whipped around and went back to kiss Lottie on the cheek.

"What was that for?" she whispered.

"Credibility," he replied. "Hey, y'all. Looks like perfect timing."

"For what?" Gabe asked as he headed across the room.

"Eddie has the bathroom all warmed up for you," Lottie answered.

"Not as hot as Lottie and Knox left it for me," Eddie told them.

Knox slipped out the door and whistled all the way to his trailer. This fake stuff wasn't so bad. He got most of the benefits without having to worry about the girlfriend getting stars in her eyes when she picked up one of those magazines with pictures of rings, cakes, and big white dresses.

He started the playlist on his phone and wiggled his shoulders to Caylee Hammack singing "Family Tree." Every lyric in the song made him think of the family dynamics of the folks that had lived or even were living at the Paradise. Mary Jane had no idea what she had started when she moved into the old brothel in a near-ghost town more than twenty years ago. She raised seven daughters there and watched all of them come back home after moving away. The words to the song talked about the roots running deep, and nothing could shake the family tree.

"Absolutely!" he agreed when the song ended. "You got that right, Miz Caylee, and I feel sorry for anyone who doesn't have the love that we are all lucky enough to share at the Paradise—even with our nosy Aunt Bernie."

***

Lottie was deep into a sexy scene in her romance book when Thomas touched her on the shoulder and startled her so badly that she dropped the book on the floor. "Damn it! Why'd you do that?"

"The washer just buzzed. You need to go transfer your stuff to the dryer so you don't hold us up," he replied.

She picked up the book, shoved it back into her bag, and stood up. "You are forgiven."

"I didn't have anything to apologize for, so I don't need forgiveness," Thomas told her.

"Okay, then, but don't sneak up on me like that when I have a book in my hands."

Thomas sat down beside her. "So, according to what Eddie told me, you really *are* seeing Knox."

"Is that a question or a statement?" she threw over her shoulder as she started toward the laundry room. "The answer is yes, no matter what it is."

"He's not your type," Thomas said.

Lottie stopped and turned around. "What is my type?"

"You ever heard that song that came out a while back by Caylee Hammack?"

"Which one? I listen to a lot of her work, and what does any of it have to do with 'my type'?" She air-quoted the last two words.

"I was thinking about 'Small Town Hypocrite,'" Thomas answered with a smile. "You usually go for losers that leave you in tears. I talked to Jack about Knox. He's a decent guy. Like I said, not your type."

"So, you're saying that no good man would be interested in me?" she snapped.

Thomas put up his palms in a defensive gesture. "Hey! I'm just tellin' it like I see it."

"Maybe I've learned my lesson when it comes to bad boys," Lottie said.

Eddie carried a brown paper bag full of food into the rec hall. "I'm making spaghetti. Who all is eating with me?"

The aroma of soap that smelled like leather followed Gabe out of the bathroom. "I'm in if it's not that stuff that comes out of a can."

"Me too, especially if you are making it with your famous poor-man dinner rolls," Thomas answered.

Lottie loved Eddie's spaghetti and the cheesy bread he made from hot dog buns, but there was no way she was turning down shrimp scampi. "I'm having supper with Knox, but you can save me some leftovers for a midnight snack."

"Are you cooking?" Eddie asked.

"If so, the honeymoon phase might be over," Thomas teased.

Lottie frowned at the whole bunch of them and muttered the whole way into the laundry room. She might not like to cook, but she could outwork all three of those guys. And she did not always have relationships with deadbeats.

Oh, yes, you do. Remember Danny and Toby and Jimmy? More than one therapist reminded her of the past boyfriends.

"I've learned my lesson," she argued.

The smell of onions frying with hamburger made her stomach growl when she came back to the rec hall kitchen. Waiting for the clothes to dry was going to last forever, especially when Eddie popped those cheese rolls into the oven, and that aroma spread across the room.

Gabe took three beers from the refrigerator, set two on the bar separating the sitting room and kitchen, and twisted the top off the third. "Everybody looking forward to going home for the big Easter weekend?"

"The kids are all too grown up to hunt eggs at my folks' place, so Mama doesn't make a big deal out of that holiday. But you can bet we'd all better be there for Christmas Day, or she'll send us on a guilt trip that will lay on our shoulders for a whole year," Lottie answered.

Eddie stirred the sauce and added the meat and onion mixture to it. "I hear you, but my kids are still young enough to get all excited about the day. My mother insists that we go to church with her, then have a big family dinner and the traditional Easter egg hunt."

"So, are you going home with Knox for the weekend?" Gabe asked.

"Of course," she blurted out, and she wished she could put the words back in her mouth.

As if a miracle fell from heaven, her phone rang. When Bernie's name came up, she answered on the second ring.

"Hello, Bernie. What's going on in your neck of the woods?" she asked.

"Easter weekend is coming up, and if you don't have plans, I wanted to invite you to come up here. We have a big to-do. The sisters all get together on Saturday to cook and get the eggs ready for the big community egg hunt, and the guys get the backyard ready for the event. The menfolks hide the eggs after our family dinner, and Mary Jane takes pictures of each family in front of the Easter bunny. That's a six-foot-tall wooden cutout that Joe Clay made for her to use as a backdrop for her photos. We set up tables under the shade trees for snacks and visiting after the egg hunt is over." She stopped for a breath and then went on. "And there's plenty of room in the Paradise for you to stay there. You can ride up here with Knox."

"Thank you for the invitation, but since Knox and I are kind of dating, he should be the one asking me, don't you think?"

"Well, praise the Lord and pass the biscuits!" Bernie shouted so loud that Lottie held the phone out from her ear. "I've done it again! Another star in my matchmaking crown."

"Don't go having that big old diamond polished and set into your gold tiara just yet," Lottie said, laughing. "We've only decided to go out with each other since the wedding, and maybe he wouldn't want me to interfere with his family time."

"Bullshit!" Bernie said. "Holidays mean family, and you are coming. Don't even try to argue with me. I've got to go now. See you tomorrow night."

"Hey, y'all!" Lottie raised her voice as she headed for the door. "Just throw my laundry on the folding table, please. I'll come back and get it later."

"Sure thing, but what's making you race out of here?" Gabe asked.

"I don't want my shrimp scampi to get cold," she answered and jogged all the way to Knox's trailer.

Chapter 4

Knox had just gotten the table set for two when the phone rang and Lottie burst through the door at the same time. He ignored the phone when he saw the expression on her face—pure fear.

"What's the matter? Are you all right?" he asked.

"Don't answer that call," she panted. "Please, don't answer it."

"Why?" Knox asked.

"I'll explain when I catch my breath," she said. "It's Bernie, and I need to tell you first."

A cold chill chased down Knox's backbone. "Is everything all right in Spanish Fort?"

"Yes," Lottie said with a nod. "She called me"—she took a deep breath and let it out in a whoosh—"to invite me to come to the Paradise with you for the weekend."

"And you ran all the way here to tell me that?" Knox asked.

"I told her we were dating," she blurted out. "I didn't want her to call and blindside you."

Once a cat is out of the bag, putting it back in is a tough job without getting clawed in the process. "So," he asked, "are you going?"

"I didn't give her an answer, but…" She slid into the booth and took a long drink of tea.

"But what? Either you are going, or you aren't."

"Shouldn't you be the one to ask me since we are dating?" she fired back.

Knox carried a basket of warm bread to the table. "Okay, then. If you aren't going home for Easter, would you like to go with me to Spanish Fort?"

She stood up and refilled her tea glass while he brought the rest of the food to the table. "Bernie and your relatives will be able to see right through our deception."

"Did Jack?" Knox asked and motioned for her to sit down.

"No, but this is your family. They know you well enough to know when you are faking it, don't they?"

"If we were in a restaurant, this is where I would pull out a chair for you, but since all we have is a booth…" he said.

She slid into the booth. "Well?"

He passed the shrimp scampi over to her. "If we can fool this crew, we can do the same with my family. And I've got a confession. I bragged that I would get a *fake* girlfriend so that Aunt Bernie wouldn't set me up with a blind date every weekend. I even told Tripp that I would leave every few weeks and spend a weekend somewhere to keep the ruse going."

"Why?" Lottie asked.

"If you could have seen some of the dates that Aunt Bernie sent Brodie and Tripp on, you would understand." He chuckled.

"Tell me about them," she said.

"One of the best stories is when she set Brodie up with this woman to have dessert and coffee at my sister Tertia's café. Brodie had been at war with his neighbor, Audrey, over his farm. She wanted to buy it because her family had owned it at one time. He wasn't selling for any amount of money. Anyway, to try to make a long story short, we had a tornado that wiped out our house. And the same storm landed a pot-bellied pig on the place. That critter got loose and tore up Audrey's aunt's flower beds. She got ahold of the animal and marched into the café with it. She set it on the table where Brodie and his date were."

Lottie shook her head and eyed Knox, disbelief written all over her face. "Are you serious? What happened? Does he still have the pig?"

"Pansy is still on the farm and has a brood of babies now. What happened is that pig upset tea on the woman, and she left in a huff. I could probably get you one of those piglets. It could be trained to the litter pan that Prissy uses, and we could take it for walks in the evening like Brodie does with Pansy," he teased. "Oh, and my brother married Audrey. That's the wedding where I met you."

"Forget the pig and buy me a candy bar or a rose." She grinned. "I've got a cat, and that's enough. Changing the subject here. This would be a fantastic dish to serve for Uncle Jack's retirement party."

"So, you like it?"

"Love it," she answered. "Even more than Eddie's spaghetti. That's what they're having in the rec hall tonight."

"Is that a compliment?" Knox asked.

"A really big one," she answered. "I try to get him to make it once a week, but he says it's only good for a small crowd. If he doubles and triples the recipe, it's not the same."

Knox finished off his plate of food and cleared both empty plates. "Now, for dessert."

"I'm way too full for anything else. Let's take a walk around part of the lake and then come back for cheesecake," Lottie suggested.

"That would be a good way to keep up appearances, wouldn't it?"

"Yep, and walk off some calories at the same time. You cooked, so I'll do the dishes," she said.

"The dishes can wait. Let's go, darlin'." He opened the door and held out a hand. "Don't you just love the smell of apple blossoms blooming in the spring?" He lowered his voice to a whisper. "Does that sound too mushy?"

Lottie stood up, put her hand in his, and together they left the trailer. "Not at all," she answered out the corner of her mouth and then raised her voice. "It's a shame that they had to cut down so many apple trees for the houses, but I am glad they saved a few. Aunt Mandy and my mama will probably make lots of pies, and maybe even some of Mama's famous apple butter when the apples ripen."

"Mmmm…" Knox said. "Biscuits fresh out of the oven, slathered in apple butter."

"Or waffles," Lottie added as they passed by the rec house.

Knox sniffed the air. "I smell spaghetti. If I had any room left, I would go in there and beg a plateful."

"It is every bit as good as it smells, but the shrimp was better."

"Well, thank you, darlin'," he said. "Maybe someday I'll serve it to you in bed."

"In your dreams," she smarted off.

"Hey, now," he protested, "those are fightin' words. My dreams are classified and…"

"And I'm not on the need-to-know basis, so I can't be read in, right?"

"That's what the file says, but if you were to let me cook breakfast for you…" He let the sentence hang.

"You can make breakfast for me every morning," she said. "I'll gladly come to your trailer before work and eat your cooking."

"You are a prickly woman, Miss Charlotte Johnston."

She nudged him on the shoulder. "Don't you forget it."

Knox sat down on the grassy bank next to the water and pulled her down beside him. "That is too beautiful for just a passing glance. We should sit here for a few minutes and admire it."

For a split second, Lottie thought he was pretending to flirt with her, but then she realized that he was looking at the full moon's reflection in the lake. The water rippled toward the shore, making the sight seem more like a slow-motion video than a picture. A few apple blossoms danced on the gentle waves, giving the whole scene even more life.

"This reminds me of a calendar on the kitchen wall at my mama's house," she finally said.

"Thomas Kinkade?" Knox asked.

"Yes. Mama likes his paintings," she answered. "I've always thought that they don't depict real life."

"My mother had a couple of his originals," Knox said. "She told me that there are two sides to life. One is dark, and one is light. Kinkade chose to see the light."

"I can believe that, but if we won't appreciate the light if there aren't a few dark moments," Lottie said.

"We're getting into a deep conversation for a fake relationship," Knox said.

"How about for a plain old friendship?"

She felt a presence behind them before Jack spoke and hoped that he hadn't heard the last couple of comments.

"I smell Stetson," she said with half a giggle.

"That's apple blossoms, not cologne, and you are changing the subject," Knox said.

Jack sat down on the other side of Knox and groaned. "Nope. It's my shaving lotion. I just took a shower and shaved. Now that I've made up my mind to retire, my knees are wanting this project to be done with sooner rather than later. Our house in Bandera sold today. The timing is perfect. By the time the paperwork is finished, we should be ready to move into the first cabin."

"That's great, Uncle Jack, but I'm not ready for this," Lottie said.

"You can come see us and your folks anytime you want," Jack said. "And think how special it is to all your family that you helped build our retirement homes. Before things get all weepy, I'm going to continue my walk." He groaned again when he stood up. "Y'all enjoy sitting out here under that lovers' moon. Did you know that in some circles it's called the pink moon or the awakening moon?"

"Are you trying to get us to bite on a late April Fool's joke?" Lottie asked.

"I am not," Jack answered. "Look at it in the water. It's pink, and the other name was given to it because right now winter is over, and spring is waking up. It's a fine time for new relationships like you kids have, and new beginnings like me and Mandy are going to have. See y'all in the morning."

"We'll be there," Lottie said past the lump in her throat.

"Are you about to cry?" Knox asked.

"Maybe," she answered. "The job won't be the same without Uncle Jack."

Knox scooted closer to her and draped an arm around her shoulders. "Change happens to us all. I thought I would never adjust after we lost our mother, but the move to Spanish Fort was the best thing that could have happened."

"Why?" Her voice quavered.

"I'm not sure if I can explain it. The closest I could get would be that everything seemed dark without her, but all three of us found a glimmer of light when Brodie bought the farm and we started over. We were able to chase our dreams—at least Tripp and Brodie were. I've always loved working in construction, and the sisters had plenty to keep me busy."

"Tripp hasn't always had a leather shop?" Lottie asked.

Knox gently squeezed her shoulder. "Nope. Tripp was the CEO of my father's oil company. When Brodie joined the military, Tripp felt duty bound to get into the family business. I was the rebel who went into construction from the beginning."

"How did Brodie go from being in the service to…"

"Organic farming?" Knox finished the sentence for her. "Mother was always piddling around in her garden or flower beds. I guess he got a love for it there. When we drove to the Paradise to meet Joe Clay, Brodie's biological father, he found a small farm for sale and bought it on the spot. Then when the whole Paradise family adopted us, it seemed like an omen that a farm just like he wanted was close by. Tripp and I agreed to help for a few months."

Lottie gasped.

"What?" Knox asked. "Do you see a snake or something?"

"No, but I see a Callahan," she whispered.

He was one of those multimillionaires that her mother talked about, and that was why she had been called a *gold digger*. She couldn't believe she had brazenly asked him to be her fake boyfriend. But then, in her defense, nothing at that fairly simple wedding said that the family were rich folks. Even Mary Jane, who had more than a twenty-year writing career of bestselling books, didn't act all hoity-toity.

"And that means?" Knox asked.

"I am not a gold digger. I am not after your money by starting a fake relationship to make you fall in love with me. Why are you doing such a manual job when you are rich, anyway?"

"I like what I'm doing. It makes me happy, and honey, if I thought you were angling to get your name on my bank account, I wouldn't be sitting here beside you." He chuckled. "Let's talk about something else. Did you stay in Aunt Bernie's trailer or the Paradise when you were in Spanish Fort?"

"I stayed in my trailer, but the Paradise is more like a small hotel than a house," she answered. "Bernie told me that the house started off as a brothel back when Spanish Fort was a booming town that got a lot of trade during the days when cattle were run from Texas up to Dodge City."

"Yep, and the whole family is working to get the place off the ghost town register," Knox said.

Lord have mercy! She had trouble wrapping her mind around the fact that he was a rich man.

"Why did you agree to do this with me?" she asked.

"It suits both of our needs. You don't want to deal with the unmarried men. I don't want to put up with Aunt Bernie and her matchmaking."

Her emotional moment at the idea of Jack leaving had passed, but she couldn't make herself scoot away. Sitting there with him in the moonlight was both comforting and exciting—even though she didn't want to admit the latter.

"That said and understood," he said, "the Paradise is kind of like a hotel, and you really ought to come around and see it at Christmastime."

"Bernie showed me pictures," Lottie said. "I bet it's the best-decorated place in the county."

"Yes, it is, and the whole town of Spanish Fort looks like something out of a Hallmark movie during the holiday," Knox replied and stood up.

He extended a hand to her, and she took it. She was surprised that the sparks didn't catch the floating apple blossoms on fire, but Knox didn't even seem to notice. He kept her hand in his, creating even more heat all the way back to his trailer.

She vowed that she would not let their relationship be any more than a passing fanciful fake one.

Chapter 5

"You are the most stubborn man on the face of this earth." Lottie pulled the trigger on the nail gun half a dozen times and then gave Knox a dose of stink eye. "No, that's not right. The earth isn't big enough. You are the most exasperating guy in the Universe."

"Whoa!" Thomas said. "That's giving him a lot of credit, and my wife, Angie, would say that he'd have to fight me for the title."

"What's the problem anyway?" Gabe asked.

"We're going to Spanish Fort for the weekend. She wants to take her trailer," Knox answered.

Leave it to a man to not explain the whole situation. She popped a dozen more nails into the supports to hold up the last wall and seethed with every one of them.

Eddie stretched up and nailed in braces to hold the two walls together. "What's wrong with that?"

"We'll have to take two vehicles," Knox answered. "There's plenty of room at the Paradise for her to stay there two nights, but she won't leave her cat alone that long."

"Why can't you ride with her?" Thomas asked.

"Because I don't let anyone else drive my truck, and

he's being a…" She couldn't think of a word mean enough to say.

Thomas glanced over at Knox. "If that means you'd have to ride in the passenger seat, then I don't blame you for taking your own vehicle. I hate it when Angie insists on driving and I'm over on the other side trying to brake by stomping the floorboard. I swear that woman should've been a NASCAR driver."

"Same with Jeannie," Eddie agreed. "She's the princess of procrastination and always leaves the house in a rip-roaring hurry. She'd be the queen, but her mama is still alive and kicking."

"Y'all are not helping!" Lottie declared. "Whose side are you on, anyway?"

Gabe laid down his nail gun and threw up both hands. "We still love you, girl, but facts is facts."

Eddie went back to work but stopped for a minute to look over his shoulder. "Is that cat worth all this, or do you just want to have your way?"

"Yes, Prissy is worth it. She's brought me through some tough times. She listens to me when I talk and never betrays me like the bunch of you. But then she's a girl and understands. I'm so aggravated with all y'all right now that we could plug one of these nail guns into my ear and run it on the electricity from my body."

"Honey, you're not mad at anyone but me," Knox told her. "If you would have let me get a word in edgewise, I would have told you that I need a vehicle while I'm in

Spanish Fort. I want to go out to the farm while you ladies are shopping, and I really want to check on Tripp at the leather shop. You could hook up your trailer to my truck if you weren't so bullheaded."

"Or I could check in on Prissy each day," Jack said as he rounded a stack of lumber. "Mandy is driving up here to pick out flooring and shop for new furniture this afternoon. She'll be staying in my trailer until Monday, but she wouldn't mind helping me take care of your cat. She loves Prissy. No need for y'all driving in two trucks and pulling a trailer behind one of them. Now get this wall up so y'all can get on the road."

"Are you sure?" Lottie hated that Knox was getting his way, but at the same time, she was tired, and it would be nice to get to catch a nap on the way.

"I'm sure," Jack said.

"Well I, for one, will not argue about knocking off work a couple of hours early. We might even get home in time for supper if I drive like Angie." Thomas chuckled.

"Hush!" Lottie growled and then smiled at Jack. "Thank you. Prissy will love to see Aunt Mandy. I'll feed her before we leave."

"I'll check on her before bedtime," Jack said. "Now, get busy and finish what you are doing before I change my mind and tell you to start building trusses."

"Yes, sir!" Lottie threw up her hand and saluted him.

"And no more arguing," Jack said with a wide grin.

"Can't promise that," Knox said. "I've got to ride with her all the way to Spanish Fort, and she's in a mood."

"I am not in a mood!" Lottie protested. "Men! Y'all are jackasses."

"Maybe so, but it's against the law to shoot us," Eddie teased.

Like a good boyfriend, Knox loaded Lottie's garment bag and suitcase in the back seat and then opened the truck door for her. When she had settled, he jogged around the front of the vehicle and slid in behind the steering wheel.

"Why are you so happy?" Lottie asked.

"I'm going home. I have a girlfriend, so Aunt Bernie can't make me go on a blind date. The weather is beautiful. We get to leave early, which means we can eat supper at the Paradise with some of the family. Is that enough, or should I go on?"

"It's enough," she answered.

Knox started up the engine and drove away from the project. He looked back in his rearview mirror at six foundations and one place with four walls standing. Had this been a real relationship with Lottie, their beginning could look like that. A few dates would equal some walls going up, and a few more would be like the roof going on the top.

"Are you changing your mind about introducing me as your girlfriend?" she asked.

"Why would you ask that?"

"Your expression went from all sunny and bright to dark.

Not quite a tornado, but a big storm on the horizon," she answered.

"No. Not just no! But hell, no! I am not changing my mind!"

"You don't have to raise your voice," she snapped.

"Yes, I do. I want you to understand that I'm in this for the long haul," he declared. "Now, do you want to stop at the first convenience store to get a cold drink?"

"Maybe we could find a Sonic and get a raspberry tea instead?" she suggested.

"There's one about a mile up the road. I like the ice they use in their soft drinks," he said.

"You are a great boyfriend." Lottie's tone softened. "I suppose I can ask your sisters and two sisters-in-law to tell me stories about you, but you could make the trip seem shorter if you would do it."

"I'll tell you a funny one about when Brodie first knocked on the door at the Paradise," he said as he slowed down and turned into the Sonic parking lot. "Every one of us was as jittery as a squirrel on espresso, waiting to see what kind of reception he would get. Bo, that's one of the sisters, answered the door, and insisted he tell her why he wanted to see Joe Clay. He said later that he wasn't sure if those seven half sisters were going to shoot us all or what, but they welcomed him as well as me and Tripp into the Paradise and into the family that very day."

"What's so funny about any of that?" she asked.

"You would have had to have been there," Knox answered.

"Brodie is the big, mean ex-special services brother who wasn't afraid of anything. Well, maybe except Aunt Bernie, but we're all afraid of her. To see him so nervous was…"

"I understand," Lottie said with a smile. "My brothers are all on that overconfident list too."

Knox pulled into the first available space and pushed the call button. A tinny voice welcomed him to Sonic and asked for his order. "A raspberry tea and a root beer, both extra-large, and an order of fries."

"Have that right out," the voice said.

"Thank you, ma'am," Knox said and turned back to Lottie. "Fries can be our appetizer. I called Mary Jane and told her we'd be there for supper. Remy and Ursula are bringing smoked brisket, so we don't want to be full on burgers when we get there."

"For good barbecue, I would give up everything else, including ice cream, and that is my weakness," she told him. "But I'll be a good girlfriend and share with you, so you can have all the brisket that you can hold."

"Thank you," he said and flashed a wink her way.

"Tell me another story, maybe one on Tripp," Lottie said.

"He's our quieter, more introverted brother, but Willa Rose has brought out a whole new side to him."

"That would be his wife, right? The one in the gorgeous vintage wedding gown, who has a little baby boy?"

"That's right. Her sister didn't want to be a mother, so Willa Rose and Tripp adopted Nicky. Tripp and I were adopted at birth too. We were lucky to get such amazing parents who loved us, and when they were gone, we were blessed to have Mary Jane and Joe Clay take us in."

The carhop brought out their order, and Knox handed her a bill. "Keep the change, and thank you."

"Thanks," the girl said. "Y'all have a nice rest of today."

"You too." Knox set the cups in the holders in front of the console and handed the fries to Lottie. His hand brushed against hers, and a few hot little sparks flitted around in the truck cab.

He silently reminded himself that they were not a real couple.

Chapter 6

"CURTAIN IS COMING UP," Lottie said when Knox turned down the lane to the Paradise. "Places. Action."

"Smiles. Jazz hands," Knox added and parked at the end of a line of vehicles.

She unfastened her seat belt. "What do you know about jazz hands?"

"My mother thought we should have a well-rounded education, and that included theater and drama classes. I was Danny Zuko in our high school musical, *Grease!*"

"No way!" she gasped. "I was Sandy in ours."

"Small world, ain't it?" Knox said as he got out of the truck, rounded the back side, and opened the door for her. "It's show time, *darlin'.* Think we can do this?"

"I have faith," she muttered, and reminded herself that she was up against Bernie.

As if on cue, Bernie came out the front door and motioned them inside. "I'm starving, and Mary Jane won't let us start eating until y'all get here, so don't lollygag around out there. You can talk after supper. If you sniff the air, you can probably smell the brisket and baked beans all the way out there."

Knox took her hand in his and whispered out the corner of his mouth. "Lights. Camera. Action."

"You are too funny," Lottie said and took a deep breath. "Lord, that smells good! I hope we can eat before Bernie figures out that we are lying."

"She's smart, but if we are good enough to fool the guys at the site, we can do this." Knox kept his voice low.

"Did you hear me?" Bernie yelled.

"Yes, ma'am, but we've worked all day and sat in a vehicle for two hours. We aren't moving fast just yet," Knox raised his voice and then added, "Everything smells wonderful, and we only shared an order of fries on the way."

Bernie picked up Pepper and held the door for them. "They just don't make young folks with the stamina I had at your age. Welcome to the Paradise, Lottie. Come on in and meet everyone." Then she headed straight through the foyer and into the kitchen. She passed Bo on the way and frowned. "Don't get to talking to them and hold up supper."

"You are here." Bo gave each of them a hug. "Hurry up and eat, or else make a plate and take it with you to the bar."

"Why?" Knox asked.

"Maverick has the flu, and I need help. Lottie, you don't have to go if you don't want to, but I am going to drag Knox away from you for the evening."

"I'll be glad to help," she said. "I've never done that kind of work, but I'm a fast learner." Getting to know one sister would be better than staying back with half a dozen more to answer their questions. Worse than that, she would have to deal with Bernie.

Bo tiptoed, gave her another quick hug, and whispered. "You can thank me later."

"For what?"

"Giving you a chance to get away from Aunt Bernie and all her nosiness." Bo's green eyes twinkled as she led the way to the kitchen, where supper was spread out buffet style.

"Joe Clay will offer grace, and then we can all dive in," Mary Jane said, "but first I need to welcome Lottie and hug Knox. Seems like he's been gone for weeks instead of days."

"Mamas and their kids." Joe Clay grinned.

Mary Jane wrapped both Knox and Lottie up in a three-way hug, then stepped back and nodded to Joe Clay. He bowed his head and said a quick prayer, and then everyone lined up to load their plates with food.

The dining room table was huge, but there were enough people around it that they were shoulder to shoulder. Every time that Knox moved, his upper arm brushed against Lottie's, and the vibes got hotter and hotter. She tried to take her mind off the attraction by studying each family member and putting names with faces. Remy and Ursula went together, along with their toddler, Clayton. Bo owned the bar where she and Knox were supposed to work that night. Her eyes shifted to Bernie, and the old gal winked. Did that mean she had invited Lottie to the Paradise to see for herself if the relationship was real?

That alone broke Lottie's concentration. Then Knox

leaned over and added to the rush of heat she was trying to avoid, and whispered, "Aunt Bernie is giddy with excitement."

"And in six weeks, we are going to break her heart. It's not going to be easy to fool her for all that time," Lottie said out the side of her mouth.

A strand of Bo's strawberry-blond hair escaped the messy bun on top of her head, and she pushed it back behind her ear. "Y'all stop talking and eat," she scolded from across the table. "Mama, can we take our dessert to go? We really have to get on the move soon as these two"—she nodded toward Knox and Lottie—"finish their food."

"I'm swallowing my food whole already, and I need to put our stuff upstairs," Knox said.

"Why are you in such a hurry?" Bernie asked. "You know very well that few people ever show up the minute the doors are open."

"If I'm not there at six on the dot, Maverick will start to work. He's not contagious at this point, but I don't want him to wear himself out so badly that he won't feel like coming to Easter on Sunday."

"Then swallow that last bite of food, Knox, and get a move on," Mary Jane said. "We'll have plenty of time to visit tomorrow. I don't want Maverick to miss our big day."

Knox swallowed, downed the last of his tea, and pushed back his chair. He laid a hand on Lottie's shoulder and said, "I'll get our things taken up to our rooms while you finish. Do you need to change or…"

"I'm good just the way I am," she said.

He kissed her on the top of her head. "Yes, you are."

"Before you get away, and I forget," Bernie said. "In two weeks, I'm having one of my senior mixer events. We're doing it from two to five on Saturday afternoon. That way it doesn't interfere with Bo and Maverick's regular hours. Can I depend on y'all to help me?"

"What do we need to do?" Lottie asked.

"Basically, help decorate and draw up free beer," Bo answered.

"Sure," Lottie answered. "I reckon I can do that."

"And do some karaoke singing," Bernie added.

"I'm out!" Lottie declared.

Knox threw up both palms. "Me too."

"She's pulling your leg," Bo said with half a giggle. "The juke box will be playing old songs all afternoon. Karaoke night isn't until the following weekend. Maybe y'all can come back then and sing a duet."

"Only if you want us to clear out the bar in record time," Knox said on his way out of the room.

Lottie felt like the only chicken at a coyote convention when the room went silent as a tomb. Everyone seemed to be staring at her, expecting a speech or, at the very least, a complete sentence. Her mind went blank, and she pretended she was alone in her trailer with her cat.

They're sizing you up, the voice in her head said.

Someone say something. Anything. About any subject. Everyone can even talk at once. Just make noise. This quietness is deafening, she screamed without making a sound.

"Are your parents in the building business?" Joe Clay finally asked.

"No, but my mother's brother, Jack, is, and he gave me a job when I was in high school. I went to college, and when I graduated with a business degree, my three brothers offered me a job in each of their businesses." She didn't tell him that she was more comfortable around a bunch of carpenters than she ever was in a dorm full of giggling and whining young women who were only interested in their makeup and shoes. Thank God, her parents had sprung for a private room, or she would have checked out after the first semester and gone straight into the construction business.

"But you liked the construction business better?" Bernie asked.

"Yes, I did," she answered.

"Okay, folks, y'all can ask her more questions tomorrow," Bo said as she stood up. "Thanks for supper. The brisket was amazing, like it always is, Remy. I appreciate you making a plate for me to take to Maverick. I hear Knox coming back downstairs. See y'all tomorrow around noon."

Knox poked his head around the corner. "Y'all ready, or are you going to stand around and talk for another thirty minutes?"

"We would have already been there if you hadn't taken time to comb your hair and put on fresh cologne," Bo fussed at him.

Knox crossed the room and took Lottie's hand into his. "Hey now, a guy has to do his best when he's got a beautiful girlfriend. All the customers at the bar will try to take her away from me."

"I've only got eyes for you, darlin'." Lottie played along with the charade with only a smidgen of guilt, but her insides were a jittery mess of tightly bound nerves.

Knox let go of her hand when they reached his truck. "I apologize for my sister dragging you into this."

"I'm glad she did. I wondered all through supper if I had something on my face," Lottie said. "And when you left, everything got quiet and…"

Knox helped her into the truck and patted her on the shoulder. "They couldn't help staring at you because you are beautiful."

She fastened her seat belt and crossed her arms over her chest. "We're alone. You don't have to keep up the fake stuff."

"I'm tellin' you the truth."

"Then thank you," Lottie said, and part of the tension left her body.

"What did Bo do before she bought a bar?"

"She spent several years in Nashville trying to break into the country music scene. When she got tired of that, she came home and went to work for Aunt Bernie in her match-making business. She fell in love with Maverick, and they settled down in Nocona to run the bar."

"Do they all have happy-ever-after stories?" she asked.

He backed the truck up and followed Bo's vehicle down the lane. "Pretty much. Some of the stories got a little stormy at times, but when the obstacles were cleared, they all seem happy now. You'll probably hear all about them tomorrow."

"We should be absolutely sure that we've got our stories straight if you're going to leave me alone with all of them." The tension got so tight in her shoulders that they ached. How did getting a fake boyfriend become so complicated?

"Just divert their attention if things get too tense. Ask them how they met their spouses. Audrey should be able to entertain you for hours. And then Willa Rose can step up and tell you how that…" He stopped talking.

"How what?"

"Those are all their stories to tell," he said.

For the next half hour, she wondered how the sisters would react to *her* story. Actually, she considered it boring. Work, a few short-lived relationships, and holidays trips to wherever her parents lived at the time, and some weekends if the job was close enough. Certainly nothing entertaining like setting a pig on the table in a café.

"You sure are quiet," Knox said as he turned into a gravel parking lot. "You have been in a bar before, haven't you?"

"Of course," she answered. "But fake boyfriends don't get to ask how many, and I didn't hear a word out of your mouth either."

"I saw a For Sale sign on a fence of some acreage between here and Spanish Fort, and an idea popped into my head." He got out of the truck and closed the door.

She didn't wait for him to help her out and had her feet

on the ground before he rounded the back of the vehicle. "Want to talk about what this new idea is?"

He took her hand in his. "Not now. I have to do some research. Plus, Tripp is the financial wizard in the family, so I would like to run it by him."

Knox let go of her hand and opened the door into a small foyer. "Bathrooms are at the end of the hallway, but there's also one for the hired help in the storage room." Waves of heat tap-danced up her spine, and his voice sounded like it was coming from the bottom of a barrel.

"Fat and Famous," by Ashley McBryde, was playing on the jukebox and seemed to fit right in with her situation. She wished all the people who had teased her and made fun of her could see her with Knox—even if it wasn't real. She might not be famous, but they would see that she had one good, sexy boyfriend even if she was a giant and boring.

"Hey! You are here," Bo waved from the back corner.

Knox went to the far corner of the room and started sitting chairs down from the tables. Lottie followed his lead and wished that she could still feel his hand in hers. She reminded herself sternly that she would not fall for him and then have a broken heart when he walked away in six weeks.

"If y'all are going to take care of that job, I'll go unload the dishwasher and get the peanuts and pretzels on the bar," Bo said. "And thank you again for helping tonight. I really want Maverick to be well enough for Sunday."

"If you need me tomorrow night, just holler," Lottie said. "They tell me we're all meeting in the dining room to decorate real eggs and stuff the plastic ones with candy tomorrow morning. But Knox and I can sneak away by the time you open."

Bo nodded. "You are a lifesaver, and I'll protect you from Aunt Bernie."

"Then the thanks go to you," Lottie set the last chair down and crossed the room to help pour peanuts and pretzels into bowls. "She didn't scare me when I went to her old bar up in Ratliff City, but with this new matchmaking thing she's got going, I've got a feeling that if Knox and I don't work out, she'll be…" She stopped for a breath.

Bo patted her on the back. "Yes, she will be all up in your business, trying to fix you up with every available man in her stable of available guys. But never fear, I'll run interference for you."

"And me?" Knox asked.

"Only if you agree to work here tomorrow night too," Bo said with a wide grin.

"I'll be here," Knox said without hesitation. "Are you expecting a crowd tonight?"

"Always on Friday nights," Bo answered. "We see our usual crowd on weeknights, but weekends are a different matter. Might be a little less crowded tomorrow since some folks will be busy with Easter stuff."

"Is it like that old television show where everyone knows everyone?" Lottie teased. "Bernie's bar, the Chicken Coop, might have been where they got the idea for the TV sitcom."

"You were there?" Bo asked.

"Yep. She poured my first legal drink when I was

twenty-one, and if I hadn't had a designated driver with me, she would have taken my keys by the time the place closed." Lottie smiled at the memory, but it faded fast when a vision of hugging the bathroom toilet the next morning flashed through her mind.

Bo pulled her hair up into a ponytail and set the bowls down the bar. "You'll have to tell us more about her sometime. She has costumes that she wears for holidays. She said that they were what she wore at her bar."

Lottie finished that job and headed for the jukebox. "You can believe her. Holidays, even the ones she made up, were a blast at the Chicken Coop. Didn't y'all ever visit her in the Chicken Coop?"

"Nope. She came down here when she could manage the time, but we all left and went to college or university right out of high school. We weren't old enough to drink, and Mama would have grounded us for eternity plus three days if we'd gone to a bar with a fake ID," Bo answered. "She supported my dream when I went to Nashville. There were times when I was living on peanuts and pretzels from the bars where I had a gig, and then I'd find a hundred dollars in my checking account. But for the most part, she let me find my own way."

"I understand," Lottie said. "My mama didn't know I had a fake ID. She thought my very first trip to the Chicken Coop was on my twenty-first birthday. Hey, you've got some of the older country music in this jukebox. I was raised on these songs."

"You *are* in a Texas bar," Knox chuckled.

Lottie brought a fistful of coins from her pocket and fed them into the slot. "I'll get the evening started."

The first two customers arrived before the second song finished playing. The woman had long, blond hair down to her waist and wore cutoff jeans so short that the pockets hung out from below the hem, and a skintight top that proved she was not wearing a bra. It was also very evident that there was a brisk, cool wind blowing outside.

The guy's jeans were tucked down into his cowboy boots, and his pearl snap shirt was undone far enough that Lottie could see a few scraggly dark-brown hairs that matched the attempt at growing a beard. Bless his heart! When he got old enough to have some real chest hair, an open shirt might be sexy, but now it looked kind of sad.

Bo pointed to a sign above the bar that read: IDs must be presented.

Lottie would bet tenpenny nails to cow patties that the driver's licenses they flipped out onto the bar were both fake. Neither of them could possibly be a day over eighteen, and that would be stretching it by a year or two.

"We'll take two longneck bottles of Coors," he said.

"No, you won't," Knox said from the shadows. "Brandon McKay, your mama will take a switch to you if she finds out you are in a bar. Bo, this is Tommy and Clarice's son. He goes to church with us, and he and his dad helped me build the new parsonage. He's not even out of high school yet. And I believe this young lady is Gabby Owens. She and my sister take care of the church nursery."

Bo set the two bottles back in the refrigerator. "Sorry, you two. You can dance, but you cannot drink in here."

"Come on, Knox," Brandon said. "Can't you look the other way just this one time?"

"He might," Bo said. "But I won't. If my brother-in-law, Gunner, stops by and finds me serving any kind of liquor to minors, he can shut down the place and take my license."

"Then we'll leave and go to the river with the other kids to party," Gabby smarted off.

Bo shrugged. "Drive safely."

Brandon grabbed Gabby's hand, and they stormed out, spewing words that could turn ice into flames.

"Thanks, Brother," Bo said. "I should have recognized both of them. If you ever want to leave the construction company, I'll hire you as a bouncer."

"I don't think so," Knox told her and made his way behind the bar. "I'm perfectly happy building houses, and besides, you have been designing one for a few months that you want me to build here in Nocona. I can't be a full-time bar bouncer and construction feller at the same time."

"Maverick and I've been looking at property, and we just about have the house plans drawn up. Nothing fancy. Just a three-bedroom ranch style with a wraparound porch," Bo said. "When you get done with what you are working on now, we'll be ready for you."

Lottie listened to the lyrics of the third song she had chosen, "I Feel a Sin Comin' On." She swayed to the words that said there was sweet temptation all over the place. She glanced across the room at Knox. *Oh, yes, I'll have to fight the desire with every fiber in my body.*

The sound of crunching gravel filtered into the building from the parking lot, and several customers arrived just as the song ended. In a matter of minutes, the barstools were full. The tables had filled up, and several folks were line dancing to "Boot Scootin' Boogie."

With a tray of beers in her hand, Lottie wove her way through the dancers to a corner table. She set the tray down, and half a dozen guys each reached for one. The line dance ended, and one of the men pushed back his chair and stood up. "I'm in love with you. Dance with me, and then we'll elope to Las Vegas."

Lottie bit back a giggle. "I don't even know your name."

He did a sweeping bow, took her hand in his, and kissed the knuckles. "I am Rusty Matthews, and I'm serious."

Not one single, little bitty spark caused a minor ripple in her hormones. She definitely did not feel anything that resembled a sin coming on. Besides that, he was so short that if he held her close for a slow dance, his nose would be buried up in her breasts.

Maybe that's what he's aiming for, the voice in her head whispered.

She pulled her hand free from him and resisted the urge to pat him on the head like a little boy. "You are a day late and a dollar short, Rusty. See that tall guy over there behind the bar? That's my boyfriend, and he doesn't take too kindly to me dancing with other men."

"The offer has no expiration date," Rusty said. "But know that my heart is broken and might never mend."

A slow two-stepping song made it easier for her to weave her way through the dancing couples back to the bar. She set the empty tray down and was loading it with margaritas to serve at a table with a bunch of ladies when Knox kissed her on the cheek.

"Do I need to go kick that guy out for flirting with my woman?" he asked.

Lottie smiled at him and said in an icy-cold tone. "I am not your woman. I am your…" She stopped herself before she let the cat out of the bag by saying *fake.*

Bo's ponytail swung back and forth when she did a perfect head wiggle. "You tell him, girl. Calling us 'woman' is fighting words."

"Well…par…don…me!" Knox's eyes twinkled.

"I can take care of myself, no matter how tall or short a man is," Lottie told him, and then patted his cheek. "That's to convince Rusty that I'm taken." She picked up the tray and headed to the table of women who were eyeballing the men in the corner.

"Y'all want me to introduce you?" she asked as she set the margaritas in front of them.

"No, but that little feller who was making passes at you sure is cute," the one with brown hair and eyes answered.

"Stand up, please," Lottie said, "and tell me your name."

"Rosalita, and why would I stand up?" she answered. "If

you are wanting to know how tall I am, it's five feet on the dot, and I like short guys."

"That's all I need to know," Lottie said and walked back to the corner table. She laid a hand on Rusty's shoulder. "See that table of women over there? That pretty little brunette with the brown eyes thinks you are sexy."

He was on his feet in a split second and hurried across the dance floor. In less than a minute, they were dancing to a slow country waltz. And surprisingly enough, the guy was smooth on his feet.

"Hmmph," she muttered. "Bernie doesn't have a thing on me. I can play matchmaker too."

After framing the house for more than half a day, driving from the lake area to Nocona, and working at the bar until the last customer finally left, Knox felt like he had been dragged through a knothole backward. He chuckled at the memory of his father saying that same thing when he came in tired from a long day in the office.

"How can you laugh?" Lottie asked. "My feet hurt. No, that's not right. My whole body is in pain. Who would have thought waiting on tables was such hard work?"

"Get Knox to give you a foot massage when you get home," Bo suggested and led the way outside. "Thanks for helping with the cleanup, and for offering to come back tomorrow night. Let's all go home and get some sleep."

"A foot massage sounds heavenly," Lottie said.

"If you can keep me awake, I'll be"—he covered a yawn with his hand—"glad to oblige."

"I'll take a rain check for a later date," she said. "I just want to find a bathroom, take a shower, and fall into a bed."

Knox looked over his shoulder at Bo and then back at Lottie. "Together?"

Lottie bumped him on the shoulder. "Not tonight, honey, and tomorrow night ain't lookin' too good either."

Bo giggled and locked the door behind them.

"Great acting back there," Knox said on the way across the parking lot.

"If we were for real dating, the answer would have been the same," Lottie told him. "I could sleep standing up in a broom closet."

Knox nodded in agreement, helped her into the truck, and hoped that he didn't fall asleep on the way back to Spanish Fort.

You are getting old. You used to be able to work all day, party until two o'clock in the morning on Saturdays, and go to church on Sunday morning.

"Maybe I was just young and stupid," he muttered on the way around the truck.

Lottie's eyes were closed when he slid behind the steering wheel, but they popped open the second he closed the door. "I'll stay awake and talk to you the whole way back. I know how hard it is to drive at night with no one to keep you from falling asleep."

"I'm not so old that I can't stay awake for fifteen miles," he protested.

"Who said anything about being old?" she smarted off. "And I'm not doing this for you. It's for me. I'd like to get there alive and in one piece, not end up lying half-dead in a ditch."

"Are you saying that you don't trust my driving?"

"I'm too tired to fight with you tonight."

"Well, damn!" He grinned. "I thought we'd argue all the way to the Paradise and then have wild makeup sex."

"In your dreams!" she snapped.

That bit of banter jacked up his adrenaline level enough to wake him up. It had been a while since he'd been to the bar, and he had forgotten how eerie a small town was at that time of morning. No vehicles on the street. Not a single store open. No people out and around. Not even a patrolling police car.

"Kind of makes you wonder if the world came to an end, and we're the only ones left," Lottie whispered.

"Would you still be my fake girlfriend if that was the case?" he teased.

"Probably not."

"But if we were the only ones on earth, and it was up to us to repopulate the place…"

He could feel her eyes sizing him up, even in the dimly lit cab of the truck. "Maybe if that were the case."

"Maybe?"

"I'd have to think about it. We would make pretty babies, but there would be no doctors or midwives, and I don't know if you could bring a child into the new, empty world. And what would we do if the kids got sick? We could raid a pharmacy, but would either of us know what to do in case of an emergency?"

"Why are those thoughts going through your head?" Knox asked.

"Because if our only job is to repopulate the earth, we would have to consider all that before we had sex," she answered. "I'm close to thirty. If I had a child every year until I was mid-forty, that would mean about a dozen kids. Then there's no one for them to marry and have families with. No thank you. I don't want to be the only two left behind."

"With that nightmare, I don't either." He noticed the For Sale sign nailed to a fence post that he'd seen on the way to Nocona, and his mind jumped over to the idea of making a group of small houses like Jack was doing down near the lake. He could start off small with only half a dozen spec places and grow from there.

"Hey!" Lottie reached across the console and touched him on the shoulder. "You missed the turn. Are you sleeping with your eyes open?"

"Almost," he replied and turned the vehicle around in Tripp's leather shop's parking lot. "I was building houses in my mind."

"Good Lord! Don't you get enough of that on the job?"

He drove a few blocks and made a right turn into the lane. "Can you compartmentalize so well that you turn everything off in the evenings?"

"I give it my best shot," she told him. "Right now, I'm thinking about a shower. Lumber, nail guns, and steel tapes aren't anywhere in my mind."

Knox parked the truck and pointed toward the huge, two-story house. "It's been a long time since someone left the porch light on for me. But back to you taking a shower. You can have the bathroom first, but only if you promise that you won't use all the hot water. I smell like spilled beer and sweat."

She unfastened her seat belt and opened the door. "Same here, and thank you."

"I am a good pretend boyfriend." He chuckled.

"Ever think about taking an acting job?" she asked as they walked across the yard together.

He opened the door for her and followed her inside the foyer. "Nope. Had enough of that by the time I finished high school. Your room is the first one on the left. Your garment bag is hanging in the closet, and your suitcase is at the foot of the bed. Bathroom is at the end of the hallway. Towels are stacked on a ladder-back chair."

"Thank you," she muttered and headed up the stairs.

She passed by him on the way to the bathroom by the time he reached the end of the hallway and opened the door into his old bedroom. He sat down in a rocking chair and dozed off while he waited for her to finish. A gentle knock on the door and her whisper woke him with a start.

"I'm all done. That is one big-ass bathroom."

"It had to accommodate seven girls." He groaned as he

stood and picked up a pair of pajama bottoms. "See you in the morning. Don't set an alarm. They won't get started until almost noon."

"Thank God," she muttered and disappeared out of the doorway.

Knox adjusted the water in the shower and shucked out of his dirty clothes. Any other time, he would have let the pulsating stream ease his tired muscles. But not that night. There was no doubt in his mind that he could fall asleep standing there. He could fall, hit his head, and drown before anyone could even find him. Or worse yet, break an arm. Then his job working for Jack would be over.

He was back in his room, under the covers and fast asleep, within ten minutes. But his night was filled with dreams of building a small, gated estate project, and Lottie was there with him every step of the way.

Chapter 7

Lottie awoke on Saturday morning to the blended aroma of coffee and cinnamon. She opened one eye and checked the time and sat up so fast that the room did a couple of spins. When everything settled, she looked over at the clock sitting on the nightstand again, and it really was five minutes past ten. She couldn't remember the last time she had slept past eight o'clock.

"Good morning!" Knox pushed through the door with a tray in his hands. "Aunt Bernie thought it would be romantic for me to bring you breakfast in bed this morning. She's in her glory right now. Too bad we'll have to break her heart in a few weeks."

She threw the covers off, slung her legs over the side of the bed, and stood up. "Give me a minute to go to the bathroom, and don't set that tray on the bed. If I spilled coffee on that beautiful chenille spread, I would be mortified."

"Does that mean pretend relationships must have a picnic on the floor rather than breakfast in bed?" Knox said.

"That's right," she replied and padded barefoot out into the hallway. One glance in the bathroom mirror made her glad that she had picked up her makeup bag on the way out of the room. Her hair looked like an old string mop that had been hung over the clothesline to dry. She quickly ran a brush through it, braided it into one long rope, and then brushed her teeth. She was halfway down the hall to her room when one of the sisters stepped out of a bedroom.

"Good morning," Lottie said as cheerfully as she could when she was wearing a faded T-shirt that covered the hem of her running shorts.

"Mornin' to you. You probably don't have all the names straight yet, but I'm Ivy, the youngest sister. I'm hoping that the adoption goes through and then I can really be number eight, but until then I'm just the foster sibling."

"Pleased to meet you, Ivy," Lottie said. "Is everyone up and ready to work on eggs this morning?"

"They are straggling in a few at a time. Mary Jane has the real eggs boiled and ready to decorate, and there's like a million plastic eggs for us to fill up with candy and bunny money."

Lottie stopped at the open door into her bedroom. "What is bunny money?"

"It's little slips of paper that have one dollar or fifty cents printed on them. The kids can take their money to the Easter store set up out in the barn and buy trinkets. Like Slinkies, coloring books, bracelets, and little things like that," Ivy explained. "Tertia and Ophelia will man the store right after the egg hunt, since it was their idea. Looks like Knox is waiting for you. We can talk later."

"Save me a seat by you," Lottie said.

"You got it." Ivy grinned.

Knox looked up from his place beside the tray on the floor. "That didn't take long."

"I'm not high maintenance. Just needed to tame my hair a little and brush my teeth. Now I'm ready for coffee and one of those cinnamon rolls. They look homemade."

"They are." Knox slipped one over onto a small plate, added a fork to the side, and handed it to her. "Tertia sent them over this morning from the café. She'll be late for the party because she and Nash will keep the café open until after supper. We'll be gone to the bar by then, so you'll have to get acquainted with her on Sunday."

"One at a time?" she muttered.

"I wouldn't say that, but after a while you will be able to put names and faces together. It took me a few weeks to get them all straight, and if they don't have their baby or babies with them, I still get Endora and Luna mixed up. There are six of the seven already here, plus Ivy, who you were just visiting with in the hallway. Plus Mary Jane and Bernie, and the sisters-in-law, Audrey and Willa Rose, and they are all downstairs right now."

"And that many guys?" She cut off a piece of the cinnamon roll with the edge of her fork and put it in her mouth.

"They've all gone to the barn to get out the tables and chairs and the props for the egg hunt." Knox picked up a second pastry with his fingers and took a bite.

"Props?" Lottie asked.

"I'll let it be a surprise. After we eat, I'll walk you down to the dining room, and then I'm going to join the guys."

"You're throwing me to the wolves?" she groaned.

"Miss Charlotte Johnston, I've seen you in action. A den of wolves wouldn't stand a chance against you." He stood up and picked up the empty tray. "See you at lunch. Even though some of us had a late breakfast, chili will be on the bar at noon."

Lottie snagged the last orange segment and popped it into her mouth. Since no one was around, she didn't expect a kiss on the top of her head, but she was still disappointed when he left without any kind of romantic gesture. She stood up, closed the door and dressed in jeans and a T-shirt, pulled on a pair of socks, and padded down the steps.

The noise of several conversations going on at once filtered from the kitchen and dining room out into the foyer. She stood in front of a coat tree and listened, but she couldn't make out individual voices. She had been to lots of church fund-raising functions with her mother, so she wasn't new to crowds. But she and Knox were lying to these good people, and that really rattled her.

"They don't bite," Bo whispered from behind her.

Lottie's soul came close to leaving her body. "Are you sure? Where did you come from?"

Bo looped her arm into Lottie's. "Absolutely sure, and I followed you and Knox down the stairs. Come on. I'll go with you into the lion's den."

"Thank you," Lottie whispered, "but I'm not a little lamb."

"No, you are not. Any woman who chooses her own path is on my hero list," Bo told her. "Hey, everyone, we are here and ready to go to work."

Bernie caught Lottie's eye and patted the chair next to her. "Come sit by me and help put this bunny money and a candy in each plastic egg."

"Or you can help my twin daughters decorate eggs," Rae said.

"I called first," Bernie argued, "and I'm the queen."

"Neither of you get to sit by the new family member," Ivy protested. "She's coming to my table with the twins, and we are putting glitter and stickers on these eggs after we dye them, right?"

Both girls raised their fists. "We want Lottie. We want Lottie," they chanted in unison.

"Only until lunch is served," Bernie agreed. "Then it's my turn."

Lottie felt like a cow being auctioned off at a sale barn, but she just smiled and sat down in the last empty chair at a square card table. "Hello, y'all know my name. What's yours?"

"I'm Daisy, and this is Heather. It's okay if you can't tell us apart. Most people can't," the little brown-haired girl said.

She was right. They were definitely identical, and had they been dressed alike, Lottie wouldn't have a clue which one was Daisy or Heather.

Heather narrowed her eyes and studied Lottie for several seconds. "Did you already kiss Uncle Knox?"

"Heather!" Rae scolded. "That's personal and a very rude question."

"But, Mama, I just want to know so I can ask her how it feels to kiss a boy, and if she's going to write his name on an egg," Heather countered.

Lottie leaned down and whispered. "Yes, I did kiss him, but I don't think I'll write his name on anything."

"Did it make your toenails curl up?" Daisy asked.

"When that happened, did your polish crack and get all ugly?" Heather whispered.

"Good Lord!" Rae gasped. "Where did you hear that?"

"At school," Daisy said with a shrug. "Our friend Brenda said that her mama told her bestie that her new boyfriend made her toenails curl up when he kissed her. We was all wonderin' if it ruined her polish."

Lottie chuckled and took off one of her socks. "Look. My polish is still good enough for church tomorrow morning, so kissing Knox didn't do anything to mess it up."

"Well, I ain't kissin' no boy, no how," Heather declared with an expression of pure disgust.

"I might if he brings me chocolate," Daisy said in a matter-of-fact tone.

"Rae, you are paying for your raising," Mary Jane said from the dining room table.

"I think I'm being charged for Bo's raising, too," Rae said.

"Mama, are the guys going to hide them chocolate eggs like they did last year? The ones that have peanut butter in the middle?" Daisy asked.

Just like that, the conversation went from kissing to candy.

"I don't know for sure, but if they don't…" Rae's blue eyes twinkled. "I saw some on the tables in the barn."

"I'm going to buy them all," Heather said.

"No, you ain't," Daisy argued. "Because I can run faster than you, and I'll buy them before you get there."

Rae held up a palm. "New rule. Each one of you can buy two. That's the limit. You have to share with the other kids."

Daisy gave Heather a dose of stink eye. "I told you."

"What'd I do?" Heather asked in an innocent voice.

Daisy folded her arms over her chest. "That permission thing."

Lottie wished for the millionth time that she had had a sister—or even a sibling close to her age. "What is the permission thing?"

"It's better to ask forgiveness than permission," Rae answered. "Where did you girls hear that?"

"At school," Heather said with a shrug and expression identical to Daisy's earlier one. "Brenda said her older sister told her, and it means to do what you want and then cry some tears, and your mama will forgive you."

"Not this mama," Rae assured them, "and don't listen to what Brenda tells you."

"Why?" Daisy asked.

"It will get you into more trouble than you can get out of," Rae said.

Lottie wasn't sure if she should butt in or not, but she

did. "Y'all know that your Uncle Knox and I frame houses. That means that we put up the outside walls and roof, and then another crew comes in to do more on the house. After that, a third one arrives to get the house in the dry. That means that even if it rains, the fourth bunch can put in insulation and drywall. We could kind of do that with these eggs. Ivy and I can dye them. Then y'all can put stickers on them, and Rae can apply the glitter. How does that sound?"

"I like it," Daisy said with a nod. "I don't like getting my fingers all messy."

"Yes!" Heather pumped her fist in the air. "Brenda's mama is taking her to the beauty place to get her nails done today. I don't want to have purple or red fingers tomorrow at church."

Daisy sighed dramatically. "I wish we could get our nails done at the fancy place. I'd have pink ones to match my Easter dress."

"Me too," Heather added.

Lottie dipped boiled eggs into water of various colors and laid them on a paper towel to dry. "If one of your aunts has some polish, I'll do your nails. We'll pretend that the sunroom is a beauty parlor."

"For real?" Daisy squealed. "We've got polish at home. Mama, will you make Daddy go get it for us?"

"On one condition," Rae said seriously, "and that is that neither of you ever do the permission thing again."

"We promise," they said in unison.

A tsunami-sized wave of guilt washed over Lottie. She

vowed she would get past the weekend, but she was never coming back to Spanish Fort again. Her conscience would not let her keep lying to all the good people who had taken her in without question.

———

"Fake or real?" Tripp whispered to Knox as they carried a six-foot wooden Easter bunny out of the barn.

"If it hops away, then I guess it's real," Knox answered.

"You know what I mean," Tripp said. "You told me that you were going to get a fake girlfriend to keep Aunt Bernie from setting you up with women. Is Lottie that, or is she a real one?"

"What do *you* think it is?"

"If it's not real, I'm going to start booking you for acting gigs," Tripp answered.

"Then I guess you have your answer, and it should make Aunt Bernie glad since she introduced us," Knox said. "Now let's get these cutouts taken out to the yard. Remember when Mother used to make Dad hide eggs more than once for us? Think you'll have to do that when Nicky gets old enough to get out there and fill up his basket?"

"Yep, I do." Tripp replied.

Knox breathed a small sigh of relief. He had not lied, but rather skipped around the truth bush several times.

"There were only three of us. There will be dozens of kids here tomorrow afternoon," Tripp answered. "But when Nicky is walking, if he wants to hunt eggs more than one time, then Willa Rose or I will hide and re-hide them until he gets tired of the game."

"If someone had told me two years ago that you and Brodie would both be married by this time, I wouldn't have believed them," Knox said, hoping to continue to keep the conversation away from his relationship with Lottie.

"Me too, and now it's your turn," Tripp said with a grin as they carried the wooden bunny to the middle of the big yard.

"Turn for what?" Brodie asked. "Dad told me to stand right here because Mary Jane wants that thing in the middle of the yard. Something about taking pictures with it."

"To get married," Tripp answered.

"Aunt Bernie is already looking at bridal magazines." Brodie chuckled.

Knox set the bunny down and pulled the stakes out of his hip pocket. "If it doesn't work out?"

Tripp took a hammer from the loop in his cargo pants and started helping his brother get the stakes pounded into the ground. "I don't think a Class 5 tornado would blow him away now." But in the same breath, he had no doubt that Aunt Bernie could melt him into a puddle with one glare if she found out what he and Lottie were up to.

"Don't put that hammer away," Remy called out from the barn door.

He and Luna's husband, Shane, eased a huge cutout of an Easter basket out the door and carried it across the yard.

"Mary Jane said this goes on the right side of the bunny," Shane said.

"And there's some eggs that are supposed to be scattered around the yard," Remy added.

"Lookin' great!" Mary Jane yelled from the back screened-in porch. "Just like I imagined."

Joe Clay brought two four-foot-tall wooden eggs out of the house and laid them in the yard. "Will you guys stand these up and then anchor them down while I bring out the other four? When we get that done, it will be time for dinner. I can almost smell that chili simmering in the kitchen."

"What about the tables and chairs that need to be put up for the leftover potluck tomorrow afternoon?" Knox asked.

"We'll get that done after we eat and take a rest," Joe Clay answered. "Remy, if you and Shane will go with me, we can make short order of this job."

"So, it's real?" Tripp asked when he and Knox were alone.

Damn it! Knox thought. Tripp was his twin, and even though they weren't identical and were even different in their thinking processes, they were still close. And Knox had never lied to him. He couldn't beat around the bush any longer.

"What makes you think it's not?" Knox asked.

Tripp pounded the last anchor into the ground and then straightened up. "My gut tells me something isn't quite right. Y'all act like you are a couple, but there's something in her eyes and yours that says different."

"So, now you are reading my eyes?" Knox chuckled.

Tripp clamped a hand on his brother's shoulder. "Do you remember when you told me that you could see that I was in love with Willa Rose? That was before I even realized it and was damn sure not willing to admit it."

Knox nodded. "I do, but what's that got to do with me and Lottie?"

"Neither of you have the twinkle in your eyes," Tripp answered. "She's got a little bit, but that could be because y'all are pulling the wool over Aunt Bernie."

"It's early in the relationship. Maybe love hasn't hit us yet. Maybe we're just barely getting to know each other," Knox argued.

"It's fake," Tripp said seriously. "If it wasn't, you wouldn't be avoiding my questions."

"Busted!" Knox finally said with a sigh. "But please don't tell anyone. Lottie only told her mother, and now I'm letting you in on the secret." He went on to tell Tripp the whole story from the time that Lottie asked him to be her boyfriend and why. "I know you and Willa Rose don't keep secrets, but I'm asking you not to tell her. We need to keep this on the down-low for five more weeks."

Tripp gently squeezed Knox's shoulder. "Your secret is safe with me, and the idea is genius. She gets to be free from advances, and you from Aunt Bernie. It's a win-win situation, until you tell the family that you've broken up with her."

"Oh, no!" Knox said. "My story is that we are having a long-distance relationship when she goes to El Paso, and I come back home. She's going to do the same."

"Even smarter, but what if you meet someone that you would really like to date?" Tripp asked.

Knox nodded toward the three guys coming toward them with the rest of the wooden eggs. "I'll cross that bridge when the time comes. Maybe that will be when she breaks my heart, and I will need someone to help mend it."

Chapter 8

Lottie figured the preacher's sermon would be on the resurrection since it was Easter Sunday, but Parker opted to speak on loving your neighbor—like Jesus did in his lifetime. According to what he had to say that morning, Jesus's birth, death, and resurrection were important times to remember, but the more vital thing was those years between birth and ascension into heaven. That was where the life lessons were.

That guilty feeling that had draped itself over her shoulders earlier got even heavier when she thought about lying to Bernie. The old gal had been nothing but kind to her and deserved more respect than that. Add in the shame of what they were doing to the rest of the family, and it put another hundred pounds onto the weight.

She hated both the shameful feeling, as well as the attraction that seemed to be growing by the hour to Knox. With Knox's shoulder pressed against hers and sending waves of heat flowing through her body, she battled two wars within her heart. She glanced up at the ceiling and wouldn't have been a bit surprised to see lightning streaking down upon her head.

Man plans. God laughs.

Lottie figured that remembering that old saying was to

teach her what impulsiveness would get her. She should have figured in all the odds when she sat down beside Knox and asked him to be her fake boyfriend. But she hadn't, and now she was in a pickle.

If she was honest with herself, she'd done that on the spur of the moment because she thought he was sexy. Now she was developing feelings for him, and he couldn't feel the same way. If he did, he wouldn't be sitting beside her as cool as a snow cone.

On more than one occasion, her mother had scolded her when she wasn't paying attention. According to her, Lottie had squirrels chasing around in her head. That meant she couldn't grab onto a thought and hold it before she was off chasing another one. Lottie thought she had overcome the inability to control her brain waves. But evidently, she was still chasing a virtual, hyperactive squirrel on a fast-moving merry-go-round that morning, because she couldn't grab one idea or memory before another one pushed it out of the way.

Squirrel number one told her that she should break up with Knox before this ruse went on another week. She turned slightly to look at him, and that thought was pushed out of her mind with the next furry critter who pictured him with water dripping from him when he got out of the shower. Her breath caught in her chest at the visual of him with a towel wrapped so low that she could see all his ripped abs. With great effort, she managed to put that image from her mind, but then he reached over and took her hand in his, and a dose of desire flooded her—right there in the church.

Ivy nudged her on the shoulder and whispered, "Wake up. Service is almost over."

She nodded and focused on the preacher.

"I sure hope that I will be preaching to a crowd this big next week," Parker said. "Now, Endora will lead the hymn, and one more thing, my mother-in-law wants me to remind you about," he said. "The community Easter egg hunt starts at three o'clock this afternoon at the Paradise. Everyone is invited, and there will be a leftover potluck afterward. Bring your half-eaten pies, cakes, and whatever else you've got, and we'll all have a picnic under the shade trees in the backyard. Now if everyone will stand and turn to page one in the hymnals, we'll close with 'Tell Me the Story of Jesus' instead of a benediction. Last verse only," Parker said.

"We should sneak out the side door," Ivy said when they finished singing.

"Oh, no!" Knox shook his head. "I want to introduce Lottie to as many people as possible. She might not be able to put faces and names together, but she will remember how friendly everyone is here in Spanish Fort."

Bernie looped her arm into Lottie's. "Not today. We're all going home instead of chitchatting. We can talk to Parker when he gets to the Paradise."

Lottie glanced over at Knox.

He shrugged and grinned. "What Aunt Bernie says is the law."

"And don't you never forget it." Bernie's tone was sharp, but the smile on her face told a different story.

When they were outside, along with an exodus of the rest of the Paradise family, Bernie leaned over and whispered. "We need to have a long conversation in private this afternoon. So, carve out a few minutes and come find me."

"Yes, ma'am," Lottie agreed.

"You kids don't dilly-dawdle on the way home," Bernie said in a shrill voice. "I'm starving, and Mary Jane won't let Parker say grace until we are all there."

"I bet we beat you," Knox challenged.

"That's your motorcycle mouth making bets that your bicycle butt can't keep. My chariot is here, and you still have to get to your truck." Bernie said as she waved and got into the SUV with Joe Clay and Mary Jane.

Knox laced his fingers with Lottie's, and she giggled.

"What's so funny? Is my hand sweaty?" Knox asked.

"No, but the salty old Bernie who ran a bar would have said that she bets that your *ass* can't keep up, not your butt. What happened to her?"

Knox helped her settle into the seat and then closed the truck door. "It's Sunday. Trust me, any other day of the week she can melt concrete with her cussin'."

Lottie fastened her seat belt and noticed a movement outside the truck window. She whipped around to see a short brunette wrap her arms around Knox's body and hug him tightly. A fireball of real jealousy landed in the middle of Lottie's heart and created a huge blaze.

Remember that this is fake and that you have no right to even a smidgen of envy or resentment. Her mother's voice was clear in her head.

"People can see him, and there will be talk that could sabotage what we have going here," she muttered.

"Sorry about that," Knox said as he slid into the driver's seat and started the engine.

"If we were really in a relationship, I would be pitching a hissy fit."

"Then thank God we are not." He drove away from the parking lot.

She crossed her arms over her chest. "Who was that woman?"

"Geneva Wilcot. She lives between here and Nocona, and I made a verbal deal with her last night to buy some land from her," he answered.

"And she had to hug you?"

Knox turned down the lane leading to the Paradise. "What's that to you?"

"People might have seen and reported to Bernie, who would tell your family, and they would catch us in a lie, and it would be so embarrassing, and…" She stopped long enough to catch her breath.

"What my family thinks or doesn't really isn't an issue. This is our pretend world, and we might have an argument along the way. But to ease your jealous mind…"

"I am not jealous," she declared.

He parked at the end of a long row of vehicles. "Sounds to me like you could be."

She turned toward him and gave him a double dose of stink eye. "Do you want to come home on weekends and go on blind dates? Shall I call Audrey and see if I can borrow the potbellied pig to bring to the café? You've got as much skin in this game as I do."

"Geneva lives in southern Louisiana and is in this area to settle her grandfather's estate," Knox said. "Roman Wilcot owned the land between here and Nocona that I want to buy. I called her yesterday afternoon, and she quoted me a good price if I would buy the whole acreage. She gave me a hug because she thought she would have to sell it off in piecemeal style and maybe have an auction for the house and its contents. Now she can go home to her husband and four kids and not stay in Nocona any longer."

Lottie should have been satisfied with that explanation, but she wasn't. "Why did she come to this church?"

"Because her grandparents attended services here their entire lives. They were both born in Spanish Fort, got married in that church, and their funeral services were held there," he answered, "and she wanted one last memory of the place. Any more questions, or are you still jealous?"

"Why are you buying a big chunk of land?"

"Because it's got a nice little two-bedroom frame house on it, and I'm tired of living in a trailer," he answered as he got out of the truck.

He was right. Knowing his business wasn't any concern of hers, and yet a nosy streak came out to replace the jealousy. "How much land is it?"

"Six hundred and forty acres," he answered.

"Why buy all…that…when…" she stammered.

"Because I can and because I want to and because I have a vision for the future," he answered as he slipped an arm around her shoulders. "I talked to Tripp, and he thinks it's a solid investment, so other than signing papers, it's a done deal. Time to get into character, darlin'. Smile and look at me like you could be falling in love with me."

Pasting on a smile and looking into his eyes wasn't difficult. "What is this vision of yours anyway?" she asked out the corner of her mouth.

"That's classified right now."

═══════════

Eggs, plastic and real, were scattered all over the huge backyard and around the barn, and Knox even hid half a dozen behind the pots of flowers on Bernie's porch. The ones that Daisy and Heather had put glitter on sparkled like diamonds when the bright sun rays hit them. He stopped and took a picture of the freshly mowed yard, now covered with hundreds of eggs waiting to be picked up. The sound of vehicles arriving, along with folks telling their kids to be patient, took his attention away from the sight. Folks who thought if you didn't arrive fifteen minutes early, you were late carried food to the tables that had been set up in the barn. Kids were blurs as they chased around in the part of the yard that wasn't roped off for the egg hunt, or else ran into the barn to check out what they could buy later with their bunny money.

This was Knox's second year as a part of the Easter celebration, and he loved it all. The excitement of the kids made him wish he had a child big enough to carry a basket all over the yard. All the elderly folks sitting in the shade and talking about the good old days brought back memories of visiting his grandparents on Sunday afternoons. He had never heard of a leftover potluck until he came to the Paradise, but he loved the idea. He was so deep in his own thoughts that he didn't hear or see Tripp until his brother was right beside him.

"Don't sneak up on me like that," Knox snapped.

Tripp nudged him with an elbow. "Seems to me like we are switching personalities. You are becoming the introvert that I used to be, and I'm getting more outgoing. What were you thinking about anyway?"

"Grandpa, and how we used to go to their house on Sunday for dinner. We would sit in the backyard with him until Nana called us to come in and wash our hands," he answered.

"I loved those times, but what on earth brought him to your mind?" Tripp asked. "This looks nothing like his house or yard."

Knox smiled and nodded toward a group of old farmers sitting under a shade tree. "No, but that did. Different place. Different time. Not as fancy or as enormous, but people are people whether they are rich or poor."

"You are so right, and it is a beautiful day for this, isn't it?" Tripp said. "Did Geneva find you after church?"

"Yes, she did, and I'm glad you think my idea is a good one," Knox answered. "The lawyers will take care of all the paperwork, but I have the keys to the place, and she said for me to feel free to move in anytime."

"I guess that means you have a real house of your own. You won't even have to stay at the Paradise when you come home for weekends," Tripp said.

"Does that make you happy or sad?" Knox asked.

"A little of both. We won't see as much of you because you'll be busy with your new project, but I'm happy that you will be doing what you love and that you'll be back close to the rest of the family. What did you do wrong?"

"That was an abrupt change of subject. What are you talking about, anyway?"

Tripp pointed.

Knox followed his brother's finger to see Aunt Bernie marching toward them like a soldier on a mission. She held down her big pink hat with fake flowers scattered around the brim with one hand. Her flowing skirt printed with bunnies swished from side to side, and the expression on her face said that she had a bone to pick with someone.

"What makes you think *I'm* in trouble? It could be you!" Knox whispered.

She reached the two grown men before Tripp could answer and popped her free hand on her hip. "I should have put ribbons on my hat so I could tie it down. Tripp, you can go. Willa Rose is having trouble keeping Nicky happy. I think he's teething. I told her to rub some whiskey on his gums, but she won't do it. Knox, you stay put. You and I are going to have a come-to-Jesus talk."

"What'd I do?" Knox muttered.

She dropped her finger and clamped a bony-fingered hand around his upper arm. "Follow me to the front porch. Everyone is congregating in the backyard, so that's a private place right now, and this is between us."

"Can we do it later?" he asked. "The hunt starts soon, and Lottie has already spread a quilt out on the ground for us to watch the kids."

She clamped a hand on his arm and pulled him along like a puppy on a leash. He felt like a petulant child who had disobeyed his grandmother and was about to get a good, solid tongue-lashing or maybe even a switching.

They hadn't taken two steps when the wind blew her hat off her head. It twirled around in the wind like a kite and finally landed beside the huge, wooden Easter basket. Knox tried to break free from her grasp, but she held on like she was a hound dog and he was a big, old soup bone.

"Aunt Bernie, I will come back. I'm just going to go get your hat before the kids all trample it flat," he said.

"It looks good layin' there, and I'm tired of fighting with it. If it gets ruined, I'll make another one next year," she declared. "We are going to have a visit right now, this minute."

"Where is that gorgeous hat you wore to church this

morning?" June Mason said as she passed them with a casserole dish in her hands.

"It's part of the decorations," Bernie answered in a saccharine tone. "But thank you for the compliment."

Knox got a whiff of sauerkraut and hoped he still had an appetite when Bernie got through fussing at him. June hurried on out to the barn, and Bernie kept dragging him toward the porch. "Was she serious about that hat?"

"No, she was not!" Bernie growled. "She told Bertha Langford that it was hideous. Bertha told Minnie Tolbert, and she whispered it to me. Don't you touch that sauerkraut she brought. Minnie says that she lets her six cats sit on the kitchen counter while she cooks. There's probably enough cat hair in that dish to choke you. And don't get me talking about Bertha's food. She always has the spring sniffles."

"Is that what you wanted to tell me?" he asked when they were on the porch.

She let go of his arm, and he sat down in a rocking chair. "Do you want me to clear off a bigger space for you to throw your hissy fit?"

She plopped down on the rocking chair right next to him and set it in motion with her foot. She smoothed back her red hair and then stared right into his eyes. "I want to know the real truth about you and Lottie. I think this is all just a show, and you are going to tell me what is going on between you two. If you aren't really dating, then why are you pretending?"

Knox laid a hand over his heart and sighed dramatically.

"Aunt Bernie! Why would you say that? If I failed in some way in my job of being a good boyfriend, then please tell me what I did wrong."

"You are trying too hard for a relationship to be so new. I can feel a touch of chemistry from her, but not so much from you. I was friends with her kinfolks for years before you ever came into the picture. If you are just using her for sex, I want you to break it off before you shatter her heart."

"I am not using her for sex." Knox's voice shot up several octaves with each word.

"Well, that much is a good thing, but I can smell a rat two miles away. And something ain't right between y'all. I'm tellin' you right now, she is a good person and comes from good people. You don't mess around with folks like that. Sweet Jesus!" She slapped her thigh. "You are using her so I won't fix you up on blind dates, aren't you?"

Knox was so stunned that he couldn't speak.

"If that's the case, you will tell her on the way back to the construction site, or else I'll call her tonight, and she'll know the truth before I hang up. I would wager that her uncle will fire your sorry ass for toying with her like this."

Knox finally found his voice. "I'm hurt that you would think that."

Bernie shook her head. "You either break up with her, or I'll tell her what you told Tripp about getting a fake girlfriend."

"How did… Why… I was only joking," he finally spit out.

"Nothing escapes me, and I won't have you messing with my matchmaking record in this family," she said.

"I've heard the stories about that, how you forbid Tertia to see Noah, and look where they are right now," he argued.

"I did, but I could see the vibes between both of them and used a little reverse psychology in that situation," she declared.

"Are you doing the same thing now?" Knox asked.

She sucked in a lungful of air, let it out in a whoosh, and narrowed her eyes until they were barely slits. "I am not. Y'all work together every day, and if this *is* real, then you spend time together at night. You have too much in common. You…"

"I give you Noah and Tertia, who work together every day in the café," Knox butted in. "I give you Ophelia and Jake, who are side by side in the winery. I give you…"

She slapped him on the knee. "Hush. Those were different cases. You and Lottie are working too hard, like bad actors on the stage, trying to make the audience believe that y'all are a couple. There's some vibes from her, but I don't feel a thing from you and mighty little from her."

He threw his hands over his eyes. "That's downright mean, calling me a bad actor when I'm just trying to impress my girlfriend."

"Hey, I lost you," Lottie called out as she walked up on the porch. "It's only ten minutes until kickoff time, and everyone is rounding up the kids to line them up. This is so exciting, Knox."

Knox could have kissed her for interrupting the conversation. He stood up and laid a hand on Bernie's shoulder. "Don't worry about me. Lottie and I know what we're doing."

"I'm not done with you," Bernie growled under her breath.

He stood up and took Lottie's hand in his. "We'll pick it up in a few weeks when we come back home and I move into my own house."

"I heard that you bought the place from Geneva. I'm glad you are settling down for good. I've been afraid you'd take that travel trailer of yours and leave. That would break up the family, and I won't have it." She shook her finger at him. "And be aware, I will be sitting on your front porch when you arrive, and we will finish this," she said. "Lottie, after the egg hunt, I want a few alone minutes with you."

Lottie waved over her shoulder. "Just come find me."

"Oh, I will," Bernie said. "But right now I'm going in the house and pouring me up a double shot of whiskey. If I have to deal with that self-righteous, nosy June this afternoon, I need some reinforcement."

The noisy crowd out back covered up the sound of the wooden screen door when it slammed. Otherwise, the kids might have thought it was the signal to run through the ribbon roping off the yard.

"What was that all about?" Lottie asked. "Bernie looks like she could chew up two-by-fours and spit out toothpicks."

"More like railroad spikes and spit out staples." Knox chuckled. "She doesn't want us to be together. She says there's no sparkle in my eyes. Have I told you today that you look beautiful?"

Lottie flipped the butterfly sleeve of her floral dress back down and shoved a strand of blond hair back into a bun at the nape of her neck. "Is that a real compliment or a fake one?"

"It's genuine," he answered. "Even if you aren't truly my girlfriend, I know beauty when I see it, and I definitely see it right now."

She led him toward the quilt and pulled him down beside her. "Then thank you. And for the record, you clean up right well too. On another note, I intend to avoid Bernie all afternoon because I can't lie to her."

"I didn't lie, but thank you for rescuing me."

"You owe me one, and I'm collecting right now. If you see Aunt Bernie coming my way, you will run interference for me, right?" she asked.

"You got it, darlin'," he said with a nod.

"Everyone, be very quiet," Joe Clay's big, booming voice filled the whole two-acre backyard. "If you are talking or noisy, you won't hear the gun go off to start the race."

Silence filled the air. Not even Rae and Gunner's daughters, Daisy and Heather, said a word, and that was a miracle.

"Okay, listen carefully," Joe Clay said.

"Does he really shoot off a gun?" Lottie asked.

"No, just a couple of firecrackers, but the kids don't know," Knox answered.

The children fidgeted, but they didn't make a sound

until the crack of firecrackers filled the air. Then the whoops and the hollers of almost a hundred kids rushing out to fill their baskets with eggs echoed off the trees.

"This has been an awesome weekend, even if it's not a real romance." Lottie leaned close to Knox and whispered for his ears only. "But can we sneak out when it's over so I don't have to deal with Bernie?"

Knox drew her closer to his side and nodded. "I had my heart set on a plate of sauerkraut and hot dogs, but I can leave it behind if it means either of us have to face off with Bernie, so yes, we can leave a little early."

"Great," Lottie said. "I'll make us some grilled cheese sandwiches when we get home."

"No need for that. We can stop at a little burger shop in Wichita Falls that I love to visit and have hot dogs for supper and then get a snow cone at another place for dessert."

"Do they have Reuben dogs?"

"Yep," he answered.

"How soon can we leave?"

"My things are all packed," he told her. "We've already taken pictures by the big bunny."

"When we break up, will Mary Jane throw the one of me and you away?" she asked.

"I doubt it. She keeps all photos forever and ever."

Chapter 9

Knox made a hard right turn and stopped the truck at a locked gate. Beyond it was a cattle guard and pastureland. Roman Wilcot must have deliberately left a few trees here, there, and yonder to provide shade for his cattle during the hot summer months. Knox didn't intend to cut down a single one of them when he started his project. He shaded his eyes with the back of his hand and could see sunlight reflecting off a gray metal roof of either a barn or a house.

"Are you in a hurry to get back to the lake? I would like to take a better look at this place," Knox said.

"Not at all, but I was more than happy to leave so I wouldn't have to talk to Bernie," Lottie answered. "Haven't you at least walked over it or taken a look at the house?"

"Nope, but Tripp did, and I trust his judgment," he answered.

"Do you have a key for that lock? The sign on the fence plainly says No Trespassing."

He pulled a ring holding two keys from his shirt pocket and dangled them in front of her. "The place isn't officially mine until we sign all the paperwork, but we shook hands on the deal, and that's binding."

"Uncle Jack taught me that the passenger has to open the gate and then close it when the driver goes through. I can't see that house from here, but I'm in no mood to ruin my best high-heeled shoes in that gravel, so you better wait on me when you drive across the cattle guard."

He reached across the console and took the keys back. "You could ruin those shoes just going to the gate. I'll get the gate while you change into your tennis shoes. They are in the back floorboard. The house has been sitting empty for six months, so the yard is probably a mess."

She removed her shoes and tossed them over her shoulder. She was tying her last shoe when he slid behind the steering wheel.

"No sense in closing it until we leave," he said. "Roman sold all his cattle to Remy when he got too sick to take care of them."

Could Aunt Bernie be right about Lottie being attracted to him even in a small way? He wondered as he swung the gate open. He shook his head at the very idea.

If Lottie had been interested in him, she would have flirted rather than bluntly asking him to be her boyfriend. This was nothing more than a business deal. He came to the end of the lane to find a white picket fence around the ranch-style house with a wide front porch. Rosebushes were leafing out and needed a good pruning. A brisk wind blew dried leaves from the pecan trees surrounding the house across the porch. Two rocking chairs with chipped white paint sat on either side of a small table with round stains in the middle—probably where coffee cups had been set while Roman and Eula Faye watched the sunrise each morning.

"That's kind of spooky," Lottie whispered.

"Why? Because it's empty?" Knox asked.

"No, because those rocking chairs are moving back and forth like someone is sitting in them," she answered.

"Maybe it's Roman and Eula Faye welcoming us," he said.

"Well, if that's the case, let's go tell them hello," she said and got out of the truck. She was halfway to the porch when he caught up to her and tucked her hand into his.

She pulled her hand free. "We don't have to convince anyone we're together out here in the boonies."

He unlocked the door and stood to one side. "Got to keep up with things or we might forget when we are around folks."

"You sure you don't want to go in first?" Lottie asked. "After all, this is *your* new home."

"Ladies first," Knox answered. "I want to see your first impression."

Lottie stepped into the house and took a deep breath.

"Does that mean you think I should raze it and build a new one?" he asked.

"Absolutely not. This is like stepping back in time to my grandparents' house. They lived on a farm, and I spent a few weeks with them every summer. Daddy moved around a lot back then with his job, so their place was my stability. I still miss them even though they passed away more than ten years ago."

He took in the living room with a sweeping glance. Spots on the walls showed where the blue paint had been brighter originally. Geneva must have taken the family pictures that had hung there back to southern Louisiana with her. An old trunk served as a coffee table, with a blue and burgundy floral sofa and matching wing-back chairs, one on either side of it.

"Does that mean you wouldn't throw out this furniture and start all over?"

"Not a single piece. It's not very masculine, but that big old burgundy leather recliner would fit your frame really well. Does all this stuff come with the house?"

"Geneva told me that she had already removed what she wanted, and the house went with the property just as it is." Knox wandered into the kitchen. Cast-iron skillets hung from hooks below shelves that held pots and pans. He didn't remember Eula Faye being very tall, so that meant there would be a stepladder hiding somewhere. The stove and refrigerator were green and matched the ivy on the wallpaper. Salt and pepper shakers sat next to a sugar bowl in the middle of a yellow chrome table with four matching chairs around it.

"What's the first thing you will change?" Lottie asked.

"Nothing for a while, other than maybe painting the walls to cover up those spots where pictures used to hang," Knox answered. "What would you make different if you had just bought this place?"

"I took a quick peek into the rooms down the hallway,

and I would put a king bed in the master bedroom, but that's about it," she answered.

Knox walked through the rest of the house and then headed back to the living room. "It will be easy to add onto the existing place by using that bedroom on the end as an office and turning the window into a doorway to a new master bedroom, a walk-in closet, and a second bathroom."

"Why would just one person need that much more room?" she asked.

"For now, the place is totally livable, and it's peaceful set back here in the woods. But the closets are small, like they were when the house was originally built. And I would want a room big enough that a king-sized bed would not take up all the floor space. I also would like a private bathroom."

"Good solid reasons," she said with a nod.

"Would you have bought it?" he asked.

"Maybe not before I even looked at it, but after being in here a few minutes, I would have written a check in a heartbeat. But to buy more than six hundred acres would take a lot more than I have in the bank," she answered.

"So, if we were a real couple, you would move into this house with me when we finish the project we are working on?"

"Maybe. I really like the place and the location, but we are not a real couple," she answered.

At the burger shop, Lottie wadded up the red-and-white-checkered papers that lined the plastic containers with their hot dogs and fries in them and tossed the two balls into the nearby trash can. "Thank you for supper and, again, for leaving early with me. And FYI, I do not intend to go with you every weekend."

"We promised Bo we would help with the senior thing in two weeks," Knox reminded her.

She groaned. "I don't make promises I won't keep, so we'll drive up in two vehicles that day. I'll come home after the event is over, and you can stay as long as you want. Besides, since I don't leave very often, I usually stay on the site to prevent any vandalism."

"You do remember that Aunt Bernie will be at the bar that day," he reminded her.

"I can avoid her for a couple of hours, but not a whole weekend," she told him.

"Well, well, well!" a familiar voice said. "Is this the new boyfriend that Thomas told me about?"

"Damn it!" She swore under her breath.

"Yes, it is," she answered. "Micah, meet Knox. Knox, Micah, who is Thomas's brother. What are you doing here? The next crew isn't supposed to be here until Wednesday evening."

Micah extended a hand toward Knox. "We finished up early, and Jack said he could use an extra hand if I wanted to help finish framing the first house."

Knox shook with him and then draped an arm around Lottie's shoulders. "We can always use an extra set of hands. Did you bring a trailer?"

"Nope," Micah answered, but his eyes lingered on Lottie.

"He usually bunks in with Thomas," she explained.

"I'll be going. See y'all in the morning bright and early," Micah said.

"We're about to get snow cones. You are welcome to join us. My treat," Knox said.

"I never turn down beer, food, or snow cones," Micah said with a bright smile. "Eddie told me that it's your turn to cook for us one day this week, Lottie."

"Yep, and I hope you all like soup and sandwiches." Never in her life had she wanted to strangle someone as much as she did Knox right at that moment. Micah was an incurable flirt, and there was no telling what he might say or do. She didn't want Knox to flare up in mock anger and cause a scene that would get him fired.

"If you'll stir it with your finger, it will be amazing," Micah teased.

Knox brought her hand to his lips and kissed the knuckles. "I keep telling her that, but she argues with me. Now, each of you name your poison and decide if you want a small, medium, or large snow cone."

"A small piña colada," Lottie said.

"Medium with cherry on one side and banana on the other," Micah answered and slid a sly wink toward Lottie.

"Y'all don't have to stand in line," Knox said. "I'll take care of our orders and bring them over to one of those picnic tables."

Lottie shrugged his arm away from her shoulders and

walked away. Forget strangling Knox. With a glancing look, she imagined him graveyard dead and his body sinking into the lake for the fishes to nibble on for supper that night.

"Thank you," Micah said and walked beside Lottie to one of the wooden tables.

Micah was a handsome guy with light-brown eyes that always seemed to twinkle. Some women would even consider him sexy with all those ripped abs stretching the knit of his shirt. But his eyes said he was a player who enjoyed the chase. Once he caught his prey and spent a night or two with her, he was finished and off on the next hunt. She had thought at one time she might be wrong about him, but he did not kiss and not tell.

Micah sat down before she did and asked, "How long have you two been dating?"

"How many women have you slept with since I saw you last?" She fired back as she slung a long leg over the bench on the other side of the table, being careful not to let her knees touch his.

"Darlin', when I'm with a woman, we do not waste time sleeping, which you would know if you would stop breaking my heart," he answered.

"No, thank you. I will not be a notch on your bedpost," she assured him.

"When you get tired of Blondie, you come find me, and I'll show you how a real man treats a woman," Micah said and lowered his voice. "And I will even throw my knife out the door of the trailer."

"I'll pick it up on the way in, and…"

Micah threw up both palms and went pale. "Whoa! Don't even go there."

"Then stop flirting with me. I'm with Knox, and I like where we are going. Speaking of which, here he comes."

"We really do have a lot in common. We both like black olive and mushroom pizza, Reuben dogs with kraut, relish, and mustard, and I see you like piña colada snow cones, too," she said to Knox.

He set all the cups in the middle of the table and sat down beside Lottie. "Folks say that people who are alike shouldn't be together."

Lottie reached for one of the piña colada snow cones and took a bite. "This is wonderful, and those people who say that are wrong." She could attest to the fact that being different did not mean a successful relationship. She and the last three guys she'd had a relationship with were polar opposites from her in every way. And every one of them was worth more cuss words than tears when everything went south.

"I agree." Micah picked up his snow cone and stood up. "I'm going to take this to go. I want to get on down to the site and get the lay of the land. Thank you, Knox. Next time, I'll treat us all."

"I'll remember that, and you are welcome," Knox said.

"You are in big trouble," Lottie hissed as soon as Micah was gone.

"Can we have makeup sex after the fight?" he teased.

"I don't sleep with dead men," she snapped back at him and took a big bite of her snow cone.

"Why are you so mad at me?" Knox asked in his best innocent voice.

"You left me alone with Micah." Lottie grabbed her head. "Brain freeze!"

"That's what you get for punishing me when all I did was let you have some time with an old friend to catch up," he said.

"Men!" she finally got out past her frozen throat.

Knox chuckled and went on. "What does that mean?"

"You did that to prove to him that you're not worried about him moving in on me. I'm no man's territory, so you don't have to do that," she answered. "Let's eat these on the way back to the lake. I'm ready to see Prissy."

"Got to disagree with you. I can't drive and eat this at the same time."

"Messy eater sure takes away from your sexy persona," she told him.

"I'd like to see you eat something with a spoon and drive at the same time," he shot back at her.

Bantering was first on the list when it came to all the things that she liked about Knox Callahan. She'd never dated a guy in reality who was so exciting, and it was all because he listened to her and always came back with a smart-ass answer.

"This is not about me." She giggled. "It's about you having a fault."

"If you think I'm perfect, then you are the only person in the whole big state of Texas who does," he said.

"Yeah, right," she countered.

He wiggled his eyebrows and grinned. "Are we fighting? If so, do we get to make out when we come to an understanding?"

"Only in your dreams," she told him.

Knox reached across the table and laid a hand on hers. "Will you be my for-real friend? I like spending time with you."

She was shocked speechless. Was he serious? Was he kidding? Did she even want to be friends with him when, down deep inside her heart, she might want more? Questions upon questions with no answers came floating down from the big, fluffy white clouds in the sky.

"Well?" he finally asked.

"I don't know where the teasing and banter stops and realism begins," she answered. "Are you joking?"

"No, ma'am, I know all this romance is fake, but I really do like you. Even though we can't be anything more, I would love it if we were friends," he replied.

"Okay then, we can give it a try for the next five weeks at least. Then you'll go home to your new house and land, and I'll go out to El Paso. We'll text a few times and then forget all about each other."

Knox spread his arms out. "You can forget something this sexy?"

Lottie finished the last bite of her snow cone, stood up, and struck a pose. "Can you forget this?"

"Nope," Knox answered. "You will haunt my dreams forever."

Lottie had trouble keeping the giggle at bay. "That's the worst pickup line I've ever heard."

Knox took the empty cups to a nearby trash can. "How many have you heard? If it's only five, then it's not so bad. But if it's a thousand, then maybe I better work on my game."

"More than ten, less than five hundred, so you *should* work on your game."

"All kidding aside, are you going to be my friend?"

"I said I would, and it seems like the least I can do since you agreed to be my boyfriend for the next few weeks," she answered and headed across the parking lot. "Are we ready to go home now? Prissy really is probably missing me."

Knox followed beside her. "That was an abrupt change of subject."

She opened the truck door before he could even reach for it. "Did you have something else to say about us being friends?"

He walked around the back of the truck and got into the driver's seat. "Not really, and to answer your question, I'm ready to go home too. This has been a busy weekend. Do friends cuddle up together for a nice nap?"

"Not friends who've only known each other a little while," she answered. "Besides, Prissy gets downright hateful if…" She let the sentence hang.

"If someone puts their head on the pillow beside yours?" he asked and backed the vehicle out of the parking space.

"Something like that, but for your information, no one has ever laid their head on the pillow beside mine, not in my trailer." A memory of the last failed relationship flashed through her mind. Prissy never did like that guy or any of the others that she brought home to meet her—not until Knox.

Wasn't it just the berries that the one man Lottie felt comfortable with was just a friend?

———

The idea that Bernie planted in his mind about Lottie being attracted to him plagued Knox all the way from Wichita Falls to the building site. He unloaded her things and then drove past a couple of other trailers, parked in the right spot, and was rounding the front of the truck when he heard a strange mewing sound coming from under his trailer. For a minute, he figured Prissy had gotten out of Lottie's place. He left his things in the back seat and hurried toward the door, only to find a banty rooster sitting on the edge of the porch.

"You did not make that sound," Knox said. "That was a cat, and the only one I know that lives in this area is Prissy. You're lucky she hasn't chased you down and eaten you for supper."

The brightly colored rooster flew up, lit on his shoulder, and threw back his head to crow. When he finally stopped, a small kitten came out from under the porch and wove around Knox's legs. The chicken spread his wings and dropped down to rub his neck on the cat's head.

Knox sat down on the top step and picked up the kitten. "Looks like you two know each other. Where did y'all come from anyway? Did someone throw you out?"

The black-and-white kitten looked up at him and meowed. Then the rooster hopped up on Knox's knee and tucked his head under his wing.

"I guess if Tripp can have a potbellied pig, I can have a rooster and a cat," he whispered. "I have a house and a lot of land, so you'll have a nice place to live. But until then, this trailer is it."

Lottie came around the corner and stopped in her tracks when she saw Knox. "What is going on here. I thought I heard a rooster, and…"

"And you did." Knox finished the sentence for her. "If he hadn't been so happy to see a human being, you might have heard a meow with the crowing. Seems like they are friends, and they're adopting me. In this case, opposites definitely do attract."

She took another step and reached down to pet the kitten. "Are you serious about keeping them?"

"Only if you don't want them," he answered.

"No, thank you. Prissy would eat the bird and pout for a month if I brought another cat into the house. Besides, you've got a house and lots of land. They'll only have to live in and around this place a few weeks."

"Some friend you are," Knox said.

"I will share some kitty litter with you and some food for the cat. The bird can eat dry cat food until you can get to the store and buy chicken feed. That should take care of them for a little while. And that"—she straightened up—"makes me an excellent friend."

"Yes, ma'am, it does," he said. "Will you go with me tomorrow evening and help me buy whatever I need?"

"I was on my way back into town to the store for a few things. I can either pick up what you need for you, or you can go with me, but I'm driving. I've got an empty boot box you can use for a little bit of litter whether you go or not."

Knox's male pride almost got the best of him, but he was out of milk, bread, and sandwich meat, so he nodded. "I appreciate the help, and yes, I would like to go with you."

Chapter 10

Knox researched information on both kittens and small roosters while Lottie drove the fifteen minutes to the Walmart store. "I'm sorry I was such bad company on the way up here, but I really wanted to find out what to feed a kitten and a rooster," he said as he slipped his phone into his pocket.

"And here I thought you thought I was such a bad driver that you didn't want to look at the road."

"Nope, not at all," he assured her with a bright smile.

She swung open the door and got out of her truck. "I bet that hurt you to say."

His feet were on the ground before she rounded the back side of the vehicle. "You'll never know how much. Now I know how Tripp felt when Pansy the pig landed on his farm, and he had no idea what to feed her or how to take care of her. How old was Prissy when you got her?"

"I didn't get her. She got me. Like the way your two new critters got you. I was on my way to my first framing job after college and pulled my new trailer into a Walmart parking lot. A car drove up beside my truck, and a hand came out the back window and dropped Prissy right out on the hot concrete. She ran up to me and climbed up the leg of my jeans. The pitiful little fur ball was so skinny I could feel every bone in her little body. I put her in the trailer and then went to the store. I asked a clerk to help me buy the essentials and point me to the nearest vet. We've been together ever since."

The automatic doors to the store opened, and they went inside together. "Welcome to Walmart. Need a cart?" The greeter—an older gentleman with gray hair, wrinkles, and twinkling blue eyes—asked the moment they passed through the second set of doors.

"Yes, please," Lottie answered.

Eldon—according to the name tag pinned to his orange vest—pulled one from the long line, swiped a disinfectant wipe across the handle, and gave it to her. Then he turned to Knox and asked the same question.

"Yes, sir, Eldon, and thank you. Have you been working here long?"

"Ever since I retired from being a lawyer four years ago. This is the best job I ever had," Eldon answered. "My advice to anyone is to only work until you can hang up your hat, then do something that requires nothing but smiling at folks."

"I'll keep that in mind," Knox said and hurried to catch up with Lottie.

"What took you so long?" she asked.

"I was getting some life hints from the greeter," he answered.

"Did you learn something good?"

"Yep, I did, but I have to wait more than thirty years to use it."

She headed toward the deli part of the store. "By then, whatever he told you will probably be obsolete. Are you stalking me or just going to the same place I am?"

"A boyfriend does not stalk his girlfriend," Knox smarted off. "And a smile is never obsolete, darlin'."

She fell in line behind two other people at the deli, and he parked his cart right behind her. "I still can't believe that you didn't think twice about keeping that kitten and rooster," she said.

"They chose me, kind of like Prissy did you. They could have gone to any one of the six trailers on-site, but they came to mine. Must be a sign in that somewhere. And besides all that, I'll be moving into my house with plenty of land after we finish this job for Jack, and the critters will be someone for me to talk to."

"With all your family living around you, I don't imagine you'll be lonely," Lottie said.

Knox thought he saw a glimmer of something in her expression, but it could have just been a figment of his imagination, fueled by what Bernie had said about Lottie being slightly interested in him.

If she was right, then damn it! I might have messed up what could have been a good thing.

"When we get through here, would you help me find the cat food?" he asked.

She moved her cart up a space. "Sure. You'll need kitten food, but don't buy a lot, because he or she will grow fast, and you don't want to waste it. But then again, you could feed it to the rooster if there's any left."

"Chickens eat cat food?"

"Birds will eat anything, including eggshells, which are surprisingly good for them. But mostly they need balanced feed if you expect to keep them healthy," she answered.

Knox eyed her carefully. "I didn't read a thing about that when I was researching banty roosters. Are you serious or messing with me?"

"My grandparents lived on a small farm," she answered. "I spent a few weeks every summer with them. They had chickens and pigs and even a milk cow. I fed the livestock and tended the garden with Grandpa and snapped green beans and canned the produce with Granny."

"But she didn't teach you to cook?" Knox asked.

She moved up in line, whipped out a list from her purse, and told the lady behind the counter what she wanted. While the woman worked on her order, she turned back to Knox. "She taught me how to make soup and sandwiches. You can tell by looking at me that I've never gone hungry."

His eyes started at her toes and slowly moved upward until he reached her eyes.

"Want me to turn around so you can check out my backside, too?" she snapped.

"Nope, I was just thinking that you should come up with a food plan for all the women in the world." He slid a sly wink her way. "Your tagline could be: Eat soup, sandwiches, and dessert, work hard all day long, and you will look great."

She put her order into the cart. "Is that a compliment?"

Knox moved to place his order. "Depends on how you take it."

"Then thank you," she said. "I'll see you when you finish."

While the lady filled his order, he watched Lottie walk away, and something stirred down deep in his heart. Not that a little flutter in his chest would do him a bit of good. The idea of something between them at this point had been ruined by a fake relationship.

===

"Are you really going to keep those animals? If so, what are you going to name them?" Lottie asked on the way home from the store. She needed to make conversation about anything or everything to ease the lingering jitters still in her body from when he scanned her from toes to eyebrows.

"If no one claims them, I am," he answered. "I hadn't even thought of giving them names, but I guess I should."

"I used to name all the chickens, the calves, and the piglets. I was almost grown before Grandpa told me that I was eating Porky for breakfast. Broke my heart," she told him.

"That rooster is way too pretty to make chicken and dumplings out of him, but then again, his feathers might look real sharp stuck in the band of my cowboy hat."

"No!" Lottie raised her voice. "He's a pet, not dinner."

"Okay, then," Knox said. "Does that mean you don't want me to skin the cat when it gets grown and make a pair of gloves out of its hide?"

"You are evil—downright wicked for even teasing me about hurting a cat." Her voice got higher with each word.

Knox chuckled and laid a hand on her shoulder. "I have a confession to make, but it's classified, so you can't ever tell anyone. I cried when a opossum had been run over in front of our house, and I was fifteen years old. I could never hurt an animal. I even swerve to keep from hitting anything on the road. Truth is, I have always wanted a dog or a cat, but until now, I didn't have a permanent home."

"That can be our secret," she whispered. "But you do need to start thinking about names."

He covered a yawn with his hand. "I'll just call them Kitten and Rooster, or Kitty and Roo for short. I don't imagine anyone who threw them away like trash wouldn't have bothered to name them."

"Maybe 'Damn It' for the kitten for getting under their feet too many times, and 'Hush' for the rooster," she said with a yawn and wished that it wasn't too late in the day to grab a half-hour power nap.

"Yep, but I figure they'll like Kitty and Roo better."

"What makes you think that?" Lottie asked.

"They told me so," he said as nonchalantly as if he was discussing the weather.

"So, you talk chicken and cat now?"

"Of course," he answered with a glint in his blue eyes. "I said, 'Where did you come from, kitty cat?' and it came right to me. I asked the rooster what he was doing on my porch, and he flew over and lit on my knee."

Lottie tried to bite back a chuckle, but it didn't work. "'Kitty' is going to be a terrible name for a boy kitten."

"You are right," Knox agreed. "The kitten's name will be 'Ballou,' or maybe 'Bally' for short."

"Why? And do you mean 'ballet'?"

"No, but it does kind of sound like that. I'm naming her after that old movie, *Cat Ballou*. My grandparents went to the movies on their first date and saw it. Granny found it on DVD and bought it for Grandpa's birthday. It's slapstick funny, but I loved the way they laughed every time we all watched it together. They passed away within three days of each other, and I inherited the movie. We'll have to watch it sometime," he said.

"But isn't Cat Ballou a girl? What if it's a tomcat? Can't you just see him out there flirting with a female and having to tell her his name is Bally?"

"She's too pretty to be a boy cat."

"All kittens, male or female, are cute," Lottie argued. "You may have to change its name if it's a boy. What about the bird?"

Knox said. "When I was a kid, my grandparents took us boys to an amusement park. There was a shop there called Cheeto's. I loved the ice cream they served, and they had this huge rooster on their sign with a triple dip of ice cream in his hand. So, his name is Cheeto," he declared.

Lottie turned into the gravel road leading to the site and parked beside his trailer. "Those seem like proper names. Need some help carrying in all your stuff?"

He handed Lottie his keys. "I can get it, but I might need you to corral Bally for me. Be careful. With all that long hair, I can't tell if she's got fleas or not, and I wouldn't want you to take home any to give to Prissy. As a precaution, I bought special shampoo to give her a bath tonight."

"You should also take her to the vet for her shots. Anyone who would dump her out like this probably did not take proper care of her," Lottie suggested as she picked up the chicken feed and headed toward the trailer.

He looped several of the plastic bag handles over his arm and followed her. "I'll do some research and see if there is one close by that stays open late. Would you go with me? I have no idea what kind of questions to ask."

Lottie opened the door and scooped up the kitten when it tried to run outside. "Sure, and you can even borrow my cat carrier. Just tell me when and where. I might even let you drive while I console poor little Cat, who is going to hate being cooped up."

"*Let* me drive!" Knox growled.

"Don't get all macho on me," Lottie warned him.

The rooster flew into the house while the door was open and lit on the edge of the sink. He leaned over and drank from a coffee cup full of water that Knox had left there on Friday.

Knox dropped all the bags on the floor, grabbed the cup

and dumped it, then refilled it with clean water. "Try that, buddy. It will taste a lot better."

"A chicken will drink out of a mud puddle," Lottie told him.

Knox picked up the bags and set them on the table. "Maybe he did in the old life he had before he got thrown in my direction. In this new life, he gets clean water."

Lottie turned the kitten over and checked it out, then handed her off to Knox. "Congratulations. You have a baby girl. Just don't bring her or Cheeto to my trailer. Prissy will eat the bird, feathers, and all, and try to murder the kitten. She's very jealous. Once, when a Dalmatian came around the site, she jumped on his back and sent him howling. We never saw him again."

She wondered if that meant if their pets didn't get along, then there could be no hope for anything other than a fake relationship.

Chapter 11

"Aha! Lottie is finally having the walk of shame?" Micah called out from a lawn chair at the corner of Thomas's trailer the next morning.

Lottie slowed her stride. "No shame, just a walk."

"Is this thing with Knox serious or just a passing fling?" Micah asked.

"Could be either." She passed by him. "This morning it was omelets, hash browns, biscuits, and sausage gravy."

"Must've been a great night for you to make breakfast for him," Micah said.

She kept walking and glanced over her shoulder. "It was, and he cooked. I didn't."

"Are you going to be my partner at the building site?"

She stopped and turned around. "Nope. I'm paired up with Knox. You can work with Eddie, Thomas, or Gabe until the rest of your crew gets here."

"Don't you know that working with someone every single day sours a relationship?" Micah asked.

"We're the exception."

"I'll be waiting in the wings to dry your tears when it all falls apart."

"Don't hold your breath," she shot back and waved over her shoulder as she went on to her trailer.

Prissy jumped off the bed and slowly made her way across the floor. Lottie picked her up and buried her face in the cat's long hair. "I know you can smell Knox's new kitty on my hands, but you have nothing to worry about. You'll always be number one in my books."

Prissy wiggled free of her arms and went back to the bed, where she washed herself thoroughly and curled up on Lottie's pillow.

"Some friend you are," Lottie said as she fixed her lunch—a sandwich, bag of chips, an apple, and two over-sized chocolate chip cookies. "What if I wanted to tell you all about the breakfast Knox made for me or, even more, how we are friends now?"

The cat raised her head and moved to the end of the bed.

"Oh, now I have your attention when it's time for me to leave for work," Lottie said. "Now you'll have to wait until this evening to hear the rest of the story, but I will tell you this. Micah is relentless, and he's already trying to work an angle that will cause a breakup between me and Knox. See you later."

Prissy let out one of those long, pitiful meows when Lottie closed the door and left her alone. Lottie almost went back inside to console her, but Knox came around the side of her trailer and smiled at her.

"You ready to start building the inside walls of Jack's retirement home?"

"I am," she answered and slipped her hand in his free one. "We've got three days to finish our part of this cabin, and then we move on to number two."

"I got the feeling you aren't wild about working with Micah. Will you be glad to get back to our original five team members on Thursday?" he asked.

"More than words can say." She sighed.

By the end of the day on Monday, Knox wished that Micah would hush for a few minutes. That man could talk the devil out of his pitchfork or a dead man into buying a new coffin.

"What are you thinking about?" Lottie asked when she caught up to him at quitting time.

"Peace and quiet," Knox whispered. "Does Micah always talk so much?"

"Yep," Lottie answered. "He's a hard worker, but when I have to work with him, my ears hurt by the time the day ends. And tonight we have pizza in the rec hall since the next crew has arrived."

"That's every Wednesday night?" Knox groaned.

"Yep, right up until we finish the last house, and then you have to provide supper for everyone," she reminded him.

"Do we have to stay very long? Can we slip away and take a walk to the lake?" Knox asked.

"As long as we just watch the sunset, and you don't say a word," Lottie whispered. "My brain has listened to so many stories the past three days that it is as tired as my body. I'm glad that I'm not going anywhere this weekend."

"Me too," Knox said.

"Oh, really? You aren't going home?"

"Nope. I need a weekend to do nothing, and besides, who's going to take care of my new livestock if I'm gone from Friday to Monday morning?"

"Anytime you want or… Whoa!" She slapped her forehead with her hand. "We promised that we'd help Bo at the bar."

"That's not this weekend, but the next one. I figure we can drive up there a couple of hours before time for Aunt Bernie's event and come home when it's over," Knox suggested. "The animals can survive a few hours without us."

Lottie stopped at her trailer. "That will give Uncle Jack two weekends away. I'm sure Aunt Mandy would love to have him at home to help her with the packing."

"What are you going to do now?" Knox asked but didn't wait for her answer. "I'm going to get my things and take a quick shower. Want to join me to prove to the next group that we really are a couple?"

"I'll be there in five minutes," she agreed with a nod.

Four new guys were in the rec hall when Knox arrived with his small duffel bag in his hand. Eddie made introductions, and Knox shook hands with each of them before he went on to the bathroom. He had soaped up his whole body and was in the process of shampooing his hair when he heard the door open.

"I thought you'd be finished by now," Lottie said.

"It takes a while to wash away all of Micah's words." He chuckled. "I'll be out in a couple of minutes."

She giggled loud enough that he heard it over the hard water spraying down on him. "That should convince the new guys that we are having fun in here," he mumbled.

As usual, when he stepped outside with a towel wrapped around his waist, she had undressed and had her towel tucked around her body. And like always, he wished he could unwrap the package and see what was hidden underneath. But *just friends* didn't do that.

"Your turn," he said as he went to the sink to brush his teeth.

"You don't have to wait on me," she said. "Jack was bringing in the pizza when I got here. If you go on out, you can save me a couple of slices of our favorite kind."

Knox waited until she was behind the shower curtain to whip off the towel and put on underwear and a pair of sweatpants. "See you on the other side, then."

No one was interested in black olive and mushroom pizza, but to be on the safe side, Knox put four pieces on a paper plate and carried it to a nearby table.

Micah sat down across the table from him with a plate piled high with slices of meat lover's pizza. "I still can't believe you and Lottie are a couple."

"Why not?" Knox asked.

"You aren't her type. She goes for tall, dark, and handsome. You look like you belong on a beach waiting for the surf," Micah answered.

"I'm tall, and some folks say I'm handsome. Apparently, she thinks two out of three ain't bad." Knox grinned.

Lottie crossed the room and sat down beside Knox. "Thank you, darlin', for saving my favorite pizza for me."

He leaned over and kissed her on the cheek. "That's the least I can do after that…"

She put her forefinger over his lips. "Shhh… What happens in the bathroom stays in the bathroom."

"Sorry," he said and kissed her fingertips.

Micah frowned, pushed back his chair, picked up his plate, and left their table. "I still don't believe it."

"Do you care if he believes?" Knox whispered in a seductive gesture.

She stared up into his eyes and said, "Not one bit, but he better shape up by Christmas. If he don't believe, Santa won't bring him a present."

Knox chuckled and brushed a quick kiss across her lips. "That should convince Micah and the newcomers."

Thomas loaded his plate with slices of meat lover's pizza and carried it over to the table where Lottie and Knox were sitting. "One down. Five to go. Before y'all came out of the bathroom, Jack told the new guys that he would be retiring after this project. I'm not sure that all of them want to work for Walter. Steve even said that he had been thinking of forming his own company. I like Walter, but Steve is going to keep his jobs closer to western Oklahoma, so I could be home more. Lottie, what would you do if he asked you to forsake Walter?"

"I'm going to El Paso," she answered. "I'm not jumping ship."

Thomas turned his face toward Knox. "If we all stick together for at least one more project, do you think we might convince you to stay on with the team?"

"Thanks, but no thanks," Knox answered. "I'm going back to Spanish Fort when we finish here. Jack only asked me for this six-week stretch because Walter broke his arm, and El Paso is too far from home to suit me."

"Walter would take on a good framer like you in a heartbeat," Thomas assured him. "And I'm sure Lottie wouldn't fuss about having someone to take showers with."

"Not one bit, but he's bought a home, and he's got livestock," Lottie told him.

"Cattle?" Thomas asked.

"No, a rooster and a kitten. Someone must have thrown them out. We found them at my trailer when we got home on Sunday," Knox answered.

Thomas wiped imaginary sweat from his forehead. "I thought I heard a rooster crowing this morning, but thought I was losing my mind. Thank God they landed on your trailer and not mine."

"Oh. My. God!" Lottie gasped under her breath and shivered.

Knox slipped an arm around her shoulders. "What? Are you okay?"

The chair that Thomas had been sitting on hit the floor

with a deafening thud when he jumped up and headed across the room. "Where did y'all come from? What a surprise!"

———

Lottie took a deep breath and let it out very slowly. She closed her eyes as she stood up, but when she opened them, her parents, Darlene and Zeke, had not disappeared. Thomas was shaking her father's hand. Jack had wrapped Darlene up in a hug.

Knox got to his feet and slipped his hand into hers. She started to shake it off but then remembered that he was her boyfriend. She took a couple of steps toward the center of the room. "I guess tonight is when you meet my parents," she whispered.

"Seems only fair since you've met mine," Knox told her.

"Mama! Daddy!" She faked a squeal. "This is a big surprise! What are you doing here?"

Darlene crossed the room to hug Lottie. "Ryan has been transferred to Dallas, and we're helping him move. We drove on up here a day early to see you. Surprise!"

"Did you tell Daddy?" Lottie asked out the side of her mouth.

"No, I did not," Darlene assured her. "But you are going to before we move into our house up here. And I mean all of it, not just that you broke up with this fellow."

"And…" Her father made it a three-way hug, "Paul is moving from El Paso to Abilene. We'll be somewhat centrally located to all the kids this way, and that will make it easier for y'all all to come home at the same time."

"Besides, I wanted to meet your new boyfriend and take a look at the cabin that has the walls up, so I can get a general idea of what to bring with me," Darlene told her as she took a step back. "Now, don't just stand there, introduce us."

"Mama, Daddy, this is Knox Callahan. Knox, my mother, Darlene, and Daddy, Zeke."

"I'm pleased to meet y'all," Knox said and extended a hand toward Zeke and then to Darlene.

"Well, we've just been dying to get to know you, and now that we will be living close, you'll have to spend some time here at Swan Song Estates with our Lottie," Darlene said.

"I'll look forward to it," Knox agreed.

Bless your heart, Lottie thought. *This is going beyond what I expected of you.*

"But for tonight, we're going to steal Lottie away to have supper with us in a little café we found between here and our hotel," Darlene said. "Jack and Mandy raved about their chicken-fried steak."

Lottie dreaded having to spend a couple of hours with them. Keeping a secret from her father was easy when they were several hours apart, but to lie to his face was a far different matter. "But we have pizza. You could eat right here."

"Not when I can have chicken-fried steak," Zeke said. "Nice meeting you, Knox. We'll see you in the morning on our way down to Dallas. We'll check out the first house that's got the walls up then and have a doughnut and a cup of coffee with all y'all."

Thomas opened the door for them, and Knox's rooster walked inside like it was his own private barn. "Well, well, Darlene." Zeke chuckled. "Does that look like a swan to you?"

"It's mine," Knox spoke up. "His name is Cheeto, and I'll be taking him home when this project is finished."

"He's our alarm clock," Thomas added.

"Whether we like it or not," Micah said from the back of the room.

Lottie's mind was on a fast-moving merry-go-round. Knox's quick peck on the cheek before she left with her parents did not even ground her. Her mother was chatting on and on about how wonderful it was going to be to live closer to all her children. Her father interjected a comment every now and then, but the only thing Lottie could think about was that she would be lying to her father about Knox.

"You've been pretty quiet back there. Is there trouble with your new boyfriend? Is he a controlling type like that last feller you brought home?" Zeke said when he parked the SUV in front of the café.

"Not at all," Lottie answered.

Her father opened the door and unfastened his seat belt. "Didn't seem to me like you wanted to leave him behind. I figured if you wanted him to join us, *you* would have asked him."

"Wasn't my place to invite him," Lottie said with a sigh. "This is y'all's party."

Darlene got out of the vehicle and opened the back door for Lottie. "Ain't no reason to get your feathers ruffled. We don't often get one-on-one time with you. Now, let's go inside this place and have a nice family dinner."

"Y'all have a seat anywhere you like," a lady called out when the three of them were inside the small café. "I'll be right with you."

The place was booming, but Zeke led the way to an empty booth toward the back of the place. "Must be good food to be this crowded."

Lottie slid into the fake leather seat and pasted on a smile. "Something smells good, and I'm starving. Do y'all really think you'll be happy living so close to your relatives that you won't even need a phone to call them? All you have to do is step out on your porch and holler."

"Honey, we each have two acres. Not even my voice reaches that far to yell at Mandy and Jack," Darlene replied with half a giggle. "Much less whoever lives in the last cabin. But it will be nice to be able to visit more and for you kids to come home for the holidays. After we get settled, I will expect every one of you to be at Swan Song Estates for Mother's Day, Father's Day, and at least one day close to Christmas."

A middle-aged woman with dyed red hair appeared with three menus and set a glass of water in front of each of them. "I'm Billy June, and I'll be your waitress this evening. I'll have the biscuits and whipped honey out here in a minute. What else can I get y'all to drink?"

"Sweet tea," Zeke said without looking up from the menu.

"Same here," Darlene added, "and some fried green tomatoes for the appetizer."

"Raspberry tea," Lottie answered.

"I'll get right on that while y'all decide what you want to eat," Billy June said and disappeared.

"You won't disappoint me, will you?" Darlene asked.

"Don't y'all have a cruise planned in May?" Lottie side-stepped the issue.

"Yes, but we'll be settled in very well by Christmas, so that's when I'm starting on the holidays. We'll have a big meal in the rec hall for the folks who live here and all their kids that can come for the day."

Zeke laid the menu to the side and took a drink of water. "And we'll all play Dirty Santa. I love that game."

"Me too, Daddy," Lottie said with half a smile.

"Were you disappointed to hear that Jack was retiring?" Darlene asked.

"Of course, but not as shocked as I was when he told us that y'all and Mandy's siblings were all moving into Swan Song Estates," Lottie answered.

Darlene reached across the table and laid a hand on her daughter's arm. "We're tired of moving, and even more so, we do not like being so far from family."

Zeke added his hand on top of Darlene's. "Honey, we've got more years behind us than we've got in front of us. We want to spend years or even moments with you and your brothers."

"And with Jack and that side of the family," Darlene added.

Lottie's eyes misted over. She had never given a single thought ahead to the days when she wouldn't have her parents. They had always been there, no matter where they lived, and she figured they always would be. Reality set in that very instant. Her dad's thinning hair was now all gray with no dark brown left, and his wrinkles had deepened. He didn't have the spring in his step that he had had ten years ago, and the glitter in his eyes had dimmed a little.

Darlene's blond hair was almost all gray now. She and Lottie used to be the same height, but now her mother was at least two inches shorter than Lottie. They had shared clothing on occasion, but these days her mother looked to be two sizes smaller than she was.

"Well, now that the shock and surprise is over, I'm glad you'll be living here," Lottie said around the lump in her throat.

Billy June returned with their drinks, a basket of steaming hot biscuits, and a plate stacked high with fried green tomatoes. "Are y'all ready to order?"

"I am," Zeke said. "I'll have the chicken-fried steak, mashed potatoes and white gravy, candied carrots, and a side salad with ranch dressing."

"Make that two," Darlene said.

"No, make it three." Lottie smiled, and this time it was real.

Chapter 12

THE QUACKING NOISE OF at least fifty ducks filled the air as they floated down from the blue sky to land on the still lake water that evening. Knox sat in the grass on the bank and watched their heads dip into the water, looking for small fish for supper. Their actions reminded him of bobbing for apples at the church festival during Halloween when he was a little boy. Tripp had been good at getting his teeth into one, but not Brodie or Knox. Most of the time, all they got was a nose full of water.

"I wonder what kind of luck Lottie had in that game," he whispered.

The ducks closest to the bank glared at him.

"Okay, even though I was here first, I will be very quiet," he said.

He wondered where Lottie was at that very moment and how things were going with her parents. He imagined her sitting at a booth or a table across from her father. She would be fidgeting because she had let him believe that she was in a semi-serious relationship. Knox knew that because he had felt the same way when they were in Spanish Fort—especially with Mary Jane and Joe Clay.

Thinking about her brought on visuals of her the past week. There she was in her overalls and braided hair, holding a board for him to nail in place. Then a picture of the wind on Easter Sunday, blowing the sleeves away from her dress and showing her toned arms. Last was a vision of her coming out of the shower with a towel wrapped around her body every evening. Lately, the desire to take the towel away had been so overpowering that it took every bit of his willpower to keep his hands to himself.

"It would be so easy to take this from friendship to the next level," he whispered.

Several ducks' heads swiveled around to glare at him again.

"Sorry, guys. It just slipped out." He chuckled.

The next picture that filtered through his mind was her holding the bouquet that Willa Rose, his new sister-in-law, threw at the wedding. She'd acted a little embarrassed since she was one of only a handful of strangers at the event. Knox didn't know her name at that time, but he had thought she was the most gorgeous woman he'd ever seen. It had probably been nothing more than what his seven sisters called *wedding fever.*

The ducks suddenly took flight and landed so far across the lake that they were nothing but dark-colored dots. He hadn't said a word or even moved a muscle, so they couldn't lay the blame on him for getting spooked like that. Was this area poor picking grounds for supper, so they left to find food elsewhere?

A movement in his peripheral vision caught his eye, and he whipped around in time to see Cheeto flying low to the ground and coming right at him.

"You are late to the party," Knox said. "The ducks are gone, and I doubt if they would have wanted to be your friend anyway. They weren't very friendly, and one of the prerequisites to getting into their club is that you have to be able to swim."

Cheeto strutted down to the edge of the lake, threw back his head, and crowed.

"No use in cussing them," Knox told him. "They are gone."

The rooster came back to his side for a moment and then headed back across the grass toward the trailers. Knox turned around to be sure Cheeto didn't encounter a snake on the way and saw Lottie. By her walk and the way she focused on the ground, she was either watching for slithering critters or had the weight of the world on her shoulders.

"Hello," he said when she was close. "How did your dinner go?"

She sat down beside him and wiped tears from her eyes. "I need a friend."

He slipped an arm around her shoulders. "I'm here."

She scooted over closer to him. "Give me a minute."

"We'll sit right here until you are ready."

The sun finally dipped behind the trees and left a final splash of color across the sky. The shades of pink, orange, and purple faded quickly in the water's reflection. The dots that were ducks took flight, and the night seemed as still and heavy as the mood Lottie was in.

"It's like life, isn't it?" she finally said.

"What?" Knox asked.

Lottie moved away from him and pointed across the lake. "The sunset. It's like life, and we take it for granted."

"I suppose a poet might say something like that," he said. "But what happened with your parents to make you so philosophical tonight?"

"I felt guilty about not telling my dad the truth," she answered, but didn't look at him.

"I figured that much, because I felt the same about my family."

"But more than that, as I was sitting there in that café, I realized that my folks are aging, and I need to spend more time with them. It's come on so gradually that I didn't even see it until tonight. Seems like only a few months ago, neither of them had a single gray hair, and they had very few wrinkles. Daddy is walking slower, and most likely the reason Mama holds on to him is so they can steady each other."

"I've been there, done that, and have the tearstained shirt to prove it."

She nodded and swiped tears from her cheeks with the back of her hand. "I'm sorry to bring my baggage to you. You lost both of your parents, and…"

"Shhh…" Knox butted in. "I know what you are going through. The difference is that my dad died suddenly, and there were no minutes or hours left to ask him one last question or to play one more game of chess with him. Mother was sick for months, and all three of us brothers spent every second we could with her, and we all regretted the years we wasted when she was in better health. You've figured this out when you can enjoy whatever days or years you can with them. That is a blessing."

"I can't go to El Paso. I need to be closer to them," she said in a monotone.

"What do you want to do?"

"Build houses. Do construction work. That's where my heart is. I'll have to see if Uncle Jack can recommend another crew for me," she answered.

"I might have a connection up around Spanish Fort if you think you'd be interested," he offered. "That's an easy two-hour drive from here."

"That would be perfect, but what about us?" she asked. "We'd have to come clean with your family and my dad."

"We've got five more weeks to figure something out. Until then, I'm sure your folks will be up this way several times since your brother will be trying to get settled in Dallas."

"And they'll want to see the actual cabin they are moving into, so Mama can figure out where she's going to put everything from Grandma's old mixing bowls to Daddy's recliner."

"Yep, and remember that old saying: 'When you close a door, another one opens.'"

"Maybe Uncle Jack can shorten that time by letting them move into the second cabin that gets finished," she said. "That way I'd be right here close by for a couple of weeks before I figure out where I'm going."

Knox almost told her right then and there what he planned to do with the acreage he had bought, but his gut told him to wait. She could be taking a ride down the old proverbial Guilt River and would change her mind about everything after spending some real time with her folks so close by.

"Even if they don't get the second one, the fact that you want them here sooner will make them feel good," Knox said.

"How long did it take you to get through the grief of losing your folks?" she asked.

"I can't answer that."

"Why?"

"Because in some ways, I'm still going through it. Little things still pop up that make me get misty-eyed. Like seeing those first little purple wildflowers in the spring. I remember picking them when I was a little kid and taking a fistful to Mother. They don't have much of a stem, but she would take the lid off a little saltshaker and use it for a vase. She would set the bouquet on the dining room table like it was a huge thing. Or at the end of the day, when I'm sitting on the porch and, for just a split second, I'm expecting Dad to get home any minute so I can get his advice on a project I want to build. Memories are what keep them alive for me."

Lottie moved away from him, drew her knees up, and locked her arms around them. "That's why Mary Jane takes so many pictures, isn't it? She is making memories, not only for herself, but for the family after she is gone. I'm going to start doing that tomorrow morning while my folks are here for doughnuts."

"Never thought about it that way, but you are right. Mama wrote in journals. We have them all in a box, but not a one of us three brothers have gotten past the grief enough to read them."

"I love that idea, so I'm going to do it too. But, Knox, aren't you curious enough to want to know what she wrote about you?"

"I know she loved me and was proud of me for my independence, even though I didn't get a degree like Tripp or put several years into the military like Brodie. That's enough for now," he answered.

"You are a good man," she whispered.

"Thank you for saying that, but what do you make of that sight?" Knox quickly changed the subject and pointed toward the middle of the lake, where a reflection of the moon became a dim spotlight for a single swan floating on the top of the water. "Oh!" she gasped. "It looks surreal."

She took her phone from her pocket and snapped several pictures. "If they turn out good, I will have one put on canvas for the rec room."

"That would sure be fitting. Wouldn't it be something if it brings more swans to the lake?"

"I'm glad you are here to share that sight with me," she said.

Knox stood up and held out a hand to her. "Me too."

"Where are we going?" she asked.

"Wherever you want to," he told her. "We can take a walk, go to my trailer and watch a funny movie, or drive into town and get a snow cone."

"Let's watch a funny movie, and thank you," Lottie said.

"What for?" Knox asked.

"For being here for me."

"No thanks necessary. That's what friends are for."

═══════════

What Knox said about friends kept coming back to Lottie's mind all evening and stuck there when she crawled into bed that night. Moonlight drifted through the lacy curtains over the small window in the bedroom end of her trailer and left shifting patterns on the ceiling. One looked like the silhouette of a young woman. The air vent moved the lace a little, and it turned into an old woman. That made her think of how much her mother had aged right before her eyes, and yet she had not seen it until that very day.

Prissy jumped up onto the bed, turned around a few times, and then settled down onto the pillow where she always slept. Lottie reached over and rubbed the cat's head. "I know you are always here for me, but Knox is a different kind of friend. I was always a loner. In college, even a few of the introverted girls shed their inhibitions and became party animals, but not me. I had a goal in mind. Get the education over with to please my folks and then build houses."

Prissy meowed, slapped a paw over her eyes, and went to sleep.

"I don't know if I'm happy with being just friends with Knox or if…" she whispered and closed her eyes.

She dreamed about him—again—that night. She was standing in front of the bathroom mirror and rubbing a little extra face cream into the wrinkles in her face. Knox came up behind her and wrapped his arms around her waist. He told her she was beautiful and sang part of the old song titled "Forever and Ever, Amen." The lyrics talked about him loving her even if all her hair fell out. She slowly turned around and laid her face on his chest, and then that damned rooster started crowing.

She left the beautiful dream and opened her eyes to see that the sun was only a tiny sliver of orange and barely sending any light at all through her bedroom window. She jerked her pillow out from under her head and crammed it down tightly over her face, leaving only her nose clear. But no matter how tightly she closed her eyes, she couldn't bring back the dream or capture the feeling she had.

Cheeto crowed again, this time longer and louder, and woke Prissy up. The cat growled and jumped up on the headboard. She stuck her head between the curtains and made that eerie sound in her throat of when she chased a cricket or that one time when she cornered a field mouse in the trailer.

"I know, baby girl," Lottie said. "I would gladly bring Cheeto's pretty head to you on a platter for breakfast, but

Knox kind of likes him. But if this keeps happening, I'll turn you outside to put an end to that bird. I could have slept another hour, but now that you are awake, I'll have to get up and feed you. Or you might claw your way through that window to end all crowing forevermore."

When the noise stopped, Prissy hopped down from the bed and headed for the kitchen. Lottie threw back the covers and peeked out the window. The rooster was sitting on the side mirror of her truck, looking at his reflection and seeming to dare that bird to try to take his new place in the world. He threw his head back to get enough air to crow again. Before he could get it out, Knox grabbed him and carried him away.

"Why couldn't you have done that before he woke me up?" Lottie grumbled as she filled Prissy's food and water bowls.

She made a small pot of coffee, poured herself a cup, and carried it out to the front steps to watch the sunrise since she was already awake. The dream that Cheeto had so rudely interrupted came back to her mind. She wanted to know what happened next. For that matter, she would have loved to have seen the past, to have known if they were married, or still friends—or maybe they'd grown old together as friends with benefits. Suddenly, she needed to see the whole show.

"Damn it!" she swore under her breath. "I don't know how far in the future—it seemed like it could have been an anniversary—but we were more than friends."

"What are you fussing about?" Knox asked as he rounded

the side of the trailer and handed her a plate piled up with breakfast burritos. "I brought a snack before we have doughnuts with the guys. I'll share if I can steal a cup of coffee."

She fought back a blush and hoped he hadn't heard what she was mumbling about. "You've made enough for an army. Sure you don't want to take them to the rec hall and share with all the guys?"

"Honey, at least three of those are mine. That wouldn't leave enough for the others to even have one each. Now about that coffee?"

"Go on in and help yourself. Is this an apology for that blasted bird of yours waking me up so early?"

"No," he said as he stepped around her. "I told him to do that so I could have an early breakfast with you."

"That's not a very good friend," she growled.

"Hey, now, I made the burritos. All you did was get up in time to eat them and put on a pot of coffee," he countered.

"Are we arguing?" she asked.

"Everyone argues sometimes," he answered. "But couples usually kiss and make up. Are you ready for that?"

Before she could answer, Micah came on over toward them. "Good mornin'. Did Knox's rooster wake you up, too?"

"Yep, he did," Lottie said. "Want a burrito? It's a while until Jack brings doughnuts to the rec room."

Micah reached for one and then pulled his hand back. "Did you make them?"

"Nope. Knox did." Lottie handed Micah the plate,

swallowed the bite she had in her mouth, took a sip of coffee, and leaned over to kiss on Knox's lips. " Does that settle the argument?"

"With him or me? What were we fighting about?" Micah took a burrito, bit into it, and handed the plate back to her.

"With Knox, not you."

"This is very good. You want to make breakfast every morning in the rec hall?"

"No, thank you," Lottie said.

Knox winked at Lottie. "I do believe that settles the question. FYI, burritos and coffee together make for good kisses."

"I'm leaving now and giving y'all some early morning privacy, but first, one for the road," Micah grabbed another and headed toward the rec hall.

"What is morning privacy?" Knox asked.

"Micah's definition and mine would be two different things for sure," she answered.

Knox wiggled his eyebrows. "I can figure out what Micah is referring to, but what is yours?"

"Not being wakened by a rooster crowing," she answered. "But then I won't complain if I get breakfast burritos out of the deal."

Chapter 13

Lottie had just finished her second doughnut when her folks arrived in the rec room that morning. "Hey, y'all made it," she called out and waved.

"Just long enough for a cup of coffee and a doughnut, and a tour of the first cabin y'all have put up," Darlene answered and crossed the room to give Lottie a hug. "The movers are supposed to be at Ryan's by noon."

"I'll team up with Knox while you show your folks around," Eddie offered.

"Thanks," Lottie said with a nod.

"Would y'all be interested in the second cabin?" Jack asked. "Mandy would be glad to have some space between her and her siblings, and I would like to be next door to you and Zeke."

"Yes, definitely," Darlene answered and sat down at the table where Knox was sitting. "Our house in Houston has a buyer. We're just waiting for paperwork, like you and Mandy. That would mean we wouldn't have to store anything but could move right on up here."

"Then consider it yours," Jack said with a grin.

"I can show you the foundations for the other six cabins,

but I'm glad you'll be moving while I'm still here for a little while. Does that mean you are making lunch for me every day, Mama?"

"Only if you help me unpack, decorate the place, and go fishing with your dad every evening," Darlene answered.

"Oh, no! I'm not good at decorating, and I do not want to argue with you about whether to put up white window blinds or wood-looking ones," Lottie said with a giggle. "I'll just eat my lunch with the guys and leave all those jobs to you."

Zeke took a seat beside his wife, reached into the box, and pulled out a doughnut with chocolate icing. "Smart girl, but I might steal Knox away from you a few times to go fishing with me. I'm bringing my boat, and your mama fries up a mean batch of fish."

"That can be arranged," Lottie told him.

Darlene nudged him on the arm. "Zeke, darlin', do you realize this means we can be moved in before we go on our cruise the second week in May? That we can come home and begin our second honeymoon when we get back."

Lottie poured two cups of coffee and carried them across the room. She set one in front of each of her parents, then sat back down beside Knox.

"It will be noisy for a while after you get here," Knox was telling them. "We'll still be working on the last couple or three cabins when y'all get here."

"How does all this construction stuff work anyway?" Darlene asked.

"Knox, Gabe, Thomas, Eddie, and I are framers. We get the first cabin ready in a week, and then those guys over there at that table"—she nodded to her left—"they come in behind us and put up the outside and roof."

"Get it in the dry, right?" Zeke asked.

"Yes," Knox answered. "It's kind of like an assembly line. We'll be framing the third cabin when the next crew comes in to do the drywall, painting, and all that."

"The fourth week, the finish guys bring in the cabinets, do all the baseboards, doorjambs, and that kind of thing," Lottie said.

"When the framers are done with the last cabin, we all go back to wherever we are needed to help get everything else up and going," Knox added. "Or if it rains and we can't put up walls and roofs, then we pitch in where we can."

"What else are you good at, son?" Zeke asked.

Her father's last word was like a sword piercing Lottie's heart. In spite of all her dreaming, the likelihood of Knox ever being a son-in-law was at that point at the .00001 percentile.

"I can do it all, from the foundation to putting up the last ceiling fan or staining and varnishing, but I enjoy framing most of all," Knox answered. "I hear y'all's cruise is going to Hawaii. I've never been, so you'll have to tell me all about it when you get back."

Zeke rolled his eyes. "Oh, we definitely will, and you'll have to sit through eight million pictures that Darlene will take on the trip."

Darlene shook her finger under his nose. "Hush, you old coot. You'll be the one who looks at the photo album more than anyone else."

Zeke winked at Knox. "Got to keep the womenfolks on their toes so they don't get antsy. A little argument is good for the soul and the marriage."

"I'll remember that, sir," Knox said. "So, you'll be at Swan Song Estates before you leave for your cruise?"

"We'll only be here a couple of weeks before we fly to California to catch the ship taking us to Hawaii for thirteen days," Zeke said. "By the time we get back, the sidewalks and landscaping should be done, and we can spend the summer either fishing in the lake or watching the sunrises and sunsets."

Lottie shoved the box over closer to them. "I'll be glad when you are here, and I can spend more time with y'all."

Her mother's face glowed, and her eyes misted over. She didn't let a single tear fall, but Lottie could tell by her expression that those few simple words meant the world to Darlene.

Darlene laid her hand on her daughter's and gave it a gentle squeeze. "Yes, and so will we."

Zeke reached into the box and picked up a second doughnut. "Absolutely. We've missed you, ladybug. I understand you only live a couple of hours from here, Knox. Do you have a lot of family up in that area?"

Lottie shrugged when Knox glanced over at her with questions written all over his face. "You tell them about the Paradise. I can't remember all their names."

"I guess that means you come from a big family," Zeke said. "Darlene said your last name was Callahan. Was your mother a Paradise?"

"Paradise is a place, not a name," Lottie answered.

"I'll try to make the story as short as possible," Knox said. "I have a twin brother, Tripp, and we were adopted. My mother had an older son, Brodie, who's about two years older than us. He doesn't belong to my father and only found out who his biological father was a few months ago. Just before my mother passed away, she told all of us about our biological fathers. Mine and Tripp's was no longer living, but Brodie's father was alive and well in Spanish Fort, Texas, living at the Paradise," Knox answered and took a sip of his coffee.

"They came to Spanish Fort to the Paradise where Joe Clay and Mary Jane live to see Brodie's blood father and decided to stay in the town," Lottie continued. "Joe Clay is retired military, and Mary Jane writes romance novels as Mary Jane Simmons. They adopted all three of the Callahan brothers into the already large family."

"I've read Mary Jane Simmons books for years. My favorites are the ones about the ladies who worked in the old brothel…" Darlene clamped a hand over her mouth. "That's the Paradise, isn't it? The one that she wrote about and where she lives."

"Yep, and if you read her biography, you know that she raised seven daughters there," Knox answered. "She and Joe Clay are in the process of adopting Ivy, a teenage girl who needed a home. So, the short version is that there are seven, soon to be eight daughters, seven sons-in-law, and my two brothers are newly married, so there are two daughters-in-law. Plus, a handful of grandkids. That means I have a very, very large family. Maybe someday you can come up to the Paradise and meet them."

"Do you think Mary Jane might sign some of my books, or would that be intruding?" Darlene asked.

"Not at all," Knox answered and pushed back his chair. "She'd be glad to sign them for you. Looks like my crew is ready to go to work. Nice visiting with y'all. We'll be putting down the sill plates this morning. Why don't y'all stop by? We could even let Zeke hold the plate or drill in a bolt so he can say he helped build his new home."

"I'd like that," Zeke said. "Hurry up, Darlene. I want to brag to all the others that I had a hand in building our cabin."

Knox stood up, took a couple of steps, and then blew Lottie a kiss. "You don't have to rush too much. We've still got to cut the boards."

She caught the kiss and pretended to shove it into the pocket of her bibbed overalls.

"Now that one is a keeper," Zeke whispered. "Don't let him get away."

Lottie's mother shot a look across the table that made her feel even worse than she already did. "He is a wonderful guy, Daddy."

"I can see that," Zeke said. "You ready to take us on the

tour of Jack's cabin and then show us all around this place? Until last night, we had only seen pictures and mock-ups of what the cabins will look like when they are finished."

Darlene got to her feet and looped her arm into Zeke's. "And we decided that the pictures didn't do justice to any part of this place. I can't wait to plant roses around my house."

"And I'm planning to till up a garden on part of my land. I've always wanted to try my hand at growing vegetables. If the apples make good, we might even make our own pies for Thanksgiving," Zeke said.

Lottie followed behind them. "I guess this means y'all are pretty well finished with traveling the world?"

"Absolutely," Darlene answered. "This cruise will be our last. We are ready to settle down and grow old together."

Lottie giggled.

"What's so funny?" Zeke asked.

"I didn't think y'all would ever get tired of traveling," Lottie answered. "But since you have, I'm glad you are moving here. Uncle Jack told me why you named the place that, but it sure doesn't go with the cabin idea."

"No, but we all loved the name," Zeke said when they entered the first cabin with only the framework finished. "Would you look at this, Darlene? It's the bare bones of what our new place will look like."

"I can see now that I'm going to have to size down a lot," she said as she wandered from what would soon be two bedrooms into an open living space for the living room, dining room, and kitchen. "But I love it. The kids can bring their trailers when they come visit since Jack already has places set up for that kind of thing. The second bedroom can be my hobby room where I'm going to make quilts."

Good Lord! Her parents who had been city people her whole life were going back to nature.

"And we can use the rec room for meals when the family is here," Zeke mused. "I'll need a shed out back for my gardening equipment and lawn mower."

"It's all going to be perfect," Darlene agreed.

Lottie hoped her mother was right. That her parents lived to be a hundred years old and died happy right there at Swan Song Estates. After the epiphany she had the night before, she sure intended to spend more time with them— even if they upset her at times—than she had in the past.

"What do y'all think?" Jack came through what would be the back door. "Sorry I wasn't here earlier. I just dropped off the doughnuts and hurried down to the lumberyard to put in an order in time to get it delivered tomorrow morning."

Darlene gave her brother a brief hug. "No problem. We love all of it. The place. The cabins. The lake. And especially the room between the places. I didn't realize how much land two acres covered."

Lottie's mind wandered off to think about the section of land that Knox had bought—six hundred and forty acres— and how many houses would fit on that big of a place. Then it jumped track to think about moving to Spanish Fort to what Knox said about having connections for her to work in that area. She would be close enough to her parents to drive down on Sunday morning, go to church with them, and then spend the afternoon visiting all her relatives.

Right away, she banished the idea from her head. She probably couldn't make enough money to survive, much less be running back and forth from Spanish Fort to Swan Song Estates.

She reminded herself that there was enough money in her savings account to live on for a while.

"Besides, a boring person doesn't need much," she whispered under her breath.

Jack nudged her on the shoulder. "You look like you are either angry or sad. Which one is it?"

"Maybe a little of both," she answered. "I don't want to go to El Paso. They"—she nodded toward her parents, who had started walking toward the place where the framing crew was already working—"aren't spring chickens anymore, and I need to spend more time with them. That means taking jobs that are closer, maybe no more than a couple of hours from here."

"If that's what the Universe has in mind for you, then a door will open," Jack said. "For now, let's go watch Zeke drill a sill plate in place. It'll be kind of like the day he proposed to my sister."

"How's that?" Lottie asked.

"That was the beginning," Jack replied. "This is another one, only this time it's also the swan song."

Lottie shivered. "Don't remind me. I already feel so guilty that I have avoided them as much as I have in the past."

"You can't change the past, darlin', but you can use it as a stepping stone to have a future where you won't ever have regrets," Jack told her.

<hr>

Knox had the cordless screwdriver in his hand when a shadow covered him. He looked up to see Zeke standing in front of him with a big smile on his face. Knox handed the tool to him and pointed to the pilot hole that he had already drilled. Zeke put in the bolt and gave the device to Lottie.

"You take this now and get to work on our new cabin. Your mother and I have to get on the road, or Ryan will be worried," he said. "But this has been special. Kind of like when your mother and I said our vows."

"How is putting a bolt into concrete like saying vows?" Lottie asked.

"We've had tough times like this slab, and we've had to use every tool that we had to keep our marriage from falling apart, but we worked at it until we got past the rough patch. Now we're in our glory years, and every day is a blessing. I hope you find someone to love as much as I do your mother."

Darlene gave him a quick hug and wiped a tear from her cheek with the back of her hand. "All these years, I thought you were as romantic as a rock, and now you spout off something poetic."

"Saving the best for last, darlin'," he said and gave her a quick kiss on the forehead. "Now let's get on the road. I've used up all my lovey-dovey for this day."

"I've been ready for an hour, but you had to help put down the first sill plate," she teased.

"Yeah, right," he grumbled and took her hand in his.

"Don't I get a hug?" Lottie asked.

Zeke reached out with his left arm and gathered her to his side. "Now, get to work before Jack fires you, and you have to move onto Swan Song Estates permanently. I've gotten used to the empty nest and do not want a kid underfoot all the time."

"If I did, you'd have a fishing buddy," Lottie told her father.

"Even that ain't worth it. You and your mother would argue all the time and ruin my peace."

"You are an old coot." Lottie covered a giggle with her hand. "Y'all send me a text when you get to Dallas so I know you made it."

"Oh, no!" Darlene protested. "We aren't going to start that nonsense. We are two independent adults. Just because we are settling down doesn't mean we are ready for the role reversal where you become the parent and we are the children."

"Yes, ma'am," Lottie said with a snappy salute.

Knox could well remember the time when his mother lost her independence and had to rely on her sons to take care of her physically, mentally, and even the estate she and her husband had amassed. He would have loved to have built his parents a lovely little cabin beside a lake and to have gotten to watch them hold hands when they took long walks.

"What are you thinking about?" Lottie asked as she bent over to drill another bolt into the sill plate.

"Probably the same thing you are," he answered.

She moved down another two feet. "That time goes by too fast, and we didn't take advantage of the moments that's already gotten past us?"

Eddie handed his drill to Knox. "Y'all are awfully poetic this morning, but I reckon a day of back-breaking working with sill plates and a nail gun in your hands will take that right out of you. I'm going to go back to my job of building a wall to put up. That is if y'all can stop being all lovey-dovey and keep up with us."

"We can work circles around y'all old, lazy men," Lottie teased.

"Are you bragging or just wishin'?" Thomas asked.

"Oh, I'm bragging for sure," she fired back. "I already heard that you are making Thomas's Terrific Thursday Tacos for supper tonight, and I intend to work up an appetite."

"It's the only time you'll get them until we get to El Paso, so you better eat all you can," Gabe told her.

"Why's that?" Knox asked.

"I cook one time at each building site," Thomas explained. "After that, it's someone else's turn to show off their talents. Micah will probably do it next Thursday, and he'll make enchiladas. That's his signature dish. But we're all looking forward to the end of the job when we get finished and you make the dinner."

"I'll do my best to make it a meal to remember," Knox said and went back to work.

At noon, Knox and Lottie carried their lunch over to the rec room and sat down at an empty table. When Gabe, Thomas, and Eddie joined them, he was reminded of grade school when the kids in the first grade never sat with the older ones.

As if she understood what Knox was thinking, she nudged him on the shoulder. "They'll be a little more friendly at supper tonight," she whispered. "Right now, they are sizing you up and deciding whether they believe that we are really a couple."

"Why would they do that?" he asked.

"Because three of them are single, and they've had bets going for the past several jobs as to which one will get her to go on a date first," Thomas answered.

"Ever since we've known her, she's declared that she would never date a coworker," Eddie said. "None of us believed it at first either. We figured she roped you into being her fake boyfriend so all the single guys would stop hitting on her."

"Why would I give up my freedom to do a foolhardy thing like that?" Knox asked.

"Who knows, but we are good with the idea of y'all being a couple now, and by the time the third crew gets here, those guys over at the other table will be, too," Gabe said.

"That said, what's everyone doing this weekend?" Thomas asked.

Jack sat down at the end of the table and took out his

lunch. "I'd like to go home to help Mandy finish packing this weekend."

"Lottie and I figured we'd stay close by," Knox told him. "We can keep an eye on things, so go on if you want to. You plan to drive?"

"Yep, and I'm not looking forward to six hours in the truck tomorrow evening." Jack bit into a sub sandwich.

"Are you afraid of flying?"

"Not at all, but by the time I drive to Dallas, worry with all the stuff at the airport, and then fly to Houston, it will take more time than driving," Jack answered.

"We have a small plane that could get you there in about an hour and bring you home on Sunday or Monday," Knox said.

"Who is this 'we' business?" Lottie asked.

"It belongs to the three of us. My brother Tripp wanted to keep it when we sold the Callahan estate," Knox answered. "I can make a call, and the pilot that he keeps on payroll will be glad to take you."

"Yes, and thank you so much," Jack said with a nod. "I can get an Uber to take me home from the airport and surprise Mandy. Maybe we'll all just call it a day at noon tomorrow. Y'all have really been keeping your shoulder to the work this week, and we're ahead of schedule."

Lottie didn't say anything until their lunch break was over and they were walking over to the job, but before they began helping build walls, she whispered, "You have a private plane?"

"It's not a jet."

"After supper, I want to hear more about this estate thing."

He handed her a nail gun and set a stud in place. "Darlin', you already know more than most of my real girlfriends have ever known."

Chapter 14

"Are you really not going to tell me about your airplane?" Lottie asked that evening before they left the bathroom. Knox had already had his shower and was wearing nothing but a towel, wrapped low enough to see the V of his abs. Asking about the plane was nothing more than her feeble attempt to talk about anything so she would stop wanting to run her hands all over his broad chest.

"Nothing to tell. Tripp wanted to keep it, so we did," Knox answered.

"Why did you have it anyway? You talk about your mother's estate, and you share a plane with your brothers. Are you rich or something?"

"Let's leave the rich story at 'or something,' but I will tell you about the plane. Tripp and my dad used it to fly to places where Dad had either oil wells or companies that he had to check on regularly. I'm a carpenter, so I never got into all that business end of things. But it has come in handy a few times since we sold the company and Mother's estate and moved to Spanish Fort," he answered and changed the subject. "Now, let's talk about why Thomas's tacos are any better than any fast-food joints."

"One more question, and then we'll talk tacos," Lottie said. "Are you really a prince in pauper's clothing?"

"Never heard it put that way before." Knox chuckled. "I'm not royalty, but I was never a real pauper, so I wouldn't know about either one. My parents raised us to be responsible and hard workers, and we never felt entitled."

"Fair enough," Lottie said. "What makes the tacos so special is that Thomas makes his own blend of spices for the meat. He makes the corn and flour tortillas from scratch, and also a special salsa. And…" She turned around to face the wall. "He does not share his recipes for any of it, so we only get them once or twice, depending on how long the construction project lasts."

Knox got dressed and then took his place in the far corner. "Martha, my mother's housekeeper and cook, used to make homemade tortillas for us. She said that we had hollow legs that she could never get filled up, no matter how much food she made."

"I'm decent now," she said. "And my mama used to tell me that feeding three boys was a lot tougher on the checkbook than one girl. I guess boys just eat more, but tonight I plan to run all y'all some competition."

Knox wiggled his eyebrows. "So, you worked up a big appetite in here with me, did you?"

"Of course," she said without a second's hesitation. "Staring at a blank wall while you cover up all those muscles takes a lot of energy and eats up a lot of calories."

"You think I'm a stud, then?" He continued to tease.

She picked up her tote bag and dirty towels and opened the door. "I did not say that."

He followed her out. "You implied it."

"Did not!" she snapped.

"Is there trouble in Paradise?" Jack asked from across the room.

"I wouldn't know about Paradise," Knox answered, "but we're all good here."

"We are not fine, Uncle Jack," Lottie disagreed. "He's not remembering my exact words."

Jack draped an arm around her shoulders and guided her over to the bar, where Thomas flipped fresh, hot tortillas onto a platter. "It's a guy thing, sweetheart. Us men have selective hearing."

"Mama says that same thing," Lottie said.

Knox handed her a plate and got in line behind her. " That's why women are from Venus, and men are from Mars. Want me to get you a beer? There's no way you can handle two dozen tacos and a bottle at the same time."

Lottie took the plate and began to put together half a dozen tacos. "What do you know about that old book about women and men?"

Knox had talked himself into a corner without meaning to do so. A woman from one of his previous short-lived relationships had quoted lines from the book when she was angry with him for not doing what she wanted. This was not the time or place to discuss the past with his fake girlfriend.

"Someone mentioned it, so I checked it out." It wasn't a

complete lie because he *had* scanned through the book after his last girlfriend threw it at him when she left the house during a hissy fit.

<hr>

Knox covered a yawn with his hand and glanced at the clock. "Would I be a horrible fake boyfriend if I leave you alone to watch the last of this episode? I can hardly keep my eyes open."

"Of course not," Lottie said. "It's an hour past my bedtime, too, and we both have to work tomorrow morning."

"You can come to bed with me if you don't want to go home," he suggested. "It's a king bed, so we probably wouldn't even touch each other."

"No thanks, but I do want to finish the rest of this episode. Go on to bed. I'll turn out the lights and make sure Bally doesn't sneak out when I leave."

Knox stood up and headed back to the bedroom end of his trailer. He pulled back the covers, and she heard a few soft snores in only a little while.

Lottie intended to watch the last twenty minutes of the final episode in the *Dark Winds* series and then go back to her own trailer. But her mind and body had different ideas when she stretched out on the makeshift couch/bed and pulled a throw over herself. She was already half-asleep when she picked up the remote and turned off the television.

"Just a twenty-minute nap," she whispered to the kitten. "Then I'll get up and go home."

Sunrays peeked through the blind slats the next morning when she awoke to Cheeto pitching a fit outside. It didn't sound like his normal wake-up-it's-morning crowing, but more like he was warning every sparrow and crow this side of the lake that something wasn't right.

She threw back the throw and stood up. "Not that I have any insight into rooster talk. How can Knox sleep through all this noise?"

Bally had managed to climb up onto the edge of the sink, and her tail was a fluff ball, and when Lottie tried to pick her up, the kitten hissed at her.

"What's going on, girl?" Lottie held her close and rubbed her fur. "What has got you and Cheeto both spooked this morning? Is a storm coming our way? I hope not, because if it is, it will slow down our progress."

She set the kitten down on the floor, and it ran under Knox's bed.

If both of Knox's animals were this upset, then she'd bet that Prissy was in a tizzy too. Figuring that she'd better not even stick around long enough to make a pot of coffee, she slipped her shoes on and peeked out the door. She expected to see dark clouds and maybe see a streak of lightning, but it looked like it would be another beautiful day without even the slightest little breeze to make the new leaves dance on the apple tree.

She had raised her right foot and was ready to step outside when she heard a faint noise like dry beans being shaken in a jar. She looked down to see a huge diamondback rattlesnake, coiled and ready to strike. She slammed the door shut, screamed, lost her footing, and fell backward. She landed on her back on the floor with a very unladylike thud. The next thing she knew, she was gasping for a breath to fill her lungs.

Then Knox was on the floor beside her, his big arms lifting her to a sitting position. "What happened? Are you all right? Did you bump your head? Do we need to take you to the emergency room?" He fired off questions, but she didn't have enough breath to answer a single one.

"Sn…sn…" She tried to get the word out, but she simply could not.

"Have you got a concussion? Can you speak?"

"Snake!" She finally managed to get the word out. She hated spiders, but she would do battle with a whole family of tarantulas before she did with a snake. Those things had been evil since the days of Adam and Eve.

"Where? Were you dreaming? Did you spend the night here, or did you see one on the way?" he asked.

She inhaled deeply and let it out slowly. "On your top step." She was so proud of herself for getting a whole sentence out that she could have jumped up and danced a jig.

"Are you sure you weren't dreaming?" Knox asked.

"Cheeto is having a fit. Bally sensed something was wrong, too, or maybe she could smell it."

"Did it bite you?" Knox's voice sounded like it was coming from the bottom of a barrel as he checked her foot and leg.

"No, just scared the bejesus out of me," she answered. "I hate snakes."

"I'm not a big fan either. Are you sure you're okay?"

The room took a spin or two when she stood up, but she made it to the sofa and sank down on it. "I'm fine, just still a little rattled."

Knox went back to the bedroom and returned with a pistol. He eased the door open, aimed, and fired. Bally had come out from under the bed and was slinking along with her little belly close to the floor when the shot sounded all through the trailer. She growled and jumped up on the sofa with Lottie.

"It's okay, baby girl," Lottie consoled her. "Knox is our hero today."

Knox put the gun away. "That snake won't bother anyone again. I'll get it off the steps soon as I get dressed. Then I'll make us some coffee and breakfast."

"I should go see about Prissy."

"You are still a little shaken up. I can hear it in your voice, and the color hasn't come back into your face. Let's get some food and coffee in you before you go."

"Okay." She agreed without an argument. She leaned back and closed her eyes, but they popped open in a hurry when a virtual picture of that snake showed up with its mouth wide open. She shivered all the way to her toes and had barely gotten herself under control when Knox came back through in a T-shirt and his faded work jeans. He went outside, and it was several minutes before he came back.

"What took so long? Was it still alive?" she asked.

"No, ma'am. I killed him dead, but I didn't want you to have to look at it, so I threw it in the lake to feed the fish," he answered. "Now, let's get some food going. How about chicken and waffles?"

"That sounds wonderful," Lottie answered.

Cheeto began his usual crowing, telling everyone that it was dawn and time for them to rise and shine. Bally hopped down from the sofa and wound around Knox's legs. Life was back to normal.

Knox made coffee and then filled Bally's bowl with food, carried fresh water and food out to Cheeto, and came back to make breakfast. "You need to be extra careful and watch your step wherever you go. That old rattler was a grandpa. He had at least a dozen buttons on his tail, so there could be more of his family members in the area."

Lottie shivered again. "I will. I promise."

"Have you never seen one on a construction site before?"

She shook her head. "Only a couple of little garden snakes, and I'm scared of them too."

"So"—he grinned as he set up a small waffle maker—"I'm a hero? Does that mean I can go from being a fake boyfriend to a real one?"

"It does not!"

"That took the quiver right out of your voice," he said.

Knox practiced what he preached as he and Lottie walked away from his trailer that morning. He scanned every which way and checked under and around Lottie's trailer while she changed into work clothes.

The rest of the guys were already at the rec hall and sipping what might have been their third or fourth cup of coffee. Thomas waved from the table where they were sitting and pointed at a couple of empty chairs.

"Did you hear that gunshot this morning?" Eddie asked.

"Sounded like it came from down near your trailer," Gabe said. "We wondered if one of your old girlfriends or one of Lottie's old flames had come back with a jealous streak and killed both of you."

"I haven't got one that would care enough to spend the rest of her life in jail," Knox said.

"Neither have I," Lottie told them.

"I figured it was some kids with firecrackers," Thomas added.

"No, it was a gunshot," Lottie said. "Knox killed a rattlesnake on his steps. I don't know how big it really was, but in my eyes, it looked like a granddaddy python that could swallow the whole trailer."

"You are terrified of snakes. What happened when you saw it?" Jack asked.

"I slammed the door, screamed loud enough to make Grandma Johnston rise up out of the grave, lost my footing, and the fall knocked the wind out of me."

"What happened to the snake? I hope it didn't crawl away and decide to live up under my trailer," Eddie said.

"Knox shot it and then threw it into the lake," she answered.

"It's fish food," Knox said. "I checked under my trailer and Lottie's to be sure there weren't any more critters, but it wouldn't hurt for all y'all to do the same every day. They're looking for nice warm places at this time of year."

"I always thought if the devil himself popped up in front of you, that you'd fight old Lucifer to the ground," Lance, one of the second crew, said.

"I would," Lottie declared, "but a snake is an animal of a different kind altogether, and they terrify me."

"Keep a sharp eye out," Jack said. "Time to get to work. If we don't get Mandy's retirement home done by deadline, I might be in some seriously hot water."

"We're on it," Knox said and extended a hand to Lottie. "We'd hate for you to start off your second honeymoon sitting in boiling water."

Lottie put her hand in his and stood up. It wasn't the first time, and probably wouldn't be the last, that he wished they were in a real relationship.

Chapter 15

Lottie was halfway from Knox's trailer to hers on Saturday night when she heard the distinct sound of a vehicle driving slowly up the gravel driveway. She slipped into the shadows between two trailers and sure enough caught sight of a pickup truck heading down the gravel road with its lights turned off.

"That can't be good," she whispered.

She pulled her phone from her hip pocket and sent Knox a quick text: Come quick. Trespassers.

One came right back: Where are you?

She typed in her location and then watched the shadow of the vehicle. It came to a stop right in the middle of the road in front of the rec hall, and four doors opened. From where she stood, she couldn't tell if the people who got out were men, women, or teenagers. But when they didn't close the pickup doors, she figured they were up to no good.

The lights around the rec hall lit all of them up enough that Lottie could tell they were all guys. The metal of a chainsaw shone when the tallest one took it from the bed of the truck. Another one laughed when he slid a suitcase of beer down from the open tailgate. A third one twirled a wrecking bar around like it was a sword, and the last one seemed to be bringing two large bottles of liquor. Even from a distance, she could tell by the shapes of the bottles that one was Maker's Mark, and the other Jack Daniel's.

"What's going on?" Knox whispered so close to her that she could feel his breath on her neck. He held a shotgun in one hand and a fistful of shells in the other.

"I believe we are about to get vandalized," she whispered. "We should video whatever is going on just in case…" A popping noise caused her to stop in the middle of the sentence. "There went the door to the rec hall."

"Chainsaw?" Knox asked as he loaded the double-barrel shotgun.

Before she could answer, the saw revved up, and music that sounded like fingernails on a blackboard and a jackhammer on steroids made Lottie put her hands over her ears.

"We have vandals." Knox handed the shotgun off to her and slipped his phone from his back pocket. He punched in 911 and told the lady at the other end what was going on.

"There are two patrol cars in that area. They can be there in ten minutes," she said.

"Thank you," Knox said. He returned the phone to his pocket and yelled above the noise. "Ten minutes, and I agree about videoing whatever they are doing."

Lottie could tell by the change in the sound of the saw that it was cutting through something. "I'm not waiting," she said and headed toward the rec hall.

Knox nodded and reached for the gun.

She shook her head. "I know how to use one of these. What's it loaded with?"

"Number 8 bird shot," he answered.

"That should sting if I have to use it," she said and kept walking.

"When I open the door, shoot into the air, and stand back in case they are armed with more than a chainsaw," Knox told her.

"Why into the air?" she asked. "I've got a good aim. I'll patch whatever holes I blow into the wall."

"Protection," Knox said. "I'll explain why later."

The door stood wide open, and four boys with scraggly beards and bloodshot eyes didn't even see them until the sound of the shotgun rang out. One of them immediately touched the screen on his phone, and the music stopped.

Knox set his phone on a nearby shelf and hoped that he was getting the right angle to film all three of them having a great time with a chainsaw and spray paint.

One of them took a long gulp of whiskey from a bottle and then threw it at Knox. It shattered on the floor right as the boy with the chainsaw finished cutting the table and turned off the saw.

"What the hell?" the kid yelled. "You didn't leave any of that for me, and I'm doing…"

That's when Lottie stepped into the room with the shotgun raised.

The kid shook the chainsaw at Knox. "This is our party, not yours, old man. Get out and take the gun with you, but you can leave the pretty lady."

The look in the boy's eyes made Lottie's skin crawl.

"Not happenin', son," Knox said. "You are going to sober up in jail for all this damage."

The teenager jabbed the saw toward Lottie that time. " Are you crazy? My old man wouldn't let that happen!"

The other boys pointed spray-paint cans sideways at Knox, like gangsters with guns in a mob movie.

"We have called the police," Lottie told them.

"So what? My dad is a lawyer, and I won't spend a single night in a cell."

"You *will* need him," Knox said as he picked up the phone and turned it around to video two holes in one wall, spray paint streaking two others, and the table that had been sawed in half.

"Turn that damned thing off, or I will saw it and you in half," the kid growled.

"Boy, you talk a big game, but…" Lottie started.

The boy grinned, wiggled his head, and took a step toward her. "Don't you call me 'boy,' woman," he yelled above the noise.

"If you want the notoriety for your deeds, then I've got the proof right here, and I'm going to keep filming until the police get here," Knox growled.

"Y'all let us leave, and I won't hurt either of you, but if

I have to cut my way out of here, well…" The kid sneered at him. "That video was taken without my permission, so it won't stand up in court anyway, so have fun."

"No one is leaving until the police get here," Lottie said and wished that she had a good old peach-tree switch to teach these kids a lesson. "Now, sit down with your back against the wall that *you* just drilled holes in. And the rest of you boys drop those spray cans and line up beside him."

The kid dropped the saw. His expression changed into that of a pouty little boy and his tone changed to a semi-whine. "We didn't do anything. You shot at us, so we ran in here for protection. All this was done before we had to take cover or be killed. Right, bros?"

"You got it, Boss," the youngest one said.

"There's another shell in the gun," Knox told him, "And I've got more in my pocket. I would do whatever she says if I was you, boys. How old are y'all anyway?"

"Don't say a word, Devon," a freckle-faced kid with a curly red mullet said.

"You idiot!" Devon's expression changed from contrite to angry in an instant. "You are never to use my name, and you know it. I'm Kingster. That's your third strike, and now you are out of our gang. You can turn in your colors, and my daddy ain't bailin' you out this time." He whipped to face another boy. "Baby D, I want you and the others to take that phone from Mister Smart Ass and smash it."

"You guys ever heard of the twenty-one-foot rule?" Knox asked, trying to scare the kids with something he picked up from a television show. "In case you haven't, it says if you are twenty-one feet or closer and you come at either of us with intent to harm with a knife, or in this case a chainsaw, we are within our legal rights to shoot you dead on the spot. You just threatened both of us. That's a crime worse than vandalism."

"And, honey, I can pull this trigger and reload so fast that I can load and fire again before you get anywhere near me," Lottie said.

The one who was about to be thrown out of the little gang threw down his paint can, jerked a purple bandanna from his low-riding jeans, and tossed it toward the almighty Kingster. "I didn't sign up for this if you're going to get one of us killed. You can have my colors. I don't want to run with y'all anymore. My mama is going to ground me for eternity if she sees that video."

Sirens sounded in the distance, but Devon didn't seem the least bit worried. He sat down on the floor with his hands laced behind his head. Three of the others followed his lead.

Red and blue lights flashed through the open door, and four policemen rushed inside, guns drawn as they scanned the room. "We'll take it from here," one of them told Knox and Lottie.

"What have you done this time, Devon?" one of them asked with a groan.

"Them two shot at us, and we rushed in here to get away from them. See that hole in the wall? I had to duck down to keep from getting hit. This place was all messed up before we even ran in here, and now they're framing us for doing it. We're waiting for you to come rescue us."

"Here you go." Knox handed his phone to the officer. "You can transfer that over to your phone. The first part they did not know was being filmed."

The officer holstered his gun and tapped the two phones together. "I'll go ahead and send it in to the lab while I'm at it," he said and then watched the video. "Looks like you boys might be in some real trouble this time. The kind that even your daddy can't get you out of."

Devon laughed at the man. "My dad takes care of me and my friends, and besides, it's their word against ours, and that can't be shown in court because…"

Knox didn't give him time to finish but butted in to say, "You will find Devon's fingerprints all over the saw that he threatened us both with. And the other three boys' prints on the paint cans. Mine will be on the shotgun shell lying out in the yard. I'm Knox Callahan, and the gun is mine. It is registered. Papers are in my trailer. This is Lottie Johnston, and we are both employed as carpenters here."

"I'm Officer Harrison. These guys are Officers Tisdale, McBride, and Lowry. We will need to take the gun for now, but you can claim it at the station tomorrow morning."

Lottie broke the shotgun, removed the shell, and handed both to McBride. "I'm the one who fired the gun into the air outside. You'll find the spent shell out there, and when you test this, you'll find that they are only loaded with Number 8 bird shot. It might sting their sorry little asses, but it wouldn't kill them."

"Maybe she didn't fire it at us, but come on, Harrison. You might as well let us go. We are all going to tell you the same story. We didn't do the damage. We just picked up the paint and saw because we was scared them two fools were going to shoot us," Devon told him.

"That's not what I saw on the video," Officer Harrison said.

Devon jacked up his chin and glared at Harrison. "You are dead wrong, and that's my daddy coming through the door behind you. And like I said, that video was shot without our approval, so it won't stand up in…"

A man in an expensive-looking sweat suit pushed his way inside the damaged rec hall and took a look around. "Don't say another word, Son. I'm Richard Adams, the lawyer for these boys. Can someone tell me what is going on?"

"Trespassing, vandalism, driving without a license—unless Devon or one of his buddies got one in the last month—drunk and disorderly, and threatening to kill these two people right here," Officer Harrison answered.

"And what do my son and his friends say about all that?" Richard asked.

Devon tilted his chin up and grinned. "Daddy, we didn't do anything, and that bi…lady threatened me when she fired that gun right at me. See that hole in the wall? That's where the bullet landed."

Knox stepped over to Richard's side and played the video

for him. "Officer Harrison not only has this on his phone, but it's been sent to the police lab to use as evidence. Lottie fired into the air while still outside. An officer already has the spent shell bagged for evidence. And, sir, if you will look closely, that hole is the size of the snout of the saw, not peppered with bird shot."

Lottie wanted to tell them that had she been firing at the boy, he would be moaning with bits of bird shot in his body, not lying about what happened, but instead she said, "The police have the gun and will find the other slug in the gun if you want to see what it's filled with."

Officer Harrison held up a bag. "This is the shell we found on the ground outside. Your son is lying, Richard. We have to take them all in for questioning, and I'm sure they'll all tell the same story. But the video shows a different one. I'm afraid you can't get them off so easy this time."

Devon glanced over at his buddies, and a wide grin covered his face. "We'll be out in a couple of hours, won't we, Dad?"

"Not this time, Son," Richard said with sadness in his tone. "Do what you have to do with the lot of them, Harrison. They're all fifteen years old, so I expect they'll spend some time in juvie. If there is any leniency at all, I will send my kid to military school. The rest of the parents can handle this any way they want. I won't represent any of them. They can get a public defender."

"You can't do this to me," Devon screamed.

"Yes, I can, and should have done it before now," Richard

said. "That truck out there is mine as well as the chainsaw. I'm sure both will be taken away to be locked up for evidence, but I would like them back when this is over. And send me a bill for all this damage. I'll pay for it." He turned around and walked outside.

"Da…dee…" Devon yelled.

"Okay, boys," Officer Thomas said, "hands behind your backs. You're going to lock up for the weekend. There's no arraignment until Monday morning, so if you have other weekend plans, they are canceled."

"Before we put the cuffs on, I'll need all your cell phones," Officer Thomas said.

The other boys handed theirs over without question, but not Devon. He glared at the policeman and said, "Over my dead body. No one touches my phone."

Harrison put the cuffs on him and then slipped the phone from the back pocket of his baggy jeans and handed it to Tisdale. "Take the phones to the lab and tell them to look at Devon's first to see what these boys have been texting about."

"It's password protected," Devon snapped.

"We've got some excellent tech guys," Tisdale said.

Lottie looped her arm in Knox's when the boys were finally in the back of the two police cars. Devon was still spitting threats and telling his buddies that his father didn't mean what he said and would have them out within an hour.

"I'm sorry that y'all have to deal with this damage," Officer Harrison said, "but it could have been much worse if they'd taken that saw to one of the buildings you are putting up. And I'm so glad you caught it on a video that we can use in court. Richard might have a change of heart and try to get them out of jail like always, but this time is going to be different since we've got proof. So, thank you for having the good sense to start filming when you walked in the door."

"How many times have they been in trouble?" Lottie asked.

"I'd have to take my shoes off to count them," Officer Tisdale said with a chuckle. "They've been hell-raisers since they were ten years old, and this won't be their first time to stand before the judge."

"*My* daddy would have let me sit it out in jail from the beginning," Knox said.

"He raised you right, like mine did," Harrison said. "Thanks again. There will probably be a plea bargain, but we'll call you if we need you to testify."

"Sure thing," Knox said. "Would y'all mind stretching some crime scene tape around the building so there won't be any problems when the insurance adjuster arrives?"

"And letting us know what happens if they do all take a plea deal? When we finish this job, we could be miles away for the next one," Lottie said.

"Of course we will, and we'll do one better than crime scene tape. Tisdale is already in there taking pictures. Just tell the adjuster to come down to the station, and we can give him copies of everything," Harrison answered. "Cell phones capture things very well, but we like to have photos taken with a high dots-per-inch ratio for court. I doubt it goes that far, but one never knows."

"Thank you," Knox said. "Then it will be all right if we use the other end of the rec room until our boss gets in touch with the insurance folks?"

"Sure thing," Harrison said.

Tisdale came out of the rec hall and gave Harrison a thumbs-up. The other two officers carried out several bags with evidence tape stretched across them. They all loaded their things into the patrol cars and drove away.

"Do you think it's safe for six elderly couples to be living in a place so far from town?"

"The police were here in less than the ten minutes the dispatcher thought, so yes, I do. Besides, we held our own against four of those little hoodlums. There will be six men and as many women living here. Plus, tomorrow I'm driving into town and getting an inexpensive security system to attach to the fence out front. After the place is finished, I'm sure there will be something more sophisticated put in to open the front gates. Until then, Jack, you, and I are going to have an alert when someone comes onto the property in the evenings," he said. "For now, though, we've had enough excitement for the night. Let's go get some sleep."

She motioned with a hand to take in the whole room. "If they could do this in that short length of time, think what they could have done if we hadn't caught them."

"It's a scary idea," Knox said.

"I'm way too wound up to sleep, and one of us needs to

be awake the rest of the night in case there are more in their little purple bandanna gang to come back for retaliation," she told him.

"What do you want to do, then?"

"I need to do something physical to get all this tension out of my body," she answered.

"I'm in the same boat. What have you got in mind?"

"We could get the floodlights out of the storage room, run a couple of extension cords out to the cabin we're working on, and build a wall or two before dawn. The little punk-ass kids won't even turn into the road if they see things all lit up," she suggested.

"I'm in," Knox agreed and followed her to the room where the tools were stored behind the kitchen.

"What kind of security are you putting up tomorrow?" she asked as she loaded a small wagon with a skill saw, two nail guns, and boxes of nails. Then she clipped a tape measure to the waistband of her jeans and tossed one to Knox.

Knox caught it, looped two extension cords over his shoulders, and picked up a floodlight on a six-foot stand with each hand. "There was one at a place where I worked years ago. It was motion-activated. Any movement could set it off, and when that happened, lights flooded the place, and a siren loud enough to wake the dead sounded. That's what I intend to buy and set up."

"It's a shame that we have to do this at all," Lottie said with a long sigh as she pulled the wagon through the rec room. "When I have kids, they are going to be taught accountability from the time they can crawl."

Knox followed behind her. "So, you are planning to have children?"

"Of course, at least three and maybe four, and all a couple or three years apart. I don't ever want to have a tagalong like I was," she answered. "Don't you want a family?"

"Yes, I do, but I was thinking maybe six to start out, maybe with a couple of sets of twins right off the bat. I loved having a brother the same age as me."

"You are crazy!" She was amazed at how much a simple giggle eased all the tension from her body. "Why would you want a family that big?"

He took her hand in his free one and led her back to her trailer. "Because I've been around Mary Jane and Joe Clay and learned how precious a huge family can be. And life is better with siblings, don't you think?"

"By the time I went to kindergarten, my brothers were out of the house, either in college or working their first jobs, so I didn't know much about that."

Knox stopped long enough to plug in the two extension cords and then strung them all the way out to the third cabin. "This will really put us ahead of schedule."

"Yep, and work some out of the anger at the same time." She connected the saw and stretched a tape over a board, marked it with a pencil, and made the cut.

When Cheeto announced the morning, they had built one wall, and another was almost ready to stand up on

Monday morning. Lottie sat down on the floor and leaned back against a stud. "Is all the anger out of your body?"

"Oh, yeah." Knox eased down beside her with a groan. "I haven't pulled an all-nighter in years. That chainsaw kid might be right about me being an old man."

"I don't think so," she singsonged and covered a yawn with her hand. "I'm so wrung out that I feel like I just walked out of a massage."

"Never had one of those, but Brodie says he's like a wet noodle when he gets one," Knox said.

"When we finish this job, we'll both get one. My treat," she said.

"I'm game. Will it be one of those couples' massages?"

"Maybe," she answered and yawned again.

"Think you can sleep now?" Knox asked.

"Probably not. Every little sound will wake me."

"I'll share my earplugs with you. Tripp snores when he's really tired, and I've learned to keep a jar of them close by."

"And you want a dozen kids?" she asked as she stood up. "What if they all get their uncle Tripp's DNA and snore? You'll have to go to the barn to sleep."

He got up on his feet with a groan. "Then I'll build a bedroom in the barn for me and my wife. Let's load all this up and put it back where it belongs."

"You mean you don't want to grab some breakfast and then work all day?"

"Exactly. I'm willing to eat cold cereal and even fall into bed without a shower."

"Then I'll make breakfast this morning." She grinned as she began to put everything into the wagon. "What will it be, plain oatmeal or with maple brown sugar? There's both kinds in the rec room. We can make coffee and eat while we look at the damage in daylight."

"Thank goodness those boys didn't have time to destroy the kitchen," Knox said.

"I might have really given them a dose of bird shot if they had messed with the coffeemaker," she declared.

Cheeto strutted across the street and flew up to sit on the side of the wagon.

"All right, pretty boy," Lottie said. "You can have a ride, but the rec room has a bad aura right now. You might not want to spend any time in there."

Evidently, Cheeto wasn't afraid of any kind of aura because he didn't leave his perch until they were inside. Then he hopped down to the floor and began to snoop. Lottie and Knox took the equipment to the storage room, put it away, and came back out to find the rooster staggering around and trying to crow, but all that came out sounded somewhat like hiccups.

"Is he dying?" Lottie asked. "Hurry, Knox, look up bird flu and see if he's got the symptoms. Maybe that's why he got dropped off. The people didn't want to kill him, but some of their other animals have it."

Knox picked up the Maker's Mark bottle that had been turned over in all the melee from the night before. "Here is your bird flu. Cheeto isn't sick. He's drunk."

Lottie's giggles turned into full-fledged laughter. She plopped down in a chair and could not get control, no matter how hard she tried. The adrenaline from the night before and working until daylight finally left her body. Tears ran down her cheeks and left wet spots on her T-shirt, but she didn't care. She was alive. Her muscles ached too much for her to be dead.

Knox sat down beside her and handed her a paper towel from the center of the table. "It's funny, but not that much."

"Thank you. I can't explain it, but that felt so good." She wiped her eyes. "I'm so…sorry… Bless…his little…heart." She hiccuped between words.

Cheeto tried to fly up on Knox's knee but misjudged and landed on the floor between him and Lottie. Knox reached down and picked him up. "I'm going to take him to my trailer and put him in the cat carrier you loaned me. He can sober up in it. I'll be back soon to have some of your famous oatmeal and a cup of coffee before I get some sleep."

"Do you think he needs to go to the vet?" she asked.

"No, but now that I know he's an alcoholic, I might make him go to those meetings," Knox answered.

That set her off into another giggling fit that she barely had in control when Knox returned with several bright orange earplugs in a small plastic bag.

Lottie traded him a mug full of coffee for the bag and stuffed it down into her hip pocket. She pointed to boxes of instant oatmeal on the cabinet. "Which one do you want?"

"You make it, and I'll eat it," he answered. "But you might want to make three of those packages. I'm really hungry."

"Since you brought me earplugs, I will make this a special meal and add two pieces of toast to the order," she teased.

He took a sip of his coffee and sat down. "That sounds amazing. I'll try not to fall asleep while it's cooking."

"Thanks for the earplugs," she said as she emptied packages into a bowl and added water.

"Darlin', I would do anything for my new friend."

Chapter 16

"HOLY HELL!" JACK SAID when he saw the condition of the rec room. "I'm sure glad you and Knox corralled those hoodlums. What is the world coming to? Why didn't you call me? I would have come right back."

"I wasn't about to have Aunt Mandy mad at me for robbing her of her time with you. We took care of it, and Knox has fixed up a security system that will do until you get the proper fence and gate installed," Lottie answered.

The door hinges squeaked, and Thomas stopped in his tracks on the way inside the room. "What happened here? Did Knox break up with Lottie?"

"No, and what makes you think that?" Knox asked.

"Well, this is what you can expect if you do," Thomas teased. "Now someone tell me who really tore this place up."

"A bunch of boys who thought they were above the law," Lottie answered and went on to repeat the same story she had told Jack when he got back to the site a few minutes before.

"First time ever in all my years there has really been a break-in," Jack answered. "But Knox has installed security so that one of us will know if anyone comes over the cattle guard after dark."

"Sweet Lord!" Thomas gasped. "Us old married guys are glad to rest after a hard day's work, but what about the single guys who stay out late at night?"

"The system is set to go off at eleven o'clock every night. If anyone forgets or is too drunk to check the time, a siren will wake all of us up, and lights will flood the place."

"And believe me when I say they will definitely suffer if they do," Lottie added.

"As in?" Jack asked.

"I will cook breakfast, and they will be required to eat it," Lottie answered.

"That would be terrible after a late night and too many beers," Thomas said.

"Then tell them to come home before eleven," Lottie told him. "Or you'll all have cold cereal and burnt toast."

Knox chuckled and wondered if Lottie truly could cook. Not that it mattered since he loved to be in the kitchen. More guys filtered into the room, and while Lottie told them the story, he went to the kitchen and started a pot of coffee. When that one finished dripping, he set it on the warmer. If he was dating for real, would it matter if she didn't cook?

He answered his own question by realizing that he wouldn't mind working all day and coming home to cook supper, too, because if this was real, she would be working right alongside him all day. So why should she have to prepare supper? Besides, there was always takeout or DoorDash if neither of them wanted to spend time in the kitchen.

He took several mugs from the cabinet, and when the

coffee stopped gurgling, he set the pot to the side and started a second one. Before everyone checked in for the morning, both would be emptied and a third and fourth one made for break time.

Lottie startled him when she said, " What are you smiling about?"

Knox poured a mug full of coffee and handed it to her. "I was wondering if you have always taken it black or if there's a story?"

"A short story. When I first started drinking it, Martha, the housekeeper that I told you about, made it so strong that it practically curled my toenails."

Lottie edged over close enough to Knox that her shoulder brushed against his. That feeling that he wanted more than friendship landed like a rock in his heart. Apparently, she didn't feel the same because there wasn't even a hitch in her voice when she went on with the story.

"I asked for cream and sugar, and she laughed at me. She said, 'Girl, life don't come with cream and sugar, and neither does my coffee. Take it like it is or leave it alone.' I didn't touch it again until I went to college. Even then I usually made something like one of those Starbucks lattes that has lots of sugar and cream in it to get me going in the mornings. Then I started working full time with Jack and the crew and learned to drink it black."

"What changed?" Knox noticed that most of the guys had gathered around Jack and were looking at the video playing on his phone.

"I found out that all coffee wasn't like drinking Grandma's stuff." She took a sip and stepped away from him. "In case you are wondering, they're all watching the video on your phone. I'm tired of telling the story."

"Me too," Knox agreed. "You probably won't need a fake boyfriend anymore after they all see how mean you were with that shotgun. They'll all be afraid to cross you or even mention going out with you."

"One can only hope, but I'm not ready to break up with you yet," she told him.

————————

Lottie spread a blanket on the grass beside the lake and watched Knox walking toward her with an old-fashioned picnic basket in one hand and a six-pack of soft drinks in the other. She had vowed that tonight she was going to tell him that she had developed feelings for him. He might say he didn't feel the same, but at least the guessing game in her head would end.

"You remembered to bring the blanket." He smiled as he motioned for her to sit down and then followed her.

"Of course. If all I have to do is rustle up a blanket to get a good supper, I can do that. Are you disappointed that I don't cook?" Her voice held an edge.

"Hey," Knox set down the basket and the soft drinks. "What bee crawled up your overall legs?"

"I'm wearing a sundress, not overalls, and I don't have an attitude," she shot back. Maybe tonight wasn't a good time to tell him how she felt after all.

"And you look gorgeous, but, darlin', you also look amazing wearing only a towel wrapped around your body."

"Good save." She finally grinned.

The aroma of fried chicken rose up from the basket when he opened it. "To answer your question, I really don't care if you cook or not. I enjoy working in the kitchen after a long day of framing houses."

"I'll tell you a secret," she said, putting off saying what was really on her mind. "I *can* cook, but when I first came to work for Uncle Jack, I figured the guys would all expect it of me since I'm a woman. I made a point of telling them, like I did you, that I can make soup out of a can and bologna sandwiches."

"But…" Knox started to argue.

"I *can* make those things, but I'm also a pretty good cook when it comes to plain old country food. I'm probably not on the scale that you are in the kitchen, but my meals are edible. My grandmother saw to that and…" She paused. "I am a crackerjack baker. I love to make cakes, pies, cookies, candy, and desserts of all kinds."

"I do have a sweet tooth, so I will make the food if you do desserts," he said. "We'll make a wonderful couple until this job ends and we go our separate ways. I won't even tell the rest of the guys that you brought a chocolate cream pie to my house."

He pulled a plate from the basket and handed it to her. "Any more secrets a fake boyfriend…no…a *friend* should know about?"

"A couple, but I'm starving, so let's eat and enjoy the sunset," she answered. "Look at that. The ducks are here. They probably got a whiff of what's in that basket."

Knox removed the lids from several containers. "Finger foods and lots of napkins."

He brought out a small charcuterie board and arranged still-hot chicken strips on one end with cheese cubes and two kinds of dip, and fresh-cut vegetables and fruit on the other. Then he pulled out a bag of corn chips, along with a small bowl of salsa, and a basket of rolls to set to the side. "I started to get a bottle of wine, but…"

"I'd rather have root beer," she said. "This is too pretty to eat and enough to feed six or seven people."

"I'm glad you think so, but I'm too hungry to just look at it. So, dive in. Like I said, I brought plenty of napkins. And honey, if there are leftovers, we can always use them for something later."

She twisted the top off a soda, set it beside her, and filled her plate. "This is more than a picnic. It's a romantic feast."

"Friends with romance. I like that." He made a sandwich by cramming two pieces of chicken into a roll, and then loaded his plate with cheese, vegetables, and fruit.

The door is open. Say something. Tell him how you feel. The voice in her head sounded like something her last therapist would say.

"I got word this evening that the papers will be ready for me and Geneva to sign a week from Saturday. I told her I would fly down to New Iberia that day so she wouldn't have to drive. Want to go with me?" Knox asked. "We could stay overnight if…"

She didn't give him time to finish the sentence. "I'd love to."

"Great," Knox said. "Now about those other secrets."

She drew in a breath, but before she could get a word out, Cheeto lit on the blanket, stole a piece of chicken from her plate, and hopped away a few feet to peck at it.

"That is more than a little bit cannibalistic, isn't it?" she said with half a laugh.

"According to my research, chickens and other birds will eat anything," Knox said.

Was that an omen to keep her mouth shut, that this was not the time or place to say anything more about their relationship/friendship? She was still pondering that when a duck came out of the lake and waddled toward them. Cheeto spread out his colorful wings, fluffed up all his feathers, and went in for the battle. The duck retreated to the water, and Cheeto went back to eating his stolen chicken strip.

"He thinks he's all that and an order of fries, but he backs down from rattlesnakes," Lottie said.

"That means he's a mean critter, but he picks his battles," Knox told her.

Lottie wondered if she looked up her name, would it say that she was mean enough to hold a shotgun on some vandalizing kids? And yet, not wise enough to back down from this battle that will only end up breaking her heart? But if she spoke up, their friendship could be ruined, and the work situation would be in shambles if he didn't feel the same way.

Cheeto finished eating and eased down to a sitting position.

"Look at that. He's guarding us," Knox said.

"He's just making sure the ducks don't come around begging for handouts that could be his later on this evening," Lottie said, glad for anything to take her mind off her feelings.

Cheeto stood up when the ducks took flight. He threw back his head and crowed, then started toward the trailer.

"We are safe now." Knox chuckled. "He told them to stay away. Hey, we were talking about secrets. I'm surprised that you can cook, but what else have you been hiding from me?"

"Why?" she asked.

"Because I believed you. Not many people can fool me."

She inhaled deeply and let it out with a whoosh. "I have feelings for you," she blurted out. "I felt chemistry at your brother's wedding, and I've tried to fight it…"

Knox set his plate down and moved closer to her. "You can't fight what you feel, darlin'. The heart wants what it wants, and it won't be satisfied with anything else."

She looked deeply into his blue eyes. "But…what about our friendship? Is this going to ruin it?"

He tipped up her chin with his knuckles. "I have been doing battle with my own feelings for you. This won't mess up what we have, but it could make it better."

She barely had time to moisten her lips before he kissed her—long, deep, and passionately. Evidently, the fake relationship was over, and they were on a new journey, but what would happen when they went their separate ways?

Chapter 17

"Five became ten, and ten is now fifteen, with another five will make twenty when they arrive on Monday of next week since we're ahead of schedule," Lottie said that morning as she and Knox had their usual breakfast together.

Knox went inside and brought out the coffeepot and a basket of muffins. "And then the final group will get here, and we'll be filling in where we're needed because the framing will be finished."

She picked up a warm chocolate chip muffin. "Yep, if it doesn't rain. In that case, we'll be helping out the other teams before we finish the last framing job. I can do whatever is needed, but that doesn't mean I like staining cabinets or putting down baseboards. My favorite jobs are when I can get the last house framed and move on to the next site."

"That's my favorite, too, but I don't mind the rest of it. Kind of keeps my skills in those areas from getting rusty, but it looks like we'll still be finished by Mother's Day."

"Kind of like reading a good book. Exciting to open the first page, and by the time the last words are read, you wish there was more. I'm going to miss you when this job is finished and I go to El Paso."

"Me, or breakfast?" he asked.

She nudged him on the shoulder, and sparks danced all around the plate of bacon, egg, and cheese biscuits sitting between them. "Why can't it be both?" she asked.

But vibes were all there were—other than breakfast and holding hands a couple of times. Three days had passed since that mind-blowing kiss, and there had not been another one. This business of being in a real relationship was turning out to be a lot less fun than the fake one.

"If you had to pick one?" Knox asked.

She held up a finger, swallowed the bite of the muffin, and took a sip of coffee. "I will miss the food, but also the company each morning and my partner on the job. My mind keeps playing the what-if game."

"And that is?"

"What if you find someone else? What if the long-distance thing doesn't work? What if that old saying about being out of sight, out of mind happens?"

"We can make it work, if we have to," he told her. "And that game only brings worry, so don't play it."

"What does 'if we have to' mean?" she asked.

"Maybe you won't be in El Paso. Thomas and our team have been thinking about starting their own business up in Oklahoma. They might talk you into helping them," he answered. "That's a lot closer than El Paso, so we could see each other more often."

The thought of working for anyone other than her Uncle Jack put a lump in Lottie's throat that she had trouble swallowing even with a couple sips of coffee. "I should help Walter out for a few months until he gets his owner sea legs under him. Do you really think that we can do the long-distance thing?"

"Depends on how badly we want it."

"Everything will be different when we leave Swan Song Estates," she said with a sigh.

"Yes, but we have today," Knox whispered.

"We are dating for real, aren't we?"

Knox reached for another biscuit. "I told Tripp that we were, and I'm sure he's spread it around the family. I hope I wasn't wrong."

"One kiss does not make a couple dating."

"How many does it take?" Knox asked.

"I don't know for sure, but more than one."

"Okay, then…" He sighed dramatically. "I'll do my best to save enough energy tonight to see if I can remedy that problem. But if you fall asleep in the middle of a round of hot making out, that's on you."

"Hey…" One of the newest single guys, Vincent, came around the side of Knox's trailer and stopped. "I heard y'all were a couple, but I'm having trouble believing it. I thought you were saving yourself for me, Lottie."

"You were a day late and a dollar short," she told him.

Knox motioned toward the food sitting on the step between Lottie and him. "Have a biscuit and muffin as a consolation prize."

Vincent reached for one of each and chuckled. "Are you as good at framing out a house as you are at cooking?"

Knox shrugged. "You can judge for yourself after you see how our team works."

"We're almost a week ahead of schedule, so that should tell you something," Lottie smarted off.

No one, especially not Micah or Vincent, was going to play passive-aggressive games with Knox—not when she was within hearing distance. She had never worked with another partner who worked as hard as he did. His expertise and, of course, working through the night after the break-in, were what had put them so far ahead of schedule.

Vincent held up his hands with a half-eaten biscuit in one and the muffin in the other. "Hey, I didn't mean anything by saying that. I've already listened to Thomas and Eddie singing Knox's praises. Are y'all going to El Paso to work for Walter when we finish up here?"

"Are you?" Lottie asked.

"Probably," Vincent replied. "I like the idea of being in a bigger city where there is more nightlife."

Knox shook his head. "Not me. I've got plenty of work waiting for me at home. With seven sisters and two brothers, there's always something for a carpenter to take care of."

Vincent finished off the last of his biscuit and asked, "What about you, Lottie?"

"Probably not," she answered. "I need to be closer to my folks, and El Paso is a very long drive from here, but I will go for the summer to help Walter out that long."

"You do know that every one of us is going to try to talk you into joining us. I can't imagine a job without you being there, so get ready for some serious conversations. Who knows, maybe your long-distance relationship with Knox will fizzle, and one of us will get lucky."

Lottie shook her head. "Knox is the exception to the rule. If things go south with him, then I'll double down on my rule not to date another coworker."

Vincent removed his cap and ran his fingers through his brown hair. "That just means I'll have to work harder to change your mind. If I hurry, I'll have time for an extra cup of coffee in the rec hall before me and my crew try to keep up with y'all. Thanks for the food. I'm keeping the muffin for break time." He waved as he walked away.

Knox turned to focus on Lottie. "Do you think we *won't* survive a long-distance relationship?"

Lottie shook her head. "Mama says you get out of any relationship exactly what you put into it. Even without a good make-out session these past few days, I'm all in."

Knox wiggled his eyebrows. "Oh, really."

"Get your mind out of the gutter. I don't go to bed with guys I've only dated for three days," she said.

"Right back at you," Knox said. "But honey, we've been together about sixteen hours of every day for two weeks. If you divide that out into four hours for each date, then we're way ahead of the normal schedule."

"How many women have you dated for only three days?"

He leaned over and kissed her on the cheek. "I'd have to take my shoes off to count them all, and that would make us late for work."

She cupped his cheeks in her hands and kissed him properly.

When the kiss ended, he whispered softly, "And that erases the memory of every one of those women."

That kiss ignited the steamy, hot sparks that were already between them. Lottie had never believed in that old crap about friends becoming lovers.

But maybe she had been wrong.

The game, as well as a few bets, was on when they reached the building site for the fourth cabin that morning. The guys working on the outside, as well as the ones who were taking care of getting drywall up and painting, had made their brags that morning that they could keep up with them.

"I don't care if we win or I lose my hundred bucks, but Jack is like a kid at Christmas with all the progress being made," Eddie said as he and Gabe built trusses for a roof. "Lottie, why don't you and Knox go on down to cabins five and six and get the sill plates down and start building walls while we put the roof on this one."

"That ought to light a fire under all of the others," Lottie said with a grin. "You are right about Uncle Jack, and if we get done early, we might have a few days to spend with our families before all you guys have to go to El Paso."

"And it will give you time to find something closer to this place," Eddie said. "Is there no way that we can make you change your mind after the summer?"

"Nope, not even if you offer me something up around Randlett, Oklahoma. I want to be close to my folks. See you guys at lunchtime."

"At this rate, I'll be home by Mother's Day for sure," Knox said.

"And we'll be back in Randlett in time to help our wives get things organized to go to El Paso," Gabe agreed with a nod. "That'll make them all very happy."

"For a little while." Eddie chuckled.

Knox had never been in a long-distance relationship. Tripp often said that all three Callahan brothers had commitment issues because they would never find someone like their mother. Knox and Brodie had argued with him, but maybe he was right.

Was the heat between him and Lottie only a flash in the pan, so to speak? Would the old saying about "out of sight, out of mind" come into play after they had been apart for a few weeks?

"Do you want to cut the boards or drill?" Lottie asked.

He slipped the right bit into a drill. "I'll do this part until you get them all laid out."

"Then I'll help finish the job. I bet we can get the sill plates down on both cabins before the rest of them finish putting the roof on number four."

"Probably so," Knox agreed, but his mind was two hours north in Spanish Fort, not at Swan Song Estates.

Once the deal was finalized for his new land, Knox intended to ask Lottie to move to Spanish Fort and help him build an estate on a little larger plan. He envisioned ten new homes with five acres of land for each one. While he was getting the land marked off, wells drilled, and electricity for each place, and all the building permits taken care of, he would begin advertising for prospective buyers. He was pretty sure his sister Bo and her husband would be the first ones to jump on the chance. The prospective buyers could design their own homes, or they could work with him to draw up blueprints.

Lottie could move her trailer to the backyard, and after a while, he would ask her to move into the house with him. If they proved that they could live and also work together, they could possibly wind up in a permanent relationship.

Knox silently scolded himself for making big plans after being only two kisses into the real deal. He warned himself to back up and slow his roll. Just because his brothers had found their soulmates was no sign that he had to jump into the fire.

Lottie laid out the first board and measured the next one. "What are you thinking about? You've got that look on your face."

"What look?" Knox frowned.

"The one that says something is going on in your mind," she replied.

"I was making plans for the future, which is crazy, because I don't even know if the plans I am making will work."

She laid the second board down. "Ain't that the truth, but what is it that has you in a turmoil?"

"I have quite a bit of equipment, but I wouldn't mind

buying some of this extra stuff from Jack when this project is finished." He didn't actually lie since he had been thinking about that very thing.

"It will most likely go to Walter since he's the one buying out the business," Lottie said with a long, drawn-out sigh. "You disappoint me."

"What did I do?"

"You could have said that you were arguing with yourself about kissing me," she teased.

He slid a wicked wink her way. "That could be arranged, but I'm not sure I could stop with one. And right now, we should probably work, and kiss later. I promise I will not disappoint you again."

"I'll hold you to that promise."

She finished laying out the sill plates, picked up a second drill, checked the battery, and began to sink the pilot holes for Knox. "Hey, I forgot to ask about Cheeto. I didn't hear him crowing this morning. Did he die?"

"How did you get from kissing to drunk roosters so fast?" Knox asked.

"I have an Oprah mind," she answered.

"What is that?"

She picked up a high-powered drill. "It means that I can multitask."

" He must still have a hangover because he didn't crow when I peeked under the towel this morning. I will let him out of his jail cell this evening. He is eating and drinking water, so I think he will live," Knox answered.

"Then I will use the earplugs tonight."

Knox followed behind her with the heavy bolts needed to hold the plates down so that the walls could be firmly attached to them. Lottie's father had been right that framing out a house was a lot like building a family. Love made the foundation firm. Sill plates were like the commitment that everything was attached to. When the house was in the dry, it became a private place of safety and peace.

Did that mean he was in love with Lottie? He liked her enough that it could possibly grow into love, just like the walls he was working on right then. She could become his soulmate, but he was in no hurry to rush the idea.

Lottie took Knox by the hand, led him to her bedroom, and closed the sliding door. "If you are right about all the hours we've spent together, we are long past due for a night together—even if we are dog tired."

"Yes," Knox whispered softly in her ear.

Desire swept through her body like a Texas wildfire when he gently pushed back her blond hair with his fingertips. She'd had an attraction to men before, but nothing like this. She wanted things to go slowly, to enjoy every single minute of this first experience with him, and at the same time, she desperately needed to feel his whole body next to hers. She slipped his shirt over his head, and he did the same with hers.

His lips found hers as their bodies pressed together. Heat had flowed between them before, but when her bare skin touched his, there was no comparison to the former chemistry. Even her toes tingled when he slipped his tongue into her mouth.

He unfastened her bra with one hand and caressed her back. She was already panting when he slipped the straps down from her shoulders, and sheer passion like she had never felt before engulfed her whole body.

Just as he started easing her sweatpants down, all hell broke loose. Sirens blasted and startled her so badly that she had redone her bra and pulled on her shirt before she even realized what she was doing.

"Trespassers," he gasped about the same time that lights lit up the area.

"Damn it!" Lottie swore and headed toward the door, tripped over Prissy, who was making a mad dash to hide under the bed, and started to fall. Knox caught her before she hit the floor, and they both fell backward back onto the bed.

"If a bunch of"—she panted—"drunk teenagers…" She sat up and tried to stand but got tangled up on Knox's shirt she had tossed on the floor and fell back onto the bed again.

He caught her a second time and held her tightly. "I have to go to my trailer to turn off the alarm, but I'll check everything out and come right back."

"I'll go with you," she said. "But this is not our night, is it?"

He picked up his shirt from the floor and jerked it down over his head. "Probably not, but it's also not our only night."

"If we have vandals, you better hold the gun tonight and

let me do the video business," she grumbled as she followed him.

"And if it's one of our own?" he asked as he jogged toward his trailer.

"Then God help them," Lottie answered.

She followed him all the way to his trailer, but waited outside, keeping her eyes peeled for intruders. Cheeto had been released from the cat carrier as soon as he appeared to have recovered from his hangover, and he sat on the top of Knox's truck, his little head thrown back and looking like he was squawking, but Lottie couldn't hear it over the shrill noise of the siren.

"It's okay, boy," she assured him. "When I find who did this, they are going to be in big trouble."

The ringing in her ears slowly eased when the noise died down and the lights went off. Cheeto gave the all-clear warning and then hopped down to the bed of the truck. Bally ran out the open front door, and Lottie scooped the kitten up in her arms.

"We've both had a very bad night, haven't we, little girl?" she crooned. "But it's over now, and someone is going to pay if one of our own caused all this."

Bally buried her nose in the crook of Lottie's arm and purred.

"Is this an omen that things are moving too fast?" she whispered.

"What the hell was that?" Thomas yelled from down the row of trailers.

Soon all the guys were standing around her and Knox in a huddle.

"The alarm works," Knox answered.

"I'd say it does." Jack chuckled.

"I'm going to do a walk-around," Knox said. "I'll be right back. Wait right here?"

She shoved the kitten back into the trailer and closed the door. "I'm going with you."

Jack nodded and said, "I'll grab a couple of flashlights in the rec hall and go with y'all."

"We'll all help," Eddie said. "We are all here and accounted for, so it wasn't one of our team that tried to sneak in. But if those lights and noise didn't scare the trespassers away, they could still be hiding on the property."

"Are you sure that none of you set that thing off?" Lottie raised her voice.

All the men looked from one to the other as if they were taking roll call, but not a single guy said a word for several seconds. None of them looked sheepish or owned up to driving into the site after the alarm was set.

"If any of you are guilty, then this is your first warning," she said. "Just speak up so we don't have to spend time checking out the whole site."

"It wasn't one of us," Vincent finally answered. "We can make short order of the search if we all get our flashlights from our trailers and get with it, rather than standing around here."

"When we catch the sorry suckers that woke me up, I

want first dibs on the bunch of them!" Thomas growled and held up his flashlight. "I came prepared."

"They are all probably running like scared little bunnies. No telling where we will find them, so check every nook and cranny." Jack raised his voice and headed toward the rec hall.

"Give me time to put on my boots," Micah called out. "I'll check out between the trailers and under them."

"I'll help you do that," Eddie said.

"If you find anyone, Thomas has to stand in line behind me to get at them," Lottie growled and jogged around the trailer to catch up with Knox. "There's lots of places for them to play hide-and-seek, but the bunch of us out here shining lights might scare them into running."

Jack came out of the rec hall and handed a flashlight to whoever needed one. "If whoever set off the alarm was in a vehicle, I imagine they put it in reverse and hightailed it away from here. But if they were on foot, they could still be on the property. Y'all go check out the first cabin. Mandy will have my hide if they use spray paint on the walls and she has to wait to move in."

Knox and Lottie both nodded and started that way.

"I'll check around the whole cabin," Lottie said.

"I'll go on in and make sure everything is safe inside. Now that it's in the dry, and it's ready for the cabinets, there's lots of nooks and crannies for hiding."

Lottie stopped at the porch and sucked in a lungful of air, then let it out in a whoosh.

"Did you see something?" Knox asked.

"No, but that alarm going off when it did…" She paused. "Could that be a sign that we are moving too fast? Do we need to slow things down?"

"What do you think?" Knox opened the door and took a step inside.

"Hey, don't shoot me," Jack yelled. "I checked all around this place, and no one is here. Y'all can go on to the next one. I had to see for myself that everything is good because Mandy is going to have a million questions. I came in by the back door. The locks will be installed on Monday when the next team gets here. That won't keep vandals from destroying the outside or breaking down the door."

"But hopefully they won't ever get this far when the lights and sirens go off," Lottie giggled nervously.

"Amen," Jack said. "Looks like there's enough lights out here to make that crazy rooster think it's daylight. With this much help, we'll have this done in no time."

Half an hour later, everyone gathered up in the rec room. Eddie reported that they had found a opossum hiding under one of the trailers and a raccoon under another. "We didn't see any vandals, not even running away toward the lake."

"Didn't find a single spray-paint can or beer can where we searched," Vincent added.

Jack scratched his head and yawned. "A wild animal, unless it was a deer, couldn't have set off the alarm. But if those boys who caused all this damage"—he waved his arm around the room—"sent their little friends back, then I hope they spread the word that we are not putting up with their crap."

"That's right, but I'm a little disappointed that we didn't find a couple of kids shaking in their boots. I would have loved to give them a big chunk of my mind for waking me up," Thomas declared. "I'm going back to bed. See y'all tomorrow morning, or maybe I should say later this morning."

"Thank y'all for helping patrol," Jack said as they dispersed out of the rec hall.

"Glad to help." Thomas chuckled. "I'm glad that we haven't been vandalized again, but I'm even more thankful that Lottie isn't making us eat her cooking tomorrow morning."

Eddie shook his fist at the starlit sky. "Let this be a lesson to all the smart-ass kids out there, and also to you party animals among us. There's no way to get back into this place without being caught unless you want to park and swim across the lake."

"My place or yours?" Knox asked when they were the only ones left in the rec hall.

"Neither," she answered. "The mood is ruined. My heart is still on overdrive, and it's not from hormones. Besides, we have to be up in a few hours, and I'm still not sure that alarm wasn't an omen."

Knox nodded and then chuckled. "Those lights flashing on reminded me of my first date. I walked the girl up to the door and leaned in to kiss her on the cheek. My palms were sweaty, and my heart thumped in my chest like a bass drum. Then her mother turned on the porch light and scared the bejesus out of me."

"Don't tell me that you see that girl every time you look at me from now on," Lottie snapped.

"No, ma'am, I will not. You don't have braces, and you aren't six inches taller than me," he answered. "I'll walk you to your door and be sure there aren't any snakes or wild critters hanging around."

"My hero," Lottie said with a long, dramatic sigh.

"Is there any way to turn down that siren alarm? It about gave me a heart attack last night," Jack asked Knox the next morning after everyone else had left the rec hall.

"I'm not sure, but I'll check the specs on it," Knox answered.

"Appreciate it," Jack said. "I hear a vehicle. Could be the cops coming to cite us for noise."

"Not way out here. I don't think we woke up anyone across the lake, and that's our nearest neighbors, but…" He nodded toward the door. "Those fellers don't look like cops to me."

Knox recognized one of the two men entering the building as the father of the gang leader who wrecked the building. "Hello, what can I do for y'all?" he called out when they were inside.

"I didn't catch your name, or maybe I did and was so angry that I don't remember. I'm Richard Adams, and I'm looking for the foreman or supervisor. This place looks even worse in the daylight."

"I'm Jack Devlin, the owner and foreman of Swan Song Estates," Jack said and extended a hand. "I didn't see it in the dark, but you are right about it being a mess."

Richard shook his hand and then dropped it. "This is my personal insurance adjuster, Ernest Whitmore. I want to be more than fair about the damage my son and his friends did to your property. Would you mind if he takes a good look at everything?"

"Not a bit," Jack said.

A short, bald-headed guy with wire-rimmed glasses took out a notepad and made notes as he walked around the room.

"While he does that, I would like to apologize for my son," Richard said. "Until he goes to military school in the fall, Devon will be doing community service, picking up garbage on Saturday and Sunday along a stretch of highway with other delinquents. He is on house arrest with an ankle device throughout the week and will have a tutor to home-school him through the rest of his sophomore year. If any of his grades drop below a B, then he has to go to juvie. I thought you should know what punishment he is receiving."

"And the other boys?" Knox asked.

"I don't know about them, but Devon can't see or talk to them anymore. He isn't allowed to have a cell phone at all, and only a computer for schoolwork. Even then, his tutor has to be sitting right beside him. I should have come down harder on him a few years ago, but I'm hoping that later is better than not at all."

Jack nodded. "I hope that this teaches him accountability."

"Me too," Richard said and turned to focus on the other guy. "Ernest, what have you come up with?"

"Primer and paint for the wall that got tagged," he answered and nodded toward the other side. "That one will need a stud replaced and at least two sheets of drywall, and more primer and paint there. Then the entire floor will have to be replaced because there's splotches of paint on some of the tiles that will never come out with cleansers. Plus, a table was cut in half, and a few chairs have paint on them. I'm not sure what your builders charge for labor, but you need to add that into the total." He tallied up a number and handed the sheet to Richard.

"We have extra tile that was left over from when we had the rec hall built," Jack said. "We can use it to replace what is ruined and won't have to redo the whole floor."

Richard set his tooled leather briefcase on one of the tables, opened it, and took out an ink pen. He wrote a number on the estimation page and handed it to Jack. "Thank you for offering to do that. Can we agree that this will cover all the labor and materials to make this right? I realize you will take some of your employees away from the jobs they are doing now, and I want to be fair. Plus, I'm going to make Devon work off every dime this summer through the week when he's not on community service. When he's not picking up trash on weekends, he will work for the gardener on my estate."

"This should take care of it," Jack agreed.

Richard wrote out a check and handed it to Jack. "Again, I'm sorry for all this."

Jack folded the check and pocketed it. "I hope all those boys have learned a lesson."

Richard snapped his briefcase closed. "Me too, because I don't know where to go next if Devon hasn't learned anything from all this. Y'all have a good day."

The two guys left, and the crunch of gravel beneath tires said they were on their way back to town. "I wish the alarm had been set, so that man could have seen and heard what will happen if his kid cuts that ankle bracelet off and comes back this way."

"Maybe we should trip it on purpose, kind of like a fire-drill thing, and video the whole thing for that little gang to see." Jack chuckled. "But seriously, with all those punishments, I bet that young Devon will be ready for summer to end. I just hope that the military school straightens him out."

"I didn't know whether to stay or go, but I hated to leave you alone," Knox admitted.

Jack clamped a hand on his shoulder. "I'm glad you stuck around. I sure wanted to unload on the man, but it's a good thing I didn't since he was so apologetic. And Knox, the check is for more than double what it will take to fix the damage. I was about to refuse to take that much. Then that video of Devon flashed through my mind to remind me what a smart ass that kid was to you and Lottie and changed my mind. I hope Richard makes that kid work off every penny of it at minimum wage."

Lottie did not believe in coincidences, but the morning after the alarm system sounded, she began to have second thoughts. Had it not been tested, she and Knox would have had sex—mind-blowing, she was sure. But now she wasn't so sure that a higher power wasn't trying to tell her to slow down and give their relationship more time.

"Sorry I'm late," Knox said when he arrived at the sixth cabin, and then he went on to tell her what had happened.

"I'm glad to hear that our intruders last night weren't the same ones, and that Devon has reached the end of his tether. Maybe he'll grow up to be a decent human being after all."

"One can hope for the best, but if I was his father, I wouldn't hold my breath," Knox said.

"Hey, y'all, got time to talk for a minute?" Micah yelled as he walked toward them.

"Sure," Lottie answered. "What's on your mind?"

"The single guys and I have decided to take turns staying here on the weekends that are left before we finish up here and move on," he said. "Lottie, do you think Jack will be offended if we offer or even insist?"

"Jack will be relieved to have some help, and that is a great idea," she assured him.

"If two of us stay at a time, we can get in some overtime by fixing the rec room, and when that's done, we can work on the cabins," Micah said. "That way, we can even get a little further ahead of schedule. I'd like to get this job finished in time to help Thomas and his family get relocated out to El Paso. We're only going to work for Walter through the summer. That will give him time to get more help hired. By fall, we plan to start up our own company."

"Who's taking this weekend?" she asked. "I'd offer, but Knox and I already promised to help his family out with an event up in that area."

"Me and Benny have signed up for the first round. We've got volunteers for all three of the remaining weekends, so no worries. Y'all already had your turn," Micah said. "I'm going to go tell Jack now, and if he gives me any flak, can I count on your support?"

"Just let me know, and I'll take care of it," Lottie answered with a smile.

She liked that Jack wouldn't be at the site alone, but her mind filtered back to what she had been thinking about before—when was really a good time to take her relationship with Knox to the next level. It damn sure hadn't been the night before.

"What would you say to us going to Spanish Fort tomorrow after work and staying at my new house?" Knox asked. "We could sleep late on Saturday, take care of our job at the bar, and spend another night in the house and then go to church with the family on Sunday. I'd like to have some time to really take a better look at the land I'm buying."

"I would love that," Lottie said.

Knox picked up the nail gun. "Really? You said before that you didn't want to go back to Spanish Fort, so I almost didn't even ask you."

She held a stud in place, and he popped several nails into it. "Things have changed. We are dating now, so I won't be lying to Bernie. She scares me a little when she stares into my eyes. It's like she's seeing to the depths of my soul and knows all my secrets. There is electricity and running water in the house, right?"

He handed the gun off to her and made a mark every sixteen inches. "Tripp went into town for me and had all the utilities put in my name. Other than signing the papers, this is a done deal."

"I would love a long, soaking bath in that claw-footed tub." She sighed.

"Together or all alone?" Knox teased.

"Depends on whether you like bubbles and bath salts."

Chapter 18

Lottie stepped inside the house, and the scent reminded her of the attic in her grandparents' house. She shivered at the memory, switched on the light, and scanned the room for spiders. As a child, she used to sneak up there every chance she got to prowl among all the stored stuff. Until the day that she backed into a spiderweb and disturbed what looked like a million granddaddy long-legged spiders. She had run screaming to her grandmother, who brushed baby spiders off her clothes and out of her hair for what seemed like a whole hour. Thankfully, there was nothing but a couple of cobwebs on the legs of a wooden rocking chair in Knox's new place.

"Are you cold?" Knox asked.

"No, but the house has a smell about it," she replied and told him the spider story.

He dropped her suitcase and tote bag on the floor and headed back to the door. "We can fix that musky smell as soon as I punch in the security code, which is 1313 if you ever need to use it when I'm not here," he said as he touched the buttons on the pad. "I'll have to get used to doing this all over again, and, honey, if there's spiders in this house, I will slay every one of them."

"My hero. Do you have a white horse to ride in on when you save the maiden in distress?"

"I can buy one if that will make you feel safer," he teased.

"Don't you dare. If it rained, I would want to bring it inside. I've worried about that rooster of yours being outside when and if it rains down at the site. I do have a couple of questions. Why did you choose that number, and why *again*?" she asked.

"Thirteen is my lucky number, so I just doubled it, and there was a security system in the house where I grew up." He finished that and opened all the windows in the living room. "There you go. The fresh night breezes should take away the smell pretty quick."

"I don't remember that security thing from the last time we were here," Lottie said.

"It wasn't here then, but Tripp took care of having it installed for me, and after what happened at Swan Song Estates, I'm glad. There's also one at the gate. Security code is the same."

"Do lights flash and sirens sound when someone doesn't enter the right numbers?"

"No, the Nocona police bring those things with them," he answered. "Do you want that long bath in the claw-footed tub or supper first?"

"Food." She headed across the room. "I'm hungry, so let's bring in the groceries, and…" She took a step forward and looked him right in the eye. "If you tattle on me about cooking to the guys at the site, you will be in big trouble."

Knox drew her close in a tight hug, then tipped her chin up with his fist. "Your secret is safe with me."

She barely had time to moisten her lips before he kissed her. Her knees came close to buckling, and she wished that he would lead her to the bedroom right then. But then her stomach growled, and he took a step back.

"We've got all weekend, and you are hungry," he whispered. "I'll bring in the groceries."

Flashing lights, sirens, hunger. What next? She sighed as she watched him go back outside. Were they doomed to never have sex? *Maybe I'm really not his type and boring.*

Lottie wandered into the kitchen and opened the cabinet doors, one by one. She wasn't surprised to find that part of the kitchen was set up for convenience, just like her grandmother's had been. Cups and mugs in the cabinets above the coffeemaker. Dishes to the left of the sink and dishwasher. But after checking out everything, she couldn't find pots and pans, or anything that resembled where staples like flour and sugar might be stored.

Knox brought in several bags and set them on the counter beside the mint-green refrigerator. "Where do you want all this? In the pantry, or have you found space in the cabinets?"

"Pantry?" she asked.

"It's out there." He took her by the hand and led her through swinging doors into the laundry room and opened a door leading into a walk-in pantry. "I found it while you were looking at the bedrooms the last time we were here."

"Wow!" she gasped. "I missed this when we were here. I

was so surprised to see a fairly new washer and dryer instead of one of those old wringer things that I didn't really come inside this room."

Knox agreed and picked up a jar of jam from a shelf. "I got a house, a laundry room, and food."

Lottie stood in the middle of the long, narrow room with floor-to-ceiling shelves on three sides and took stock of what was stored there. Jellies, jams, and canned food were on the shelves on one wall, pots and pans on the other, and staples in see-through containers at the back. "I love this," she whispered. "I wonder why Geneva didn't take some of this stuff with her."

"She said that she got what she wanted out of the house, gave the personal things to a women's shelter in Wichita Falls, and didn't want to have a garage sale or deal with the rest. I guess all these canned goods are the rest. This is elderberry jam. I wonder if the berries grow somewhere on the property."

Lottie took a large pot off a shelf to boil water for noodles and a smaller one to make spaghetti sauce. "These will work perfectly, and I know a little about elderberries."

Knox set the jar back on the shelf and raised an eyebrow.

"Don't look so surprised." She brushed past him on the way out, and sparks danced again. "I helped my grandparents pick and clean blackberries, strawberries, and also elderberries. I whined the whole time when it was time to work in the elderberries until Granny poured some of the thick syrup that she made with them over ice cream that night for dessert. Then I realized that it was worth every single second that we dealt with those BB-sized berries."

He followed her into the kitchen. "Are we going to harvest them if we find them on the property?"

"What is this *we* business?" she asked. "Do you have a mouse in your pocket?"

"Nope," he answered, and quickly changed the subject. "What can I do to help with supper?"

She filled the bigger pot with water, set it on the stove, and turned on the oven to preheat. "You can set the table and pour each of us a glass of sweet tea. I saw the perfect pan in the pantry for the peach crisp that we're having for dessert. When I get back, I want you to tell me some more about who all is included in the *we* that will be helping you pick elderberries."

"Who do you want it to be?" he asked.

"I hope it's not some other woman who you have hiding in the background." She brought a glass pan out and set it on the cabinet. Then she opened and poured two cans of tomato sauce into the smaller pot and added spices.

"Truth is, all of us Callahan brothers have had—or in my case have—commitment issues, but I have never been unfaithful. Then again, I've never found someone like you, Lottie. You can rest assured, darlin', that no other women will come out of the woodwork. Besides, not even one from my past short-lived relationships would even know what an elderberry is."

"What about long lived?" she asked.

He made a zero with his forefinger and thumb. "How many lasting ones have you been in?"

She stirred a few more spices into the sauce and set it on the stove. "I really like to start with fresh, ripe tomatoes to make my marinara, but it has to simmer all day. This will be faster. To answer your question, only a couple, and they ended because"—she hesitated—"they weren't worth fighting for, and I don't like anyone trying to control me."

"That would be like trying to cage a lioness," Knox said.

"Thank you," she said and poured a can of peaches into the glass pan. "Are you are planning on your brothers or sisters helping you with the elderberry harvest?"

"Not really." Knox filled two glasses with ice from the refrigerator and then poured tea into them from a gallon jug. "I'm hoping that *you* will. Remember when I told you that I could probably get you a job up here in Spanish Fort?"

"Yes, and I'm sure thinking about moving here," she answered.

"Well, as soon as the papers are signed, I'm planning to turn this property into a place somewhat like Swan Song Estates, only on a little larger scale. I envision ten plots with five acres for each home, and I'm offering the first one to Bo and Maverick. The lots will be for sale right at the beginning, and I'll hire a good construction team from the local folks. Joe Clay has offered to help me with that. I'm hoping that by the end of summer, we'll be ready to start framing on the first house. I'll have to get the land surveyed, plots laid out, utilities checked into, power lines run, wells drilled, permits taken care of, and all that kind of thing before we can lay foundations.”

"And a rec hall?” Lottie asked.

"That will be the first item on the list,” Knox said. “Will you be the mouse in my pocket?”

"A mouse…oh!” she gasped. “You are asking me if I want a job helping build the houses? I am the *we*.”

"Yes. You can live in this house with me—no strings attached—either in a shared bedroom or your own room, or you can park your trailer in the yard. You choose when and where we take the steps along the way.”

"It's a little early to ask me to move in with you.” Her mind spoke, but her heart disagreed.

"Maybe so, but you can make that decision when the time is right for you. I'm all in when it comes to this relationship.”

"Can I think about it for a few days? I told my folks that I would give them the summer to get settled in before I moved closer, and I planned to work for Walter out in El Paso for three months to kind of get him started.”

Knox handed her a glass of tea. “Take all the time you need. This house isn't going anywhere, and neither are my plans.”

"Do you really think we could survive a long-distance relationship?” She was still worried that he would find her boring after a while.

"If we can't last three or four months, how would we ever make it through fifty years?” he asked.

She almost dropped the butter that she was blending

into oatmeal to make the crispy top on the peach crisp. "You are thinking that far ahead?"

"Yes, ma'am, I am." Knox took a sip of tea and then brushed a sweet kiss across her lips. "Sometimes it works out like I see it in my mind. Sometimes it falls flat."

Lottie's hands shook a little, but she managed to get control of her roller coaster of emotions while she slid the dessert into the oven, opened a box of angel hair spaghetti noodles, and worked them down into the pot of water. "Are you disappointed when it doesn't work?"

Knox set the table and even folded a paper napkin into a little tent for each of them. "Of course, but disappointment doesn't kill a person. At least it hasn't in the past. I'm not sure about the future because I haven't lived in that time capsule yet."

Lottie could hardly believe that they were having this conversation. She would have a place to live, either with Knox or in her trailer. If she got really mad at him over something, she could always get over it in her own place. And she had until the end of summer to decide all of the above.

"Well?" Knox finally said.

"My first concern is that if we do this, what happens if we break up?"

"That bridge can be crossed or burned when the time comes. My mother used to say that worrying about tomorrow sucks the joy out of today. Tonight, we eat the supper that smells pretty amazing, and you take that long soaking bath."

"And then?" she asked.

His grin lit up the whole room. "We'll see what the future holds for us."

<hr>

Lottie draped her clothing over a ladder-back chair in the bathroom, added a few more bubbles and bath salts to the warm water, and used an oversized clamp to hold her hair up in a messy bun. She stepped over the edge and sighed as she sank down into the sweet-smelling water. She had never been in a bathtub where she could stretch her legs all the way to the end, or have water up to her neck.

"Pure luxury," she said. "This tub could be the deciding factor in whether I take the job Knox offered and if I live in this house or in my trailer."

"Then I won't take it out if and when I ever remodel," Knox said.

Lottie's eyes flew open, and she jerked her head around to be sure she didn't imagine his voice. He stood in the doorway wearing no shirt, no shoes, and a big smile.

"What are you doing in here? Did you decide to join me?"

"Maybe tomorrow, but tonight I'm going to treat you like a queen," he answered.

"Are you serious?"

He set a wicker basket full of products on the seat of the chair. "Yes, ma'am. I have searched this kingdom high and low for the proper things to help me on my quest."

"Don't ever tell me that you aren't romantic," she said with half a giggle.

Knox slid a sly wink toward her. "Of course, I'm romantic. How else would I have ever convinced the queen to spend a weekend with me? Now, if you will sit up, I will begin."

She slid up to a seated position. "I've never been a queen. How will I know if you are doing a good job?"

"Listen to your heart."

"First I have to take away your crown." His warm breath caressed her neck in a way that sent goose bumps dancing down her spine.

"I would hardly call a hair clip a crown," she said.

"Darlin', crowns come in all sizes and shapes."

He pushed the bubbles away so he could fill a stemmed wineglass with water and gently poured it through her hair. He kept up the procedure—time after time—until her hair was thoroughly wet and her whole body tingled with desire.

She was amazed that the heat her body gave off didn't cause the bath water to boil when he massaged shampoo into her scalp.

"That feels so good," she whispered.

"Has no one…"

She butted in before he could finish. "Never. No one has ever washed my hair for me except a few times in a beauty shop, and never a sexy man. Sweet Jesus," she groaned when he started rinsing the soap from her hair.

"No, darlin', I'm just plain old Knox Callahan, the king

of this castle." He leaned down, strung kisses from the tender spot on her neck to her lips.

"What makes you a king?" she asked in a breathless tone.

"I'm a king because you are the queen," he answered.

After he rinsed the soap from her hair, applied conditioner, and slowly rinsed it out, he piled her wet hair up on top of her head and used the clamp to hold it. She thought he had finished but not so. He filled his hands with bath oil and worked the knots and aches from her neck and shoulders, stopping every now and then to kiss her again.

"If this is how a queen feels, I don't ever intend to give up my crown. Have you ever done this before?"

"No, I've been waiting for a woman who makes me feel like a king," he answered. "That's what makes you a queen, darlin'."

"Lord have mercy!" she moaned. "That's the most romantic thing you have said yet."

"Then you have been dating fools. Now, I want you to stand up so I can take you to the bedroom to see if we can have better luck tonight than we did before."

She rose up out of the water, feeling every bit the queen that Knox told her she was. For the first time, all her inhibitions about being boring and awkward disappeared, and in that moment, she was beautiful. He wrapped an oversized towel around her body, picked her up like a bride, and carried her to the master bedroom. Her legs were like rubber when he set her down and kicked the door shut with his bare foot.

"No one else is in the house," she said.

"There will be someday, so we might as well get in the habit now," he whispered.

Chapter 19

Knox propped up on his elbow and fought back the desire to brush Lottie's silky hair from her face. Touching her, even lightly, might wake her, and she deserved to sleep until she was ready to get up and face the day. The idea of opening his eyes to see her beside him put a smile on his face. She could so easily be *the one* if everything worked out right. After a few minutes, he eased out of bed, got dressed, and tiptoed out of the bedroom, down the hallway, and into the kitchen.

While a pot of coffee perked, he stared out the kitchen window at dawn pushing away the darkness. Was Lottie his dawn? Would she be the light of his life forevermore?

"I'm a carpenter, not a poet," he whispered. "I build houses, and my romantic side only comes out when I'm with Lottie."

A deer with twin fawns caught his attention when the little family wandered out of the woods at the back side of the house. If things worked out with Lottie, would they have twins at some time in the future? No answers drifted through the window, and the doe must have sensed a presence because she turned tail and bounded back into the dense thickets. Both of the babies were nothing but blurs as they flashed their little white tails and disappeared with her.

Is that one of Lottie's omens? he wondered as he poured a mug full of coffee and carried it out to the front porch. He sat down in a rocking chair and appreciated the fact that the house faced the east so he could watch the sun come up every morning. In that moment, he decided that all the plots and houses in his new gated community would face that direction. The folks who lived in them could watch the sunrise from their front porch and the sunset from the back.

A chattering squirrel took his attention to a low limb of a pecan tree. "Enjoy it while you can because in a few weeks, I'm bringing a cat and a rooster to live here," Knox told the critter. "And I may get a few chickens so Cheeto will have some company."

The old, wooden screen door squeaked when Lottie opened it and must have put some fear in the squirrel because he twitched his tail a few times and then scampered up the tree trunk. Knox turned to see her wearing a short, silky robe tied in the middle. She looked like a statue of a Greek goddess with her hair flowing down her back.

He raised his coffee mug. "Mornin' to you, my queen. You look lovely this morning."

She touched the mug in her hand to his and sat down in the chair next to him. "Good morning, Your Majesty, and you look sexy as hell this morning."

"We make quite the pair." He chuckled.

"Yes, we do," she agreed. "Royalty in a house that got stuck in the seventies."

"It can be remodeled and refurnished," he suggested.

"No, sir!" she declared. "We might ruin the peace if we did that."

"I agree about the peacefulness, especially with no sirens or flashing lights, or folks coming by the trailer while we have breakfast. But answer me this," he said. "Just how sexy is hell?"

"I'd say it can be described in one word, and that is hot."

"Will you miss our hot nights when you are in El Paso?" he asked.

"More than you will ever know," she answered and moved from her chair to sit in his lap. "But last night could have been a one-trick pony."

"Oh, honey, that was just the opening act. The concert will last for years and years," he teased as he set his coffee on the porch, and then did the same with hers. His lips found hers in a string of kisses that didn't end when he stood up with her in his arms. He carried her into the house and back to the bedroom to prove to her that the previous night was only the tip of the iceberg—which could and would be melted before breakfast.

Even sucking on a lemon could not wipe the smile off Lottie's face, or the semi-blush from her cheeks when she thought about the day so far. Sex before breakfast, and shower sex afterward. Then dozens of hot little kisses as they walked around the property. And now they were crossing the parking lot of Bo and Maverick's bar. Simply holding hands seemed like more of an intimate act than it ever had before.

"Are you ready for this?" he asked.

"Yes, and I'm ready to face Bernie now that we aren't fake anymore," she answered.

"Have I told you how beautiful you look in that cowgirl getup?"

"Just a dozen times, but I'm not complaining, and you make a fine-looking cowboy in your boots and pearl snap shirt. Do all of Bernie's events have a theme?"

"Oh, yes, but she says the Wild West is the one the folks like best—all the way from the younger crowd to the elderly folks that we have here this evening," Knox answered and kissed her on the forehead. "That's just to hold me until this is over, and I can really kiss you again."

Bo unlocked the door and motioned for them to come inside. "I'm sorry if you've been waiting a long time. I tried to keep a watch out for you, but we were fighting with Aunt Bernie. She's determined to crawl up on the ladder and hang the garland around the ceiling."

"Enough said." Knox chuckled. "Reinforcements have arrived."

Bernie stood in the middle of the bar floor with her hands on her hips and glaring at Maverick. "I am not so old that I can't climb a ladder."

Maverick did not back down an inch from the daggers shooting from her eyes. "I don't doubt that you can climb this ladder. You could probably figure out a way to hang your skinny body from a thumbtack, but if you fall and break a hip or, worse yet, hit your head and die, I'll be to blame. Mary Jane would never forgive me, so *you* are staying on the ground."

"You are not my boss!" she declared as she set one foot on the bottom rung of the ladder.

Knox slipped an arm around her shoulders. "Aunt Bernie, if you fall and die, you will fail your mission in helping me find a wife. You know your soul won't be at peace until you get that job done. You might have to sit on the steps leading up to the heavenly gates for many years, waiting on me to give up my bachelorhood."

"Okay, then." She removed her foot. "But that's the only reason. It's not that I'm old and feeble."

"Of course not." Knox led her away from the ladder and over to a table. "You know how us guys are all thumbs when it comes to decorating tables. Looks like the boxes right here are full of stuff for that job. Maybe you three ladies could get that done while we put the garland and twinkle lights up around the ceiling and bar."

She shook his arm away and gave him a double dose of stink eye. "Don't patronize me, Knox Callahan."

"I wouldn't think of it," Knox assured her.

"Bernie, I'll be glad to help you get the tables ready. Don't the doors open for this shindig in less than an hour?" Lottie offered.

"And I'll go get the boxes of centerpieces from the storage room," Bo said.

"What are y'all waiting for?" Bernie snapped her fingers and clapped her hands. "Chop. Chop. We've got a party to get ready for. When you guys finish the garland, you can go to the storage room and bring out those boxes of cowboy and cowgirl hats. I'll sit at the table to take tickets or sell to the folks who didn't already buy them and give out hats to anyone who hasn't got one."

She pulled the first tablecloth from the box and turned to Lottie. "I'm glad you are here. You and I never did get that visit on Easter, so while we work, we will have it today. We'll work together to get these on the tables. Bo can come behind us and fix the centerpieces."

"Sounds like an organized plan to me." Lottie ripped open a bag and laid the red plastic cloth on the first table.

Bernie did the same with a table right beside that one. "Okay, now tell me the truth about you and Knox. Is this relationship just a sham or is it real?"

"What do you think?" Lottie asked.

Bernie studied her for a few seconds and then sighed. "I'm of two minds about it. I was sure he had talked you into pretending so that I wouldn't set him up on blind dates. But there's something different between y'all tonight than there was at Easter."

"What is it that's so different?" Lottie asked another question without answering.

"The glow in your face. You are either having sex with Knox or you are pregnant," Bernie said.

"Well, I'm definitely not pregnant, but we are really

dating. You really did kind of introduce us since you took me to Tripp and Willa Rose's wedding, so I suppose you get the credit for us," Lottie answered truthfully and attempted to change the subject. "We spent last night at his new house. It's so peaceful out there. You have to come see it."

"Oh, I definitely will, but I've been in that house before. Eula Faye, Roman's wife, was in our Sunday school poker club and hosted the game a couple of times before she passed away." Bernie straightened the last disposable cloth.

"Sunday school poker?" Lottie giggled. "I never thought I'd hear those words in the same sentence."

"Maybe so, but I sure miss those Friday night games." Bernie pulled out a chair and sat down. "Now, tell me something. Just how serious are y'all?"

"Well, he asked me to help him with this new housing project he wants to build." Lottie followed her lead and pulled out a chair for herself. "We've really become a team in the framing business."

"Does that mean you'll be living here when you get done with the job down south?" Bernie asked.

"After the summer"—Lottie paused—"if I take the job. I haven't given him an answer yet."

"Well, damn it! That means I might fail in this mission." Bernie groaned.

"Hey, now, don't go jumping to conclusions. I'm seriously giving it a lot of thought. I'm kind of committed to help a friend get his construction business off the ground out in El Paso—at least for the summer." Lottie glanced over her shoulder to see Maverick and Knox both giving her a thumbs-up sign.

Bo set the last jar candles on the table and fluffed out a bit of white illusion with twinkling lights around each one. "I'm so glad that Knox bought that land. We looked at it, but the owner wanted to sell the whole place, not a little piece of it. I squealed when Knox told me that he thought he had the perfect place to build our new house. We're coming out to the land after church tomorrow to pick out our five acres. We have our house plans ready to go, so we get to be your first new neighbors."

"You mean *Knox's* new neighbor, don't you?" Lottie asked.

Bo's green eyes flashed when she looked up at Lottie. "I said what I meant."

"What makes you think that?" Lottie asked.

"Knox looks happier than I've ever seen him. Kind of reminds me of the way Tripp changed when he met Willa Rose. And you did catch the bouquet at the wedding."

"And Knox caught the garter. That sealed it all!" Bernie pumped her fist into the air. "And I get the credit."

"When are you going to retire from matchmaking?" Lottie steered the conversation away from herself.

"On my ninetieth birthday, I will hang up my matchmaking hat and pass the job onto whoever wants it or close down my business," Bernie answered. "If this works between you and Knox, then I have completed my major goal."

"Tell Lottie about your first match while I go to the

supply room and get the bowls for peanuts, pretzels, and chocolate kisses," Bo said.

"You mean between Clara and Nash? That was before I retired from the bar business and moved down here to Texas," Bernie said.

"I'd love to hear about it," Lottie said. "We've got the tables ready, so we have a few minutes to visit. Who is Clara?"

"That would be my grand-niece. She and Nash and Hershal, who was an old flame of mine, walked into my bar one night."

"Is this a joke?" Lottie asked.

Bernie raised her right hand. "I swear to God it's a true story, and honey, at my age, I don't take such things lightly. Clara was weeping. Hershal had one of them round fish bowls in one hand and a Chihuahua in the other, and Nash—well, if I'd been forty years younger, Clara wouldn't have had a chance. When everything was settled, I sold half my bar to Nash and gave the other half to Clara. Evidently, the heat was pretty hot between them because the bar burned to the ground a few months later. They're married now and living up in the northern part of the state."

"I'm glad the Chicken Coop was still around when my folks were living in that area," Lottie said.

"Y'all ain't foolin' me one bit." Bernie shook a finger at her. "You are keeping me talking, but I been keepin' an eye on those two guys. They're not getting that garland and lights up perfectly. But the senior citizens all probably wear trifocals anyway, so they won't notice."

"Nothing got past you at your bar, and I can see that you haven't lost your bluff one bit since you moved to Spanish Fort," Lottie said.

"Don't you ever forget it," Bernie said with a wide grin that deepened the wrinkles around her mouth. "Let's go help Bo put out the snacks. It's only ten minutes until we open the doors. I'll tell all my matchmaking stories with the family another time."

Lottie stood up and followed Bernie to the bar. "I'll hold you to that."

"Thank you for getting her out of that mood," Bo whispered and handed Lottie a bag of Hershey's Kisses. "These go in the red bowls. Pretzels in the pink ones, and peanuts in the white."

"I didn't do a good job. She figured out what I was doing and will probably blame Knox and Maverick for not doing a perfect job since we distracted her," Lottie said out of the corner of her mouth.

"You are probably right," Bo said, "but for the record, whether she really was the matchmaker that got you and Knox together or not, I'm glad that it is happening."

"Thank you," Lottie murmured and sent up a silent prayer that the relationship didn't die in its sleep while she was in El Paso.

Lottie had never seen so many elderly folks come through the door and hit the floor to two-step to "Livin' on Love" by Alan Jackson. They looked like they had just stepped out of a western wear store in their fancy boots, jeans, and hats.

And for the next hour, they didn't slow down, not even a little bit. She even wondered if they had a secret pill in their medicine cabinet that gave them more energy than that little pink bunny had on television commercials, because they were still crowding the dance floor six songs later.

"If that's the case, I wonder where they compound the little buggers and if they'll sell me a few," she muttered as she carried another tray with half a dozen red plastic cups filled with beer across the room.

"What was that?" Knox asked when he passed her.

She told him her idea about the pills, and he chuckled. "Darlin', at their age, they save up all their energy for good times like this. We have to use ours to frame out cabins."

"And other more important things," she said and wondered where the awkward Lottie went, but not for long. She liked this new person in her body a lot better than the old model.

Knox leaned in and whispered for her ears only. "Hang on to that thought for when this gig is over, and we can go back to our castle in the woods."

"I don't feel much like a queen right now," she told him.

"And I feel more like a stable boy than a king, but when we get home this evening, all that can and will change." He held up a roll of quarters. "My new orders are to put more money in the jukebox. Got any requests?"

"Play more oldies. They seem to like them best," she suggested.

"Will do." He gave her a quick kiss on the cheek. "See you later."

"The Gambler," by Kenny Rogers, brought several more senior citizens to the dance floor for two-stepping. The lyrics seemed to be speaking right to Lottie when the words said that the secret to survival was knowing what to keep and what to throw away.

Lottie wondered if she was playing with fire. Could this really be the new her, or was she just playacting at being what Knox wanted her to be? She really needed a sign to tell her if this was real or if it was time to walk away.

She set a cup of beer around to each of six older ladies sitting at a table. "Why aren't y'all out there on the dance floor?"

"We're sittin' this one out and givin' the other ladies a chance," the one with Emma on her name tag answered. "And we got a little winded on that last line dance. I remember when I carried an extra pair of shoes in case I wore the leather down to nothing in the ones I had on."

"I'm Beverly," another one pointed a bony finger with a bright red nail to her name tag. "And honey, we've done a head count. There are only half as many men here as there are women. We are the best dancers in the whole place, but we aren't greedy. So, we sit one out every so often and give the other gals a little boost to their egos when they are asked."

"But, darlin' girl, if I was thirty years younger…" Emma fanned her face with her hand, "I would give you a run for your money with that hunky chunk of sex that keeps his eyes on you."

"Thirty, my saggy ass," a third one with Myra on her tag snorted. "You'd need to be fifty years younger, and you'd probably need a how-to book to drag something that sexy into the bedroom."

"Sex is like riding a bicycle. It all comes back to a person when it's time," Emma argued.

Beverly laughed so hard that she spewed beer all over her fancy western shirt.

"Good Lord, Beverly," Myra fussed. "We can't take you anywhere."

"You ain't sittin' where you can see them two bartenders." She wiped the beer away with a napkin and looked up at Lottie. "You might as well draw up six more. Most of the women are starin' at the sex on a stick at the jukebox and the other one behind the bar. We'll all be worked up enough that we'll fight over who gets Henry for the night when we get back to the assisted care center."

"Oh, no!" Emma declared. "I've already told him that I would meet him in his room and tell him all about tonight."

Lottie picked up the tray. "Why didn't he come with you?"

Emma rolled her eyes toward the ceiling. "He won't miss his Sunday football, not even if he's seen the game before—not even for dancin'—but it will be over when we get back. And he's got a whole bottle of them little blue pills."

Lottie blushed. "You ladies have a good time, and I'll be back with another round in a few minutes. It appears that Miz Emma does not need a how-to book at all. And bless your hearts. I hope they don't quit making those pills when I'm"—she looked at Emma and winked—"fifty years old."

"God love your precious soul," Emma said. "Now go flirt with that feller that you are sleeping with."

"What?" Lottie gasped.

"You heard me. A woman has a different look about her when love is brand new and the sex is hot," Emma said. "I'm not so old that I don't remember how I felt when Warren and I were sneaking off to the barn before we tied the knot."

"I didn't know it showed," Lottie said.

"Maybe not to everyone, but us old birds see everything, say what we damn well please, and live the way we want. We're the generation that burned our bras, honey, and we don't give a flip what anyone says," Beverly said. "Enjoy your youth. Make good memories and then be happy and content if you get to live as long as we have."

"Yes, ma'am," Lottie said with a nod and headed across the floor.

Bernie stopped her after she'd taken a few steps and handed her a second empty tray. "Would you take this back for me?"

"Sure thing," Lottie said.

"I'm going to make the rounds and visit with the folks. I saw that you met Emma and her crowd. She's my age and still feisty as hell. But I got to admit, I'm glad I've got family and don't ever have to live in a care facility."

"With your big clan, I don't think you ever have to worry

about going anywhere, but those are some spicy ladies, no matter where they live," Lottie said.

Bernie reached up and laid a hand on Lottie's shoulder. "Yep, but not a one of them can hold a candle to me."

———

Knox opened the truck door for Lottie and helped her inside, then rounded the front end of the vehicle and slid in behind the steering wheel. "How about dinner at the Dairy Queen before we go home?"

"Yes, please," she answered. "I'm a hamburger junkie, and I'm starving."

He drove away from the bar's parking lot, made a right, and in only a few minutes, he parked near the front door of the Dairy Queen in Nocona.

"That was fast. I didn't even notice this place was here when we drove to the bar," Lottie said.

Knox unfastened his seat belt and turned to face her. "We were talking."

"We don't have to worry about your family knowing about our relationship. I told Bernie and Bo that we are really dating," Lottie blurted out and felt so much better after she said it. "And that table with those six ladies who drank enough beer tonight to take a bath in—they know too."

"How?"

"They said by the way you looked at me," she answered. "I want to grow up and be just like them and Bernie. I know my body will get old, but I want to stay young in my mind."

And sassy like I am with you instead of being the wallflower at every function, she thought.

"We'll still be building houses together when we are their age," Knox said.

"Oh, really, and will you still be able to pick me up and carry me to bed? Will you still look at me like you do right now?"

"I want your gorgeous face to be the last thing I see before I close my eyes and step into eternity," he said and started a song on his playlist. "Listen to the words of the song that's about to play."

Lottie knew what the song was when the first guitar licks of "Forever and Ever, Amen," filled the bar. "Are you trying to tell me something?"

"I can see it happening in the future, so keep that in mind," Knox said.

"You really are the most romantic man I've ever known."

"Well, it's all because you bring it out in me," Knox said as he got out of the truck and whistled as he walked around the front end to help her out just as the song ended.

She had been down the euphoria path before, the one lined with pretty unicorns and lots of glitter dust. Granted, not one of her previous relationships had been anything like what she had with Knox, but still, she *had* known those first few days or even weeks of happiness before everything went south.

She was deep in thought about the words that Randy Thomas sang about in his song. But all that disappeared in a flash when she heard someone yell Knox's name. She turned to see Knox's older brother, Brodie, and his wife, Audrey, walking toward them.

"Hey, is the mixer over?" Brodie asked.

"Yep, it is, and you should help with one sometime. Those old folks can put us younger ones to shame when it comes to having a good time. Y'all out for a date night?" Knox asked.

"Yep, want to make it a double?" Audrey asked.

"Sure," Lottie answered, glad for two reasons: One was so that she could get to know Audrey better, and the second was that having others around might help erase the doubts that kept popping up in her mind. The other shoe would eventually drop. It was just a matter of time, just like it always had been.

After they had ordered and found a booth in a back corner, Brodie asked, "Is this for real? Bernie has been fussing about you living up to your promise to find a fake girlfriend to keep her from setting you up on dates."

"I didn't find her." Knox chuckled.

"I found him," Lottie answered, and went on to tell them the story, ending with, "But it turned into something real."

"Did she figure it out?" Audrey asked.

"Yep, she did," Lottie replied. "I'm dying to know how you and Brodie met. I've heard there's a story involving a pig."

"I wanted to buy his land to reunite my family farms, and when all else failed, I married him and got a potbellied pig in the deal. Now, she's got piglets. Want one?" Audrey asked.

"Maybe. Knox, can you keep one out on your new property for me?" Lottie batted her eyes at him in fake flirting.

"Of course," Knox said.

"Believe me, Pansy the pig was only one little piece of the war between us before we finally admitted that we were in love," Tripp said.

The waitress brought their food, and for the next hour, Audrey and Brodie entertained Lottie with the stories of how they had started off as enemies and finally realized they were falling in love.

"And honey," Audrey looked across the table at Knox, "if we can survive all that, y'all don't have to worry about a thing."

"We work together eight to ten hours a day, then spend our evenings in the same trailer," Lottie said and wished she could put the words back in her mouth.

Knox slipped an arm around her shoulders and drew her close. "So far, so good, but I have no idea how we'll survive with a potbellied pig in the mix."

The doubts were back in her mind—with or without a pig.

She told herself to shake it off and enjoy what time they had together, but that wasn't easy to do.

Lottie locked eyes with Knox and saw something that looked a lot like love, respect, and happiness there. She reached up and gave his hand on her shoulder a squeeze and decided to quit second-guessing every move as well as the future.

Chapter 20

"Are we limited to only five acres?" Bo asked.

"Family can choose anything they want," Knox answered.

"Then we want ten acres," she said. "We've planned a sprawling ranch-style house, and we want plenty of room for kids to run and play."

"You said you were thinking about the places facing the road for easy access, but we'd like to have a strip toward the back," Maverick held Bo's hand as the four of them slowly made their way across the pasture filled with blue bonnets.

"I'm fine with y'all choosing any place you want," Knox answered. "But you might want to choose a place far enough away that Cheeto, my rooster, or all the construction noises won't wake you at the crack of dawn."

"You have a rooster?" Bo asked.

"Oh, yeah, and a kitten named Bally," Knox answered. "They were thrown out at the worksite and chose my trailer to make their new home."

"I'm just glad that whoever dumped them on the building site brought a cat and a bird. If they'd thrown out a baby elephant and a monkey, Knox would have probably taken them in," Lottie said.

"Not in the trailer," Knox argued.

"I can't wait to get a cat," Bo said.

"And a couple of dogs," Maverick added.

"This is it!" Bo stopped walking at the southwest corner of the property and plopped down on the ground. A slight breeze whipped her strawberry-blond hair to one side. She tucked it back behind her ears and seemed to take in everything around her.

Lottie took a picture of Bo. "You look like a cover model for a romance book, sitting there with all these pretty blue flowers around you. I know Mary Jane would love to have a copy of this."

"I'm pretending that I'm sitting in my bedroom right here," Bo said. "I'm looking out at all the trees through the sliding glass doors that open out onto a patio. And I'm listening to the birds when I wake up every morning."

Maverick sat down beside her. "I thought the first thing you would see was me propped up on an elbow and staring at you, not trees."

Lottie snapped half a dozen pictures of them together. "I'm putting this on the wall of our rec hall and adding to it as we build more houses."

"We'll be the first ones with our photographs on the wall, Maverick," Bo said. "And I love that you're always the last face I see before we go to sleep, and the first one I see in the morning. And after we move into our new house, I will look at trees right after I get my good morning kiss."

People didn't really turn green with jealousy, but if they

did, Lottie figured she looked like a leprechaun with so much envy pouring out of her skin. Bo and Maverick were way further down the path than she and Knox, and she needed to be patient and let things work out like they were supposed to. But at that moment, she didn't want to wait four months for it.

Lottie sat down a few yards from Bo and didn't even realize that Knox was taking pictures of her until he eased down beside her and showed them to her. "Look how beautiful you are," he whispered.

"Only in the eyes of the beholder," she said.

"Hey, you are sitting in my living room, which means you are our first guests. Welcome to our home," Maverick said.

"Thank you. When it's a reality, I'll bring the first bottle of wine," Knox told him.

"Oh, no!" Bo disagreed. "That's Ophelia and Jake's job. They own the winery. Y'all can bring chicken eggs."

"Count it as a promise." Knox grinned. "Now, tell me, how do you want your acreage? In a rectangle or a square?"

"I'm thinking that since we've designed a sprawling ranch-style house, we'll want it rectangular. How many feet across the front of five acres wide and two deep is that?" Bo asked.

"There's a little more than two hundred feet across one side of an acre." Lottie stopped and did the math in her head. "That means you will have four hundred feet on each end, and a thousand feet across the long end."

"That sounds great. Like Bo said, we need room for…" Maverick paused.

"Our kids to run and play. We might even install a small swimming pool in a few years, and definitely a barn to store stuff in before that," she finished for him. "We are waiting for Mother's Day to make the big announcement, but we are pregnant, and evidently, I got the twins gene because we're having two at once. We want plenty of running room for our children, and we can't thank you enough for letting us pick out our place first."

"And giving us the piece of land that we want," Maverick said. "But now it's time to talk money. How much is five acres as opposed to ten?"

"You are the only ones in the family who don't have a real house. So, consider this your wedding gift," Knox answered.

"Well, damn!" Bo laughed. "We should have said we wanted fifteen acres."

"More than ten would have cost you," Knox teased. "And congratulations on the babies. Rae won't have a thing on you now."

"I don't know what to say," Maverick said.

"Thank you isn't enough, but we'll make it up to you some way," Bo added. "And, Brother, Rae got her two girls when they were already sleeping all night and potty trained. I don't know how Mama did it with two sets of twins in only a year," Bo said.

"My mother said one set was a handful," Knox said, chuckling, "but I loved having a brother my age and one that was a little older."

"Actually, I'm glad we aren't having triplets," Maverick

added. "At least for this first time. Three might be nice next time around."

Bo air slapped him on the arm. "Five babies, all under the age of three? Who's going to help run the bar?"

Maverick scooted over and wrapped his arms around her. "We'll turn the storage room into a nursery and hire a nanny. Or we will hire a cute little bartender, and you can be a stay-at-home mommy."

"Storage room and nanny, yes. But cute little bartender…" She shot him a dirty look. "Over my dead body."

Maverick laughed. "I didn't figure that would float too well."

Building a new home from scratch, having babies, and planning a big family—all things that Lottie had dreamed about more than once, but had completely given up on after her last relationship went down the tubes.

Later that afternoon, Lottie looked back over her shoulder and watched Knox close the gate and reset the alarm code. "I don't want to leave," she muttered under her breath.

Because you love this place, or because you are falling in love with Knox? the niggling voice in her head asked.

"Maybe a little of both," she answered, "and I'm still waiting for that other shoe to drop."

"I love my work at Swan Song Estates," Knox said as he got into the truck, "but I already miss this place. It's my first home that's not on wheels since the tornado wiped out our house on the farm. And to be honest, that was Brodie's, not mine."

"I'm trying to picture what it will look like with ten more homes out here," Lottie said.

"So am I, and…" He paused and turned out onto the highway headed toward Nocona.

"And what?" Lottie asked.

"At first, I thought maybe I would extend it to a few more, but now I'm thinking that will be all that we offer. I don't want to get so fenced in that it scares the squirrels and deer away…" Another long silence. "And I want lots of room for children."

"Folks are going to say that you got wedding fever from Tripp and baby fever from Bo and Maverick." Lottie wasn't sure she had not been afflicted with the same thing. That's why the trip to El Paso would be a good thing.

"Maybe the baby fever, but not the wedding," Knox said. "I was determined not to let Aunt Bernie use me for a statistic, and then this gorgeous woman sat down beside me and asked me to be her fake boyfriend."

"Oh, really?" Lottie giggled. "What did you think of that?"

"We…ell…" He drew out the word. "I thought she was an answer to a prayer."

Lottie whipped her head around to look at him.

He said, "I told Tripp that I was going to get a pretend girlfriend to keep Aunt Bernie from setting me up with blind dates."

She crossed her arms over her chest. "You rat! Why didn't you tell me in the beginning?"

He raised one shoulder in a half shrug. "You only asked me to be your boyfriend. You didn't ask me if I wanted a fake girlfriend. So, tell me the truth. Did you get baby fever when Bo said she was pregnant with twins?"

"Maybe a little," Lottie admitted. "How about you?"

"Nope, not a little, but a lot," Knox said.

Chapter 21

"Okay, y'all listen up," Jack said on Monday morning when everyone had gathered in the rec hall.

Lottie let out a long sigh. She had been ready for what was coming next for more than a week, and she didn't like it.

"Thomas tells me the framing crew will finish the last cabin by noon today," Jack said. "When that's done, I want all five of you to move down to number one this afternoon and help get all the finish work done this week, so Mandy and I can move into it the middle of next week."

"Sure thing, Jack," Eddie agreed with a nod.

"I appreciate all of you working so hard, from framers to you finish carpenters who only arrived today. If everyone can keep at it until Mother's Day weekend, I believe all six of the cabins will be ready to move in. That's all. Have some doughnuts and coffee, and if this project is done a week early like I think it will be, everyone will get a nice bonus," Jack said.

"So much for being ahead of schedule," Lottie grumbled under her breath. If it wasn't for leaving Knox, she would have much rather hooked up her trailer and been on her way to El Paso.

"Don't mind her," Gabe told Knox. "Jack saw to it that she learned to do everything from holding a nail gun to staining cabinets, but…"

"I'm standing right here," she barked, "and I don't hide the fact that I don't like any of the business except but framing work."

"Why?" Knox asked.

"Framing is fast, and I can see results on a daily basis. Finish work is tedious and slow and tests my patience," she admitted. "But if it will help Aunt Mandy and my folks get moved in quicker, I'll do it."

"Without complaining?" Gabe asked.

"Nope. I'll be grumpy until the last cabinet is installed and the final door is hung." She turned her focus toward Knox. "Think you can live with that?"

"We'll have to wait and see," he answered. "We still have separate trailers that we can escape to each evening. Hopefully, the trip to New Iberia next weekend will sweeten your mood."

"What is New Iberia?" Thomas asked.

"It's a town in southern Louisiana. I've bought some land between Spanish Fort and Nocona, and I need to go to where the owner lives now to finalize the deal," Knox answered. "Lottie and I are flying down there for the weekend, but we'll be back Sunday night to help finish up this project. I would really like to be back at home for good on Mother's Day."

"If we can get it done, that will give us a week to spend

with our families before we head to El Paso. Has anyone heard from Walter?" Thomas headed back toward the equipment room with the other four of their team behind him.

"Not me," Lottie answered.

Usually, the framers finished their job and left the site the next day for the next job. They barely had time to drive from one place to another. Forget about having a day or two for anything like visiting parents or a short vacation. Only twice in the years she had worked for Jack had she been asked to help by doing the finish work, and she'd hoped it would never happen again.

"I'll call him tonight," Eddie said. "I wouldn't be surprised if he wants our team there as soon as we can make it."

"We are the first responders, so to speak," Gabe said. "Nobody works until we get the framing done. And this job is a big one even for us. Ten two-story houses in an exclusive community with all kinds of rules. I understand that there will be monthly inspections to be sure they are up to code. It's going to look like the Hamptons from the pictures I saw, and it will take at least a year to get everything ready."

"They better hire gardeners," Thomas said as he headed across the lawns toward the last cabin, "and have sprinkling systems. El Paso's temperature is definitely not like the Hamptons'."

Lottie remembered how sweltering hot the weather had been when she visited her brother in that part of Texas the summer before. Forget about sitting outside in the evenings. The sunsets might have been beautiful and peaceful if a person could withstand the swarms of mosquitoes. Add that to sweating gallons of water in the sweltering heat, and she swore she would only come back to that place in the winter.

She figured she was going to have to eat her words as she helped Knox put together the last four trusses for the roof. She bit back a groan when she thought about all those weeks without Knox. If she was honest, she would even miss Cheeto's crowing in the mornings.

Having grown up with only brothers, Knox was not an expert on women. He had learned a little about sisters when he moved to Spanish Fort with Brodie and Tripp, but even that much wouldn't fill up a small coffee cup. He was wise enough to read Lottie's expression and know that the best thing to do that morning was to let her work out her anger on her own.

Legally, he had been hired to help frame out six cabins, so if he wanted, he could load up his kitten and chicken and go home at noon that day. But Jack had been good to him in the past, and he couldn't treat him that shabbily. Besides, even if she was moody, he wanted to spend the next couple of weeks with Lottie. When all six cabins were completed, he might not see her until fall—and that seemed like an eternity.

They finished at noon with hardly any words between them except for the few times someone needed a nail gun passed to them. They took their equipment back to the rec hall and went to their own trailers for a noon break. Knox was in the process of making two thick sandwiches when Lottie opened the door just a crack and peeked inside.

"Am I welcome?" she asked.

"Of course. I made lunch for both of us in hopes you would be over your snit," Knox replied, and motioned for her to take a seat.

"I owe you an apology," she said. "After that amazing weekend, and last night in my trailer, you don't deserve the cold treatment I've given you all day, so I'm sorry. There's no excuse, but I was hoping we would be done today and could spend a few days at your place before I had to head to El Paso. But evidently, we'll be helping out all the way until Mother's Day weekend."

He set the plate of sandwiches on the table and got two bottles of sweet tea from the refrigerator. "That will give you time to spend with your folks in the evenings before they go on their cruise."

She took a bag of potato chips from the cabinet on the way across the floor. "Yes, it will, and I should not have been such a whiny baby this morning. Mama called when I got to my trailer. She was so excited that she and Daddy would have some time here before they leave. That way, they won't have to put everything in storage. I felt super guilty for only thinking about what I wanted."

He sat down beside her. "We do have the weekend in Louisiana to look forward to all week when we are putting in door facings and baseboards."

"And laying floor tile and doing the finish work on the cabinets. The place where Uncle Jack gets them custom made does not do stain and varnish. Are you any good with a spray gun?"

"I'm not too shabby," he answered.

"Do you like that kind of work?"

He wiggled his eyebrows. "I love anything that means I get to work with my hands."

She giggled for the first time that day. "I'll remember that treatment in the bathtub when I'm helping get Uncle Jack's cabin ready for them to move into in a week."

"Oh, really?" Knox asked. "Will the visions in your head make you breathless?"

"Probably so, but the thoughts of my reward at the end of each day in one of our trailers will really make me pant," she answered.

"Save some of that for the afterglow," he teased.

She slid over closer to him and nibbled on his earlobe. "There's always plenty in storage for that. Want a sample before we go back to work?"

"I would never turn that down," he said, "but first we better finish our lunch, or we'll run out of energy before five o'clock."

"Then eat fast," she said.

After lunch, when they all met in front of the first cabin, Eddie grinned and asked, "What happened to you over the past hour?"

"What makes you think anything happened to me?" Lottie fired back.

"You don't look like you could chew up two-by-fours and spit out toothpicks," Gabe answered.

"I had lunch, played with a couple of cats, and worked out my frustrations. Are y'all ready to go to work, or do you want to stand out here and analyze me all afternoon? If you want to play like therapists instead of carpenters, then we'll have a go at it. But remember, what's good for the goose is also good for the gander. If you pick my brain, then I get to do the same with each of you."

"Including Knox?" Thomas grinned.

Knox threw up both hands in a defensive gesture. "Not me. There's no way I'd attempt to try to figure out what's in a woman's mind. I'd rather try to outswim a hungry alligator."

Chapter 22

"Hello!" Lester waved from the steps of the plane and stood up. "Y'all are right on time."

Knox raised a hand. "It's good to see you, but I thought you'd retired."

"I did, but I couldn't stay away from the pilot's seat. The wife told me to go to back to work or find a new place to live. I like her cooking too well for the latter," he said as he headed toward them. "I'll help you get that luggage onboard. Just you and this lovely lady?"

"Yes, sir," Knox answered and slung the handles of a tote bag over his shoulder. "This is my girlfriend and partner in the construction business, Lottie Johnston."

Lester rolled two suitcases toward the plane. "Pleased to meet you, Miz Lottie. You got your job cut out for you with this one."

"Don't I know it," Lottie said, "and the pleasure is all mine. How long have you been flying?"

"About fifty years, but only thirty for the Callahans After Tripp got his pilot's license, he flew some of the trips, but when he had to stay home, I was drafted," Lester answered. "I'll be taking y'all to Louisiana and then coming right back to fly Tripp up to Wyoming to an auction for some prime leather goods. Then I'll come back to get you on Sunday at noon. I've planned to have a car waiting for you at the airport. It'll be a busy weekend, but I'll get to see two of the brothers. Haven't seen Brodie in a while. How's he doing?"

"I'll catch you up on the flight," Knox said as he motioned for Lottie to go up the steps ahead of him.

In his bibbed overalls and with a long, gray braid down his back, Lester looked like he belonged on a tractor rather than in the pilot's seat. "I'd love to hear all about him and Tripp both," he said as he settled into the seat. "Buckle up. We'll be taking off in a minute. When me and Mr. Callahan flew alone, he always sat up here in the copilot's seat beside me. We had some roustin' good talks on those flights. He'd tell me how proud he was of all you boys. He didn't know all the particulars about Brodie, but we'd sure get a good laugh when he'd say that old line." Lester lowered his voice to a growl and said, "'I'd tell you, but then I'd have to kill you.'"

"Then we'd go on down the line and visit about Tripp and how he was going to take over Callahan Oil Company someday, and then he'd tell me all about whatever project you were working on at the time. Three different kids all raised in the same house and following different dreams."

The plane taxied down the runway and was in the air, and Lester kept right on talking. "I appreciated your folks lettin' you boys each go down your own path…" He paused for a breath. "All but Tripp. I always thought he was pleasing his folks by taking that job as CEO of the company instead of what his heart wanted him to do. I'm glad to see that he's settled down into his leather shop. Is he doing well?"

"Yes, he is," Knox answered. "We all are, and we really like living in Spanish Fort."

"That's great," Lester said and told stories about the Callahan family the rest of the way to the airport in Lafayette.

When they deplaned, Lester helped unload the baggage and put it into the rental car. "You kids have a great weekend. I'll be here to pick you up at noon on Sunday."

Knox gave him a sideways hug. "Thanks for everything, Lester. We'll see you in a couple of days."

"You keep him in line, Miz Lottie," Lester teased and waved over his shoulder as he walked away.

Lottie raised her voice. "I'll do my best."

Knox opened the door for her. "I probably owe you an apology. We didn't get to say two sentences to each other on the whole flight."

She laid a hand on his cheek. "No problem. I learned more about your family in a little more than an hour than you've told me in all these weeks."

"Lester does like to talk." Knox grinned and then bent forward and kissed her on the cheek.

———

Lottie sat beside Knox in the conference room of the hotel that evening and watched him sign his name dozens of times to the papers that Geneva's lawyer kept pushing across the table. When Knox had a question, he talked to his own representative that he had on speaker.

When everything had been signed, sealed, and finished, Lottie glanced at the clock. The entire process had taken five minutes less time than it had taken for her and Knox to fly to Lafayette and drive the short distance to New Iberia and bordered on being both boring and anticlimactic.

There's that word you hate again, although you need to grow up and get over it, the voice in her head said.

Some things you don't get over. You just live with them, she protested.

"Thank you for coming all this way, and most of all for taking the whole acreage off my hands. It sure simplified everything," Geneva said as she shoved all her copies and proof that the payment had been transferred into her bank account into an expandable folder. "And I'm glad to get to meet you, Lottie. Has anyone ever offered you a job as a model?"

"No, ma'am." Lottie blushed. "I like food too well to do that."

"Well, you would be stellar at it. Y'all have a safe trip home," Geneva said.

"Thank you, and it was nice meeting you," Lottie said.

"If you are ever up north again, stop by and see us." Knox snapped his briefcase shut. "I already feel at home on the place. Are you sure you've gotten everything you need out of the house and barn?"

"Absolutely," Geneva said. "I'm glad you are the one who

bought the place. Good luck to you and Lottie. I hope y'all find as much happiness there as my grandparents did."

"I'm sure we will," Lottie said.

"For real?" Knox whispered when Geneva had disappeared out of the room.

"We already have, but you do realize we have to survive our first big argument before this can be considered long lasting, don't you?" Lottie asked.

Knox picked up the briefcase and laced the fingers of his free hand with hers. "Do you already know what we are going to argue about?"

"No, but it has to be good enough for both of us to want to throw in the towel and never see each other again." She pushed the up button on the wall beside the elevator, and the doors slid open immediately.

He followed her inside. "And how do you know all this?"

"Because I've never been in a relationship that has recovered from such a thing. If we can do that, we might have a chance at living on your new property until we are old and gray. Have you ever had a fight too big to survive?"

Knox nodded. "No, can't say I have. Mostly, it was all rainbows and romance at first, then it died in its sleep, or else she got angry over money."

"Why over money?"

"One relationship lasted a whole two weeks. She knew I had money. She wanted me to buy a big diamond engagement ring. I wasn't ready for that step," Knox answered. "But this weekend is for relaxing and the two of us having a good time. So, let's put this conversation about arguing on a back burner. Maybe we won't even turn the heat on under it, so it won't boil over."

"I agree. The papers are signed. You are the owner of a big chunk of land, plus a house. What is next?"

"There's a Cajun place not far from here, and I'm starving," he answered. "I'll put this briefcase in our room, and…"

"Maybe we could just DoorDash a place that makes shrimp po'boys and have dinner in our room," she suggested.

The elevator doors slid open, and an older couple stood back to let them exit first. "Y'all have a nice day," the guy said.

"You too," Lottie replied with a smile.

"Folks are friendly in this area, and I love their accents," she said as they made their way to the room.

Knox fished the key card from his pocket and tapped it on the lock. "Ever worked with Jack on a project in this area?"

"Nope, but I researched this place when you invited me to come with you. Tomorrow, I want to go to the park and see the Bayou Teche, and would love to have breakfast at the café where Dave Robicheaux ate," she told him.

"You read James Lee Burke books?" Knox asked.

"Yes, I do," she answered, "and although I didn't bring any with me, I have eaten at Victor's Cafeteria, and it was a really neat place."

He set the briefcase on the floor beside the minibar and gathered her into his arms for a hug. "You amaze me."

"Why? Because I read mystery books, or that I want to have you all to myself and not share you with a restaurant full of people?" she asked.

"Both of the above," he answered. "Have I told you how beautiful you look in that dress you are wearing?"

She stepped back and leaned in for a kiss. "Four times, and I've loved every one of those, but right now, we need to order food. I need energy for dessert."

"Oh, really?" Knox grinned as he took a couple of steps back and slipped his phone from his pocket. "I thought I would get some beignets for dessert."

"You can do that, and we'll have them after the dessert we are going to have before supper gets here," she teased, liking the new Lottie more with each passing hour she spent with Knox.

He put their food order into DoorDash, and the app told him delivery would be in half an hour. He placed the phone on the nightstand and drew her close to his chest again. "We have thirty minutes. Think we could celebrate being landowners"—he slowly unzipped the back of her dress—"by using up a little of what energy we have left after our busy day"—he slipped her dress down over her body, letting it puddle on the floor at her feet—"and before the food gets here?"

"And reboot for another session after we eat?" she whispered.

"That would work just fine"—he unfastened her red lace bra, eased the straps down over her shoulders, and dropped it on the floor—"and after that, we might need some sugar from the beignets to help us be able to sit out on the balcony and look at the stars."

"Or something else," she said as she slowly began to unbutton his shirt.

———————

Knox awoke to the knock on the hotel door and the sound of his phone ringing at the same time. He hurriedly put on the white hotel robe, grabbed his wallet, and padded across the floor.

"DoorDash delivery," the young man said. "You paid with a card when you ordered. Have a nice evening."

Knox handed him a generous tip. "You, too, and thank you."

He set the bags on the small bistro table for two and picked up his phone to find a voice message telling him that the delivery person was in the elevator.

Lottie pulled the sheet up under her arms when she sat up. "Where did you get that robe?"

Knox opened a closet door and took the extra one over to her. She threw her legs over the side of the bed, stood up, and he helped her put it on. "Have you used up all your energy? Do I need to feed you supper, or can you do it yourself?"

She giggled as she knotted the tie. "I've just barely got enough to get the sandwich from the table to my mouth. How about you? Do I need to feed you?"

"I think I can manage," Knox said with a fake sigh. "If

you'll get a couple of bottles of water or sweet tea from that little fridge, I will get our food out and ready to eat."

"If I faint dead away on the way across the room, you will give me mouth-to-mouth, right?"

"With pleasure." He chuckled.

He could not even begin to imagine an argument so intense that he and Lottie couldn't work it out, and he didn't want to think about a time when she wouldn't be in his life. He loved every minute he had spent with her, including the days when they were just pretending.

She carried two bottles over to the small table and then took her place across from Knox. "I hope this tastes as good as it smells."

Knox bit into his sandwich and nodded. "Twice as good."

"I'm not looking forward to summer," she blurted out.

"That's an abrupt change of subject, but neither am I," Knox said.

"I didn't mean to say that out loud."

"It's what's on both our minds, but we'll have to make the best of what time we have together and look forward to September."

Those words stuck in Knox's mind that night as he went to sleep. How did he make every minute count when so much dread was tucked away in his heart?

The next morning, Lottie took a dozen pictures of the wall decorations about the character, Dave Robicheaux, who appeared in James Lee Burke's novels. Then she took even more at the Bayou Teche that ran through a lovely little park.

She and Knox sat at a picnic table and fed the birds, and she even snapped a photo of a rare solid-black squirrel.

"This is a wonderful vacation," she said as she scrolled back through all the photographs on her phone. "I'm already dreading going back to the construction site. How about you?"

He picked up her hand and kissed the knuckles. "You aren't wired for that much adventure. You'd get bored after two days, but any *weekend* that you want to get away, I'll call Lester. We can fly anywhere you want."

"Are you saying you'd be bored with me after two days?" she snapped.

"Hey, don't twist my words." Knox could hear the edge to his words in his own voice.

She dumped the rest of the corn they had bought to feed the animals on the ground. "I'm ready to go back to the hotel for a nap."

"Yes, ma'am," he said through clenched teeth.

How in the hell had things gone from hot romance to a cold shoulder in a split second? he wondered as he followed her back to the rental car. Was it because he mentioned the word *bored*? By the time he came to the end of the short path, she was already in the vehicle, had fastened her seat belt, and had her head turned to look out the passenger window.

"I did *not* say you are boring," Knox said as he started the engine.

She didn't even answer him but continued to stare out the side window all the way to the hotel, where she jumped out of the car the minute that he had parked, beat him inside, and didn't even wait at the elevator for him. When he reached their room, the bathroom door was closed and locked.

Who would have ever thought our first big argument would be over a single word? He got a bottle of water from the mini-bar and took it out to the balcony. What was so wrong with *bored* anyway? And it came about so fast. Was this the first stage of failure for them, or just flat out **THE END**—all in caps and bold print?

He heard the bathroom door open, but he sat still. In his eyes, he had done nothing wrong, so he didn't owe her an apology. If she wanted to explain her actions, she could very well start at any time, and he would listen.

The door out into the hallway opened and closed, and he still didn't jump up and run after her. Half an hour later, he got a text from her: I'm going home. An Uber is taking me to the airport in Lafayette, and I'm flying to Dallas. Uncle Jack is picking me up. Don't worry.

He sent one back: Can we talk tomorrow?

He waited an hour, but nothing came back. Finally, he called Tripp.

"What's going on? Aren't you in Louisiana with Lottie? Why are you calling me?" Tripp said without even a simple hello.

"I did something wrong, and I can't figure it out," Knox replied and told him the whole story of what went on in the park.

"I would guess that she's sensitive to that word, but why she wouldn't even talk to you about it seems out of character for her. My advice is for you to go home tonight. I'm not leaving until tomorrow, and Lester is still here. I can have him fly down there and have you home before dark. You need to get this straightened out for your own peace of mind. If it's over, then pack up your trailer and come back to Spanish Fort. You've finished your part of the framing job, right?"

"Yes, I have," Knox answered. "I'll get my things together. Text me the time when you talk to Lester. He'll have to file flight plans and all that."

At seven o'clock that evening, the small plane landed at the airport, and Lester met Knox at the rental car. "Things didn't go so well, I guess?"

"No, and I have no idea what I did wrong," Knox told him. "I thought things were going in that forever amen direction and then boom! She was mad at me and left to fly back on a commercial flight."

"Well, son," Lester laid his hand on Knox's shoulder, "when we are dealing with the womenfolks, it's not easy to figure out where or why we stepped in a big old mess, but you crawl up here in the copilot seat, and we'll see what we can figure out. I might have some advice to give you, and I might not. I'm still doin' my best to figure out my wife, and I been married to her forty years."

"I'll take any help you've got to give me," Knox said.

Chapter 23

"Wʜᴀᴛ ʜᴀᴘᴘᴇɴᴇᴅ?" Jᴀᴄᴋ ᴀsᴋᴇᴅ Lottie. "Your red and swollen eyes mean that you have been crying. Was it out of anger or sadness? Do I need to fire Knox Callahan or shoot him?"

"A little of both, and now I'm embarrassed about the way I managed it," Lottie said as she got into Jack's truck. "We've been kidding about"—she opened the glove compartment and took out a McDonald's napkin—"our first big fight, and then it happened, and I was so angry that I just took off."

"Then I guess you need to talk to Knox about that, not me," Jack said. "Hungry?"

"Yes, but I can't swallow," she answered.

Jack made a right-hand turn off the highway onto an exit with a sign advertising an ice cream store. "This must be serious. You eat when you are happy, when you are sad, and all in between. I've never known you to pass up food. I'm going to get a chocolate milkshake. What flavor do you want?"

"Vanilla."

Jack got out of the truck and went inside. Tears flooded Lottie's cheeks and soaked the paper napkin in her hand. "I *am* boring. I'm like a plain old vanilla shake—nothing fancy for me like salted caramel or even orange pineapple," she whimpered.

You are acting like a pouting child. Her mother's voice popped into her head.

"Better to face the pain now, than later after…" She fished the last napkin from the glove compartment and dried her face. "The other shoe has dropped—just like it I figured it would."

No, it didn't drop. You took it off Knox and tossed it out the window. You made that choice, and now you can pay for the consequences.

"You could take my side. I'm your daughter," Lottie argued.

Jack startled her when he tapped on the window. She rolled it down and took her milkshake from him and put it in the cupholder. "Drink that. Don't look at it," he said when he was back in the truck. "I'll get after mine as soon as we're back on the highway, and I didn't order a vanilla. Last time I checked, you liked that one that tastes like an orange creamsicle, so that's what you've got."

"Thank you," she muttered.

It seemed like Uncle Jack even knew she wasn't boring.

Jack picked up his shake. "Your expression tells me that you are arguing with someone. Is it Knox?"

"No, it's… I don't want to talk about it," Lottie said as she removed her shake from the cupholder and sucked down enough to give her a brain freeze.

" You might as well get it off your chest," he said. "I'm a good listener. Is it Knox?"

She grabbed her head with her free hand. "No, and my head is about to explode."

"Don't drink so fast," Jack told her. "You made the decision to make a big deal out of something small, so now you have to pay the price."

"How do you know it was a small thing?" she asked.

"Because you said that you were embarrassed by what you did. If you were right about the fight, then you would stand your ground and do battle until the death. I know you, girl. I was there when you were born and have been in your life almost as much as your folks. Only you can make this right, so what are you going to do?"

"Knox sent a text asking if we can talk tomorrow. I haven't answered it." She held up her cup. "And thank you for this. I didn't realize how hungry I was."

"You are welcome, and it's time for you to let Knox know if and when you are ready to tell him why you acted like you did."

She took her phone from her purse and sent a text with only one word: Yes.

———————

Cheeto flew down from the roof of the trailer and landed on Knox's shoulder before he even closed the truck door. "Thank you for the welcome home. Seems like a month has passed since last night." He gathered up his suitcase and briefcase from the back seat and carried them to the trailer. "We may be going home to Spanish Fort tomorrow, so stick close by."

The rooster gently pecked him on the cheek and flew back to his perch on the roof. Knox opened the door, and Bally jumped off the bed, ran across the floor, and tried to climb up the leg of his jeans. Knox set his luggage on the floor and picked her up.

"Somebody missed me and still loves me."

She snuggled down on his shoulder and purred. He sat down on the edge of his bed and sighed. "This is the first time I can ever remember being in trouble and not even knowing the real reason why."

Bally changed places from his shoulder to his lap and looked up at him with her green eyes as if she understood every word. "She said that we can talk tomorrow, but do I go to her place, or wait for her to come to mine?"

The kitten growled and hopped down off his lap. She jumped up on the cabinet, looked out the window, and slapped at it like she was fighting a monster, and all the while, Cheeto was fussing about something up on the roof. Knox slung the door open, expecting to see a flock of birds trying to steal Cheeto's roost and tormenting Bally through the window.

Not a bird in sight, but Lottie stood on the bottom step.

"I was trying to get up enough courage to knock," she whispered.

"It's not Sunday," Knox told her.

"I understand," she said and turned to walk away.

"But it's only a few hours until midnight," Knox raised his voice, "and there's no way I can sleep."

She turned around, and even with only the dim moonlight, he could see the anguish in her eyes and feel the pain in her body language. "Then may I come in and talk to you?"

He swung the door open, and she came inside. "May I sit down?"

"We've had an argument which I don't understand at all, but you don't have to ask for permission to come in or to sit down." He couldn't control the flat tone. "Can I get you something to drink—water, tea, a beer?"

"Beer, please," she answered and sat down.

He took two from the refrigerator and twisted the tops off, then sat down, but kept a couple of feet between them. "Do you want to tell me what I did wrong?"

She took a long sip of her beer. "It wasn't you. It's me."

"Seems like I've heard that line right before a lady told me that an old boyfriend had resurfaced."

"It's not anything like that," Lottie's voice came out in half a groan.

"I'm listening."

"We were talking about whether we would survive a big fight, and…" She paused.

Knox waited for a full minute before he said, "Go on."

"I couldn't bear the pain of not being with you, and then there was the *boring* thing, and I just lost it. My mind said 'just get it over with.' Cut your losses and face the heartache now. My heart said something different and…" She paused again.

"What's going on with this boring thing and you?"

"I've never talked to anyone about it, not my mother, or Uncle Jack or even the school counselor." She kept her eyes on the beer bottle as if it mesmerized her. "When I was in elementary school, I was taller than all the other kids, even the boys. Since I was towered above them, the other kids got it in their heads that I had to be older than any of them and was held back a couple of years. They called me 'dummy' and whispered behind my back. Always loud enough that I could hear them, but low enough that the teachers didn't. Somehow, I knew that if I tattled, things would get worse, so I kept my mouth shut. To top it all off, I grew so fast that I was clumsy. I'm not telling you this for pity. I don't want that, but I do want you to understand."

"I'm ready to make a bunch of grown adults pick up highway trash to pay for their sins as children," Knox said through clenched teeth.

"I learned to be a loner. When the recess time rolled around, I sat alone and read books. Then I got into junior high school, and things got worse. I didn't fit in with any of the cliques. My grades were so good they couldn't call me dummy anymore, but I became Loser Lottie, because I didn't have friends. After that was high school, and I'd already been tagged a misfit that couldn't even be in one of the other oddball groups, so I became Boring Lottie."

Knox scooted over closer to her. "I'm so sorry."

"No one knew me in college, but part of that was my fault. I didn't know how to be a friend or have one either. I was just the awkward girl who only went to a couple of parties and felt so out of place that I spent the twenty minutes I was there hiding in the shadows. Now fast-forward to my first boyfriend. I thought I was in love, and when we broke up, he told me that he couldn't stand to be with someone as boring as me. That stung because that's what the popular girls in high school called me.

"The next one said nothing about me was exciting, and he couldn't tie himself to a woman that was boring. The third one was a loser, but by then I figured that he was the only kind of guy a person like me could catch. He wouldn't work, and when he left, he cleaned out my bank account and left me with a couple of maxed-out credit cards. I refuse to be a victim, so don't pity me."

"I'm not," Knox said. "I was thinking that you are pretty damn strong to survive all that."

She took another long drink of her beer and stared at the bottle a while longer before she went on. "I planned on us only being in a fake relationship, and then I started liking you, and that turned into love, but I kept telling myself that pretty soon that other shoe would drop. Just thinking about it hurt so bad that I couldn't breathe. When you said that I would be bored if we went on anything but weekend trips, it triggered something inside me, and I ran."

"Why didn't you tell me all this before?" Knox asked.

"I was afraid you would figure out that I am awkward

when it comes to relationships and boring, and that"—another pause—"you could do much better than being saddled with a giant sunflower when you could have a petite little rose. I shouldn't have left without giving you a chance to explain."

Knox moved over until his shoulder was against hers. "No, you shouldn't have. Now it's my turn to talk, but I want you to look at me."

She turned her face toward him, and he could not only see the pain in her brown eyes, but also feel it radiating from her whole body. He tilted her chin up with his fist and barely blinked when he started to talk.

"Don't let your past define what we have. I have always felt like the lucky one in this relationship. To have a gorgeous woman like you beside me seems surreal. At the end of the day, to be able to talk to you about my dreams and have you really listen when I'm all up in a discussion about two-by-fours and trusses is a blessing. You understand me and, honey, the other shoe—or, in my case, a work boot—is never going to drop. You are not boring, and anytime you want to take a week off and go anywhere, the mountains or beach or out in the middle of a desert, I'm ready to go with you. We can fly or road trip in a vehicle or even in one of our trailers so that we can take Bally and Prissy with us. I don't think Cheeto would travel too well, but if that's what you want, we can cage him up and take him too."

"Are you sure?" she asked with a weak smile.

Knox kissed her on the forehead. "I'm damn sure."

"Then you will accept my apology?"

"Of course, but from now on, let's be honest and talk to each other when we have a problem."

"I promise," she said.

That time, the kiss was on her lips.

Chapter 24

Swan Song Estates was looking more like a group of small cabins or a tiny, gated community rather than a construction site the evening that the moving truck was supposed to arrive with Mandy and Jack's belongings. The gate had been installed with the name of the place painted around a swan swimming on the lake. The siren and lights had been replaced with a new security system linked to the police station in Wichita Falls.

"Hey, everyone," Jack yelled to the teams that were still there. "I just got a text from Mandy that they are five minutes out."

"Then our showers will wait until after we help y'all get unloaded," Knox said.

"But Knox and I have first dibs after we get through," Lottie called out.

Thomas gave her a smart salute. "Yes, ma'am. Now, let's all get out on the cabin porch and give Mandy a proper welcome."

The big moving truck pulled up in front of the house with Mandy right behind it in her SUV. She got out and waved at the crowd. "I'm home!" she yelled.

"Welcome!" everyone shouted, and they were at the back of the truck by the time the driver lowered the ramp.

"Oh. My. Goodness!" Mandy gasped. "I wasn't expecting this much help."

Jack draped an arm around her shoulders and kissed her on the forehead. "I'm glad you are here and that we can be together for the rest of our lives."

Lottie came close to swooning when she heard him say those words. She wished that she could truly believe that she and Knox would someday still be in love.

We have made great progress today. You just admitted that you are someone Knox can love. Her therapist from years ago popped into her head.

Lottie ignored the voice and picked up a box marked Cookbooks and carried it into the cabin. "Aunt Mandy, I've never known you to measure anything. Why did you bring all these?"

Mandy led the way into the house. "Because one belonged to my grandmother, another to my mama, and the rest are from churches we attended. Seemed like there was always a committee to raise money for the missionaries by making a cookbook, and I have recipes in them. You wouldn't believe how many I gave away when I downsized."

"When you make out your will, I would love to have one with your recipes in it," Lottie said.

"Why? You don't cook," Eddie said with a smile.

"Not one time did I say I could not cook. I said I can

make canned soup and sandwiches, and that is not a lie," she shot back at him.

"All these years," Thomas growled.

"Yep, all these years, but now I'm not going to work with y'all anymore, so I figure the secret can come out." She grinned.

"You are downright mean," Gabe said.

"You are learning," Mandy told him. "She's a fine cook. Her grandmother and mother saw to that, but she always liked a hammer more than a frying pan."

Lottie put the box down on the counter and popped her hands on her hips. "I smell rain, and there's dark clouds down in the Southwest. Are you going to stand around here and argue with me, or get that truck unloaded? I'd hate to see Aunt Mandy's furniture get soaked."

Mandy tucked a strand of gray hair back into her ponytail. "Put those cookbooks on the top shelf. I'll have to get a step stool to get at them, but then they are more keepsakes than something I use very often." She waited until the guys were all back outside before she said, "Tell me about you and Knox."

"What about us?" Lottie asked.

"Jack told me that y'all hit a rough spot. Did you get through it, or is it still going on?"

"We talked it out, and we're fine," Lottie answered. No way was she going into the particulars of the argument with so many guys coming in and out with furniture and boxes. Learning that she could cook was enough for them to know in one day, or forever for that matter. Like the old saying about Vegas, what happened in New Iberia stayed in New Iberia.

"That's good, but honey, it will not be the last time you argue. That sofa that Knox and Thomas just brought inside is proof of that. Jack wanted a leather one to match his recliner, but I like a soft fabric that's warm when I sit on it. We finally compromised. I picked out what I wanted, and he got the chair he wanted," Mandy told her.

"Truck is unloaded. Thank all of you for the help," Jack said above the noise of dozens of conversations. "I'll help Mandy if…" His phone rang, and he stepped into the utility room to answer it.

When he came back out, Eddie was holding the door open for several of the guys to go on outside. "If you're going to keep from getting wet on your way to the trailers, you better jog instead of walk. I felt a little mist on my face a minute ago."

Lottie laced her fingers with Knox's and said, "We're the lucky ones. We don't have to move anything but two cats and a rooster when we leave this place."

"One cat and a chicken until you finish up the summer in El Paso," he answered.

Jack yelled before the crowd dispersed. "Would all y'all take a few minutes and meet me in the rec hall? I just now got a phone call, and I need to discuss something with you."

Thomas made an abrupt turn. "Anyone have an idea what this is all about?"

"Nope," Lottie answered, and then a chill danced down her spine. Had something happened to her parents? Had they decided to give up their cabin and live in Dallas?

"Are you okay?" Knox asked.

"Why are you asking?" Lottie frowned.

"You look worried, and you shivered. Are you getting sick?"

"Just worried. Let's see what the news is before I panic. Uncle Jack could be going to hand out our bonus checks early, and my imagination has run wild for nothing."

Jack raised his hand to get their attention when Lottie and Knox made it inside. "I've just gotten off the phone with Walter's wife. There's two things y'all need to know. He has had a mild heart attack and has decided to retire for good. Gracie says that he is doing fine, but the doctor says he has to eat right and avoid stress."

"That eating right business won't be easy." Thomas chuckled. "He loves his food and has a sweet tooth that a candy factory couldn't satisfy."

Knox gently squeezed Lottie's hand. "Does this mean we don't have to be separated for the summer?"

"Maybe," she whispered. "But we still need…"

Jack butted in before Lottie could finish what she was saying. "You are right about Walter and his sugar, but it looks like he's going to have to curb that a lot. The second is that the project out in El Paso has gone under because several of their investors have pulled out. With the economy what it is, I can't blame them. They have already built the rec hall, but a senior citizens' group has offered to buy it. That means there will be no Hamptons in Texas. I hate to tell y'all this when I know you were depending on that job, but I wanted you to know as soon as possible."

Thomas raised a fist in the air. "Yes! That is great news. My family wants to start up our own business, and this means we can do it earlier than fall. And any of y'all who are here and want a job, come talk to me. We will be located out in western Oklahoma and will try to keep our projects close enough that we can go home at night."

"I'll talk to you when we finish the last cabin," Vincent said.

"What about you, Lottie?" Thomas asked.

"I don't think so," she answered. "That's too far from right here. I want to be close to my parents and other relatives."

"If you change your mind, I'll always have a place for you," Thomas said.

"Thanks," she muttered.

"That's all," Jack said. "I've got some calls to make to the teams that have already left. Thanks for all the help unloading the truck, and I'll see you in the morning."

Eddie shook his head. "Mandy might not say as much, but you should be in the cabin helping her. We've got that last cabin covered. And thanks for telling us the news as soon as you heard. We'll all be calling home to let our families know there's been a change in plans."

"Oh, one other thing," Jack said. "Lottie's parents, Zeke and Darlene, will arrive Friday morning. If you have that last cabin finished, would you stick around and pitch in and help them like you did for me and Mandy before you leave the grounds?"

"You got it, Boss," Gabe said.

With the news, Lottie seemed to be in limbo as she picked up their tote bags carrying clean clothing for the shower. She needed to be ready if Knox asked her to live with him. Her mind said, *Go for it*, but her heart said, *Don't rush*.

"I'm going to stick around down here until my folks leave for their cruise," she blurted out and immediately wished she had given the idea some more thought before she said anything.

Knox led the way to the bathroom. "That's better than the whole summer. I can live with that."

Lottie was on the verge of being offended. If he truly felt that they belonged together, shouldn't he fight for her to go to Spanish Fort with him as soon as the job was finished? "I wasn't expecting that answer," she said with a crisp edge to her tone.

He closed the door and adjusted the water in the shower. "Hey, I will never, ever stand in your way if you want to spend time with your family. I only wish I could have a week with my parents at this time in my life. Like I told you before, I want you to come to Spanish Fort. I even want you to live in the house with me, but all that is your decision to make. I will not pressure you into anything. Now strip out of those clothes and I'll massage your back."

She dropped her jeans and shirt on the floor, and he

unfastened her bra. "Why do you have to be so sweet about everything?"

"It's just the way I am." He grinned. "I *can* get all riled up, but it would be selfish of me to try to talk you out of spending time with your family. You will make memories you will cherish forever after they are gone. That said, I will miss you something fierce when we are apart, no matter how long it is."

"I bet I miss you even more."

"Not possible," he said as he stripped out of his clothing and led her into the shower stall.

Chapter 25

"Are you out of your mind? Why are you still here?" Darlene asked Lottie the morning after they had arrived at Swan Song Estates. "We've got everything unpacked and arranged, and we're leaving in a couple of days."

"I'm going to spend the time with you and Daddy," Lottie answered. "How does that make me out of my mind?"

"Your dad and I are doing a road trip rather than fly. We're going to go through Las Vegas, then on out to California and play a day or two before we get on our cruise," Darlene said, "and even if we weren't, you should be hitching up your trailer and going with Knox. That's where your heart is. I saw the expression on your face when he drove away."

Lottie turned away and wiped a tear from her eye. "I'll miss him, but I want to be here with you and Daddy."

"Darlin', you cannot ride two horses with one ass. It just ain't possible," Darlene told her. "You want two things, and you are torn. Your dad and I will be here for the rest of our lives, and we're only two hours away from Spanish Fort. We can drive up there for a Sunday afternoon, or we can meet in Wichita Falls for dinner some evening. Right now, though, you need to go be with Knox. So, give me a hug, and get going."

"Are you sure?" Lottie asked.

"As sure as I am about this being the right move for me and Zeke," Darlene answered.

"Did I hear my name?" Zeke came through the back door.

"I'm telling our daughter to go be with Knox," Darlene replied. "Where have you been?"

Zeke slipped an arm around Lottie's shoulders. "Listen to your mama. She's a wise woman. Let's go hitch up your trailer. It looks lonely now that it's the only one out there. Almost as unhappy as you do."

"It kind of does," Lottie agreed.

In less than an hour, she had everything locked down in the trailer, Prissy in her carrier and seat belted into the back seat, and had left Swan Song Estates in her rearview mirror. In only two hours, she would be home.

Home!

That was a word she hadn't used very often since she was an adult.

"I'm going to raise my kids right there on the property so that they have a permanent childhood home to come to when they are grown," she muttered. "I've learned that home isn't really where you hang your hat. It's where your heart is content. I've learned from visiting the Paradise that I want to be like Mary Jane when I grow up."

One traffic accident and a five-mile stretch of road construction slowed her down a bit, and then there was a stop at the grocery store in Nocona. So, it was about three hours before she reached the house, and no one was there.

She made sure she entered the right code at the gate and parked her truck and trailer behind the house. "We're here, Prissy. You've never known anything but a cramped trailer, and you might be a little bewildered. There's plenty of room for you and Bally, so I expect you to play nice or else find a hiding spot."

She unloaded all her things through the back door and kept an eye on the two cats. Surprisingly enough, Bally decided that Prissy was her mother and followed her around as she snooped through every corner. Finally, Prissy curled up on the sofa with Bally right beside her.

"Well, I'll be…" She giggled. "There's my sign. If Prissy is happy to have a little sister, then everything is going to be fine."

***

"Hey, anybody home?" Knox yelled as he stepped inside the leather shop.

Willa Rose came out of her father's apartment located inside the store. "Only by a few minutes. It's closing time, and we're about to go home."

Knox reached out his arms to take the baby boy, Nicky, from her. "He's twice as big as he was a week ago."

Tripp came from the back of the store and clamped a hand on Knox's shoulder. "He's already four months old and has two teeth. Are you home for good? Where's Lottie?"

"She'll be along soon. She wanted to spend some time with her folks," Knox answered. "I unloaded my livestock at the house and came straight here."

"Livestock?" Willa Rose asked.

"Remember, I told you I have adopted a rooster and a kitten. Cheeto is checking out the yard and warning all the squirrels that he's the king. When I left Bally, she had a case of the zoomies, running in circles around the coffee table, down the hallway, and back again to tackle one of her toys. She's been used to living in a trailer, so she probably thinks she's moved into a castle."

That last word brought back to mind the weekend that Knox teased Lottie about being his queen and the old farmhouse being their castle. They had only been apart for a few hours, but it already felt like a whole week, or maybe a month, but at least it wasn't for the entire summer.

"Come home with us and have some supper," Willa Rose said.

"Thanks for the offer, but I want to make the rounds and then go on back home." Knox handed Nicky to Tripp and led the way outside. "See y'all at church tomorrow morning. Mother's Day is only a week away. I'll need to do some shopping for Mary Jane. Has she mentioned anything?"

"Not to me," Tripp answered, "but Audrey will find something special. Got to admit, this is the time of year when I sure miss Mother."

Knox swallowed the lump in his throat and nodded, unable to say a single word.

His last stop was at the farm to see Brodie and Audrey. He found them in the barn with Pansy and her litter of tiny potbellied pigs.

"Welcome home," Brodie said. "Where's Lottie?"

"She'll be along in a little while. She hung back to visit with her folks," Knox answered for what seemed like the hundredth time. "When are the little critters going to be ready to join my livestock collection?" he asked and went on to tell them about Bally and Cheeto.

"You could take them right now, but you probably should get a pen built and some kind of shelter. Pansy seems to be happy with her setup here. She's got the barn in bad weather, and when the sun is out, she can use the pet door to go out into her run," Audrey replied. "Want to pick out which one or ones you want? She's got five, and we're keeping the black-and-white spotted one to give her some company. Rae's twins want one, but they are arguing about which one. That leaves three."

"I'll let Lottie decide, but when she sees them, she might want more than one," Knox chuckled. "Let Rae's girls choose first, and then we'll most likely take the ones that are left."

"I've got chili in the slow cooker. Want to stay for supper?" Audrey asked.

"Thanks, but I'll get on back to my place. It'll take some time to get used to not living in a trailer," Knox said and headed for the open barn door. "See y'all tomorrow. Are you taking Mary Jane a piglet next week for her Mother's Day present?"

"We offered her the pick of the litter, and I won't repeat her answer." Brodie chuckled.

"On Mother's Day we plan to give her the news that we're

blessing her with a grandbaby in six months. We waited to be sure the first trimester is over before we told the family," Brodie said.

"That's great! I'm going to be an uncle again!" Knox gave them both a hug.

"Yep, and the family grows some more," Audrey said. "Don't tell anyone until Mother's Day."

"My lips are sealed," Knox promised.

Thinking about both Bo and Audrey making announcements the next day, he wondered if by next year he and Lottie might be able to tell the family the same thing on Mother's Day. Brodie's new baby would be—he stopped and did the math—maybe six months old. If he and Lottie had a child by the following Christmas, he or she could grow up with a couple of older cousins, plus all the extended Paradise family.

He was so deep in thought that he drove right past the lane to his house and had to turn around and drive back. He entered the code, and the gate swung open and closed behind him when he drove over the cattle guard. Cheeto was sitting on the back of a rocking chair and having a staring standoff with a squirrel. The silly animal was stretched out on the side of the pecan tree as if he was wearing camouflage and Cheeto couldn't see him.

Knox was on the porch when he noticed that the front door stood wide open. He knew he had set the alarm and closed it when he left, so he eased it open and yelled. "Who's in here?"

The aroma of fried chicken wafted out to meet him, but no one answered. Had his youngest sister, Ivy, felt sorry for him and came over to cook supper?

"Hey." Lottie appeared in the archway separating the kitchen from the living room. "I was hoping you would be home soon. Supper is about ready."

"If I'm dreaming, don't wake me," he whispered.

She crossed the room and wrapped her arms around his neck. "I'm home to stay, and I'm not living in the trailer. Will you be my real boyfriend?"

"Depends." Knox hugged her tightly to be sure that she was actually there. "The fake one was supposedly only for six weeks. How long is a real one for?"

"Until you aren't my boyfriend anymore, but my fiancé, and then my husband, but I'm in no hurry for all that. For now, I just want to be your girlfriend who lives with you and works along beside you as a carpenter."

"Then my answer is yes," Knox answered and tipped her chin up for a kiss.

Epilogue

10 years later

"Good Lord. Have you seen *your* youngest daughter, Knox? Janie was completely dressed for the birthday party, but she's been out there in the pigpen. She has rolled in the mud with those new piglets," Lottie fussed.

"How come when Janie does something wrong, she's my daughter?" He chuckled as he took four-year-old Janie by the hand and led her to the bathroom. "Now, you'll have to wear your least favorite Fourth of July outfit because you have completely ruined this dress."

"But, Daddy," she whined. "Do we have to wash my hair, too?"

"You look like you have muddy hair," Lottie fussed.

Janie's big blue eyes filled with tears. "I don't want muddy hair."

"We'll have it fixed in a jiffy," Knox said and winked at Lottie. "You think this is a hot mess, wait a month until the next one gets here. It's a boy."

"Yes!" Eight-year-old Amanda pumped her fist into the air. "I want a brother like Garrett. Two sisters is enough."

"I want twin brothers. Amanda says that she will get to hold our brother all the time and I don't, and that's not fair, but if we have two, then one can be mine," Six-year-old Mia declared.

"No arguing, or we won't go to Aunt Bernie's party, and y'all all know that will make her cry," Lottie said. "Go sit on the sofa until your daddy gets Janie cleaned up. And your aunt Bo and some of her sisters can have twins. I can barely keep up with one child at a time."

In a few minutes, Knox emerged from the bathroom with a little girl in a cute red-and-white polka-dotted sundress, her curly hair still damp. Lottie nodded at him and then toward the suitcase.

"I married a smart woman," he said.

"We have to be prepared," she said and leaned out over her enormous belly to kiss him on the cheek. "Dirt seems to reach out and grab them. But maybe if we're lucky, they'll be clean long enough for family pictures. Mary Jane has hired a professional photographer, and I'm hoping we can get a good one. Let's herd them out to the SUV."

The broiling-hot sun poured down on them like it was coming right out of an oven. The SUV had barely cooled down by the time Knox parked at the Paradise. The photographer had set up his equipment on the porch and was taking pictures of Bernie.

A decade hadn't changed her very much. A tiara was perched on top of her freshly dyed and styled red hair. Her hot-pink ball gown would make any queen jealous, and someone—probably Mary Jane—had draped a wide 90th Birthday ribbon across her body.

She waved at Knox and Lottie and yelled, "You all are the last ones here, so come on over here and get your picture made with me, and then one with just your family. Ain't this a grand day to celebrate Independence Day and my birthday at the same time? I am officially retired now, and I'm going to get me a new Chihuahua puppy to celebrate my ninetieth. I miss Pepper…" She rolled her eyes toward the sky. "God rest his precious little soul."

"Happy Birthday, Aunt Bernie!" Amanda squealed as she bailed out of the SUV. "You are gorgeous."

"Of course I am, and you will be, too, when you are ninety," Bernie said. "You and Mia can stand on either side of me and hold my hands. Janie can sit in my lap and kiss me on the cheek for one of the pictures. When we are done here and y'all get your picture done, Mary Jane wants the whole family to gather round me out by the Christmas sleigh, only it's a Fourth of July one today."

Lottie eased out of the truck with Knox's help. "Was she really born on Independence Day?"

"Who knows when she was born?" Knox answered and led her up on the porch. "She changes it to suit her whim, as well as how old she is. Mary Jane says she is past ninety by a few years, but we humor her."

They lined up behind and around Bernie, and the photographer snapped half a dozen pictures. When he finished, Bernie popped up out of the chair with the agility of a sixteen-year-old. "It's y'all's turn now. You girls smile at the camera. Mary Jane is going to make me an album with pictures from today, and I want to remember you with smiles as pretty as your dresses. I'm going on out to the sleigh, but when you are done, Knox needs to help me up on the seat. I could climb up into the seat myself, but I might snag my dress. We need to get these pictures and dinner all done so I can get this thing off and put on my red-and-white overalls for the rest of the holiday," she said.

As soon as the photographer finished taking several shots of his family, Knox hurried out to the sleigh, put his hands on Bernie's waist, and set her up in the seat. Someone must have been watching from the window because he had barely gotten that job done when Mary Jane and Joe Clay led the long parade out of the house.

Joe Clay helped Mary Jane up onto the seat beside Bernie, and he took his place on the other side.

Mary Jane motioned toward the photographer. "I want the eleven children in order of age and their spouses to be standing, and the grandkids all sitting in front. You tell them what to do, and no boyfriends or girlfriends. This is a family picture that is going to hang above the fireplace. You never know how long romances will last."

"Granny Mary!" Daisy, one of Rae's older twins, groaned.

"Hush!" Rae said. "She's right, and that's the reason I only wanted my four kids in our family picture."

Several minutes passed before the guy was satisfied with the dynamics, but he finally got everyone lined up just right.

Twenty-five adults, counting Bernie, Mary Jane, and Joe Clay. Thirty-eight grandchildren and three more on the way before the end of the year.

After the pictures were taken, Joe Clay helped Bernie and Mary Jane down off the sleigh and looked around at the family. "Okay, kids, let's all dance out to the barn where our dinner is waiting. I'm starving. How about all y'all?"

"Yes!" The cry went up from all of them.

Mary Jane laced her fingers in Joe Clay's, and they led the troops that were old enough to walk to the barn where hot dogs, hamburgers, and smoked brisket, along with all the trimmings, were ready to be served.

"Remember what that fortune teller told you?" Tripp asked Willa Rose.

"She said I would have five sons, and she was right. I didn't expect to adopt them all, or that there would be two sets of twins." She smiled as her two boys who were fraternal twins and her set of identical boys with bright red hair and freckles followed Joe Clay and Mary Jane across the massive backyard.

"I knew it would come about," Bernie declared and held out her arms for Knox to help her down from the seat. "She also said I would live to be a hundred, and when I do, I will wear this dress again, and you will all give me another party. By then, we should have great-grands in the mix."

"Shhh…" Rae groaned. "I'm the one with the oldest kids, and they're about to go off to college in another year. They've already got boyfriends, and I'm not even ready for that!"

"I can't imagine my ten-year-old girls being in high school, much less graduating from high school," Endora said with a sigh.

Bernie shook her finger at all of them. "They grow up in the blink of an eye. Don't take a single second for granted. Not even you, Ivy, with the youngest baby here today."

"I promise I won't. Seems like only yesterday Mary Jane and Joe Clay adopted me. Best thing that ever happened to me."

"Ain't life grand?" Knox hugged Lottie to his side.

"Absolutely," Lottie agreed, "and it's only going to get better, but honey, this is our last time around the maternity ward."

"I'm good with that," Knox agreed and lowered his voice. "And, darlin', I'm so glad that you asked me to be your fake boyfriend. Just look at all the happiness it brought into our lives."

"It was only fake until it wasn't. Our kids and this one"—she laid her hand on her belly—"are proof that it is very real."

Chapter 1

THE SOUND OF A freight train coming right at him was so loud that Brodie could barely hear his brothers, Tripp and Knox, yelling from the cellar door. A chunk of ragged wood stabbed the ground right in front of him. He dodged it, and a hog spun through the air above his head so close that he could smell it.

When pigs fly, he thought as he ran toward the storm shelter.

"Get in here!" Tripp's voice came through the noise.

A violent wind pushed him hard from behind, and suddenly he was being thrown forward with such force that his feet left the ground. He groped for balance, and then Tripp hugged him like a bear. The next thing he knew, he was sitting on the bench that lined the back wall. An oil lamp on an old wooden table dimly lit up the room. Brodie clasped his hands together to keep them from shaking.

"Pigs *were* flying," he whispered.

"What did you say?" Knox hollered above the noise. "With all the pounding out there, you've got to speak up."

"I saw a full-sized hog flying through the air," Brodie answered between bouts of catching his breath.

"Everything was flying." Tripp raised his voice. "Even you. If I hadn't caught you when I did, you'd be halfway to Arkansas by now. Thank God we've got a storm cellar."

"Thank Ira," Brodie said. "He's the one that built this storm shelter."

Brodie's heart was still pounding, and he wasn't sure his legs would support him if he tried to stand up. From the sound of things, the cellar door was taking a severe beating. Knox, the carpenter in the family, might need to build a new one next week. Audrey Tucker and her ninety-year-old aunt were his neighbors who had shown him nothing but disgust because he wouldn't sell his farm to them, but he hoped they were safe.

"Oh, no!" he whispered, but evidently neither of his brothers heard him. "What if this storm blows the Paradise away or hurts one of my seven half sisters, or my biological father?"

"I can see your lips moving, but I have no idea what you are saying," Knox shouted.

"Nothing," Brodie said loudly and shook his head.

Would his heart ever stop pounding, or was this his new norm? Did the force of the wind cause a problem in his internal organs? Brodie was no stranger to destruction. He had done a couple of tours in countries with bombed-out buildings. He had seen—up close and personal—what an IED could do. He'd served on the Bandera, Texas, Volunteer Fire Department and seen and been through atrocities that gave him nightmares. But coming so close to being swept away in a tornado affected him worse than anything he had ever experienced before. If he had been a child, and not thirty years old, he would have definitely needed years of therapy.

"Are you alright?" Knox asked.

Brodie glanced over at his brother. "Why do you ask?"

"You've been staring at the lamp with a blank stare on your face," Knox answered.

"I thought I was a goner," Brodie admitted.

"So did I when that piece of wood flew out of the air and stuck in the ground right in front of you," Tripp yelled.

Suddenly an eerie silence filled the place. The lamplight flickered a couple of times before it went out completely, leaving the cellar in darkness so heavy that made Brodie shiver. He stood up and felt his way around the shelving to his right. He moved slowly toward the thin streak of light on the steps, possibly coming through a broken board on the weathered old wooden door. A sticker in the palm of his hand was payment when he searched for the rusty bolt that would unlock the door. He ignored the stinging pain and slid the bolt to the side. Then he pushed hard with his shoulder, but it did not budge.

"Need some help?" Knox asked.

"Only if y'all want to get out of here," Brodie answered.

Even with three strong men giving it all they had, the door would not open. Brodie was so winded on the third try that he sat down on the step and groaned. "We are stuck until someone comes along to help us from the outside."

"Everyone may just drive by and think that we were blown away like you nearly were," Tripp groaned.

"Brodie! Tripp! Knox!" Voices blended together, but in among all of them, Brodie recognized Joe Clay's.

"In here. In the cellar," he yelled.

"Hush! Everyone be quiet!" Mary Jane's voice sounded like it was coming from the bottom of a barrel.

"We are trapped," Brodie shouted.

Shadows covered up the tiny streak of light, and the scraping sounds of something being dragged off the wooden door filled the cellar. Brodie didn't realize how tight his chest had been until he could actually take a deep breath without pain.

"Anyone got a chain in their truck?" Joe Clay's voice came through plain and clear.

"I do," Shane answered. "I'll get it so we can drag this tree away. Looks like the tornado ripped away the electrical wires to the house, but they're not lying around anywhere. Remy is calling the power company now to get them out here to fix things."

Brodie sat down on the top step. "I hope that's not one of the apple trees on the door."

"We're working on things out here," Mary Jane yelled. "Are y'all safe?"

"We are fine," Tripp called out.

"That's good," Joe Clay said. "We're wrapping a chain around the tree and using my old work truck to pull it off the doors. Y'all might want to stand back away from everything in case the wood splinters and flies. If this don't work, we'll go back to the Paradise and get chain saws."

"We'll get you out of there," Mary Jane assured them in a worried voice.

The crunching sound of the tree being dragged away was deafening, but immediately a beam of light flowed into the cellar. Joe Clay's face appeared first when he opened up what was left of the splinters and shattered doors.

"Are y'all sure you are all right?" he asked.

Brodie was the first one out, and Joe Clay grabbed him in a fierce bear hug. "When we saw that the house was gone, I thought I'd lost you."

"I'm fine except for a splinter in my hand," Brodie assured him.

When the other two brothers came out of the cellar, Joe Clay left Brodie and wrapped them up in a three-way hug. "We are so lucky that you made it to shelter on time."

"Brodie just about didn't," Tripp said and then pointed toward where their house used to be.

Disaster lay all around the place. The roof, all except for shingles scattered around the yard, was gone. Three walls of the house, along with everything but the bathroom fixtures, had been blown away. The water hose, hooked up to the well house, was still coiled up like a sleeping snake. How could a storm so violent that it picked him right up off the ground not even disturb a lightweight hose?

Brodie closed his hazel eyes, but when he opened them nothing had changed. He stood to the side of the cellar steps, looked out across the farm, and stared at broken boards and shingles scattered every which way.

"What do we do now?" Tripp asked.

His brother's voice sounded as if it was coming from a mile away.

Lightning lit up the sky behind Brodie and thunder rolled. The tornado had left a chilly wind, drizzling rain, and shock in its wake. Now it was traveling north toward the Red River, most likely destroying whatever got in its way.

"We will rebuild." Knox's statement seemed flat and unsure.

"That will take months," Tripp said.

"I've already got the plans drawn up," Knox said. "We were going to build a bigger house this summer, anyway. Until we get it ready to move into, we can live in my travel trailer."

"We don't have anything but the clothes on our backs," Tripp snapped.

"We'll go to Nocona this evening and get whatever we need—toothbrushes, soap, and that kind of thing. We'll figure this out," Knox said.

"Thirty minutes?" Brodie whispered.

"I can't build a house in half an hour," Knox declared.

"I know," Brodie said, "but half an hour ago Tripp was…" he paused and glanced over to see if the grill was still there—it wasn't. "Tripp was grilling T-bones."

"We can buy more steaks," Knox barked. "We can buy anything we need or want. Three pieces of meat are the least of our worries right now."

"And what are we going to do for supper tonight?" Tripp asked.

"We'll eat at the Dairy Queen, buy what we need, stay

in that little hotel east of town, and figure things out tomorrow," Knox answered.

"We need to see if we still have a truck that will take us to Nocona," Brodie finally got the words out, but his feet wouldn't move.

A cardinal lit on a bare pecan tree branch above him and began to sing. His mother Jolene always said that when a cardinal lands close by, it means that someone who has passed away is thinking of you. If that was true and his mother was thinking of him, then why would there be a song in her heart? She should be weeping, not putting out a joyful sound.

Somewhere off in the distance the sound of more vehicles coming down the dirt lane drowned out the bird's happiness. Dark clouds covered the sky to the northeast, but to the southwest, the sky was clear blue, and the sun was slowly making its way toward the western horizon.

None of it made any sense.

The noise of lots of trucks and cars took his attention toward the road, where they lined up like a funeral procession, which seemed fitting to Brodie at that time. Family members were hurrying out of seven more trucks and coming toward him.

"Family," he muttered.

"Are you guys hurt?" Parker asked as he and Endora ignored the rain and ran across the yard, sidestepping all the debris.

"We're fine, but we don't have a home anymore." Brodie could talk, but his feet didn't work anymore. "Did the tornado hit any of y'all's places?"

"We are all safe and our homes are still standing. Houses can be replaced," Mary Jane told him. "Sons can't."

But I'm not your son. Neither are Tripp and Knox. Brodie was glad he had just thought the words and hadn't spit them out.

He still hadn't moved a single step when all seven of his sisters surrounded the three of them, all talking at once and getting soaked by the drizzling rain.

"When we drove up and saw that the house was gone, we were scared that y'all were in it when the tornado came through," Parker said.

Mary Jane gave Brodie an extra-tight hug before she turned him loose. "Y'all are coming home with us. There are seven empty bedrooms at our house. You have a place to go."

"Knox has a travel trailer…" Brodie paused.

The sun was in front of him. The storm clouds behind him. Did that have some significance? How was he supposed to look forward when all he had to do was glance over his shoulder to see nothing but destruction. Then he looked over to his left and saw that Audrey Tucker's place was still standing. It didn't look like even a single shingle had been disturbed.

Of all the luck, he thought. *She's been a thorn in my side ever since I bought this place, and all she has is some debris lying around in her yard and a few blooms blown off a rose bush.*

The oldest sister, Ursula—the tall one—draped her arm around his shoulder. "Did it take your vehicles? We've got an old work truck y'all can borrow if it did."

Remy pointed toward the edge of the orchard. "There's three all crammed up together at the edge of the orchard.

They look like they've been in a losing battle, but they might still run."

"Thank you, Ursula. We might take you up on that offer if our trucks aren't running when we get all that trash off them."

He wondered how he sounded so calm and collected when he wanted to shake his fist at the sky and demand that God explain to him why this had happened. He wanted to stand in the middle of the place where the house used to be and scream until his voice gave out.

Mary Jane raised her voice above all the clamor. "Okay, everyone, let's dig these boys' trucks out enough and see if they are drivable. Once we do that, they are all three going home with us until they can rebuild."

"We could drive into Nocona and get motel rooms," Tripp suggested.

"Or live in my travel trailer. It's tiny even for one, but we can make do," Knox said.

Joe Clay shook his head. "Family takes care of family, and besides there's not a one of y'all—me included—that will go up against Mary Jane."

"That's the truth," Ursula said with a smile.

Too bad that family included Aunt Bernie, Brodie thought when he was finally able to take a step forward. He followed everyone to the three trucks that had been pushed up against a barbed-wire fence that separated his farm from Audrey Tucker's.

Considering all the experiences Brodie had had in the past, he should have been prepared for anything life could throw at him. But he kept replaying the events of the past hour in his mind—the funnel cloud coming right at them, hearing what sounded like a freight train passing over the old cellar, then coming out to find total destruction just plumb knocked the wind right out of him.

"We are three lucky dudes," Brodie whispered as he threw pieces of boards and bits of shingles away from Tripp's truck.

"Our house is gone," Tripp looked back over his shoulder at the place where their home used to stand. "Where's the luck in that?"

"We are all three alive, and it looks like the storm left us with three vehicles," Brodie reminded him. "And only a few leaves are blown off my orchard trees. From what I can see, the gardens look good. That makes us lucky."

"And we are about to move into the Paradise," Knox whispered for Brodie's ears only. "Where Aunt Bernie is in and out all day with her matchmaking business. Still think your lucky Irish blood is calling the shots? She's going to have you standing at the front of the altar waiting on a woman in a big white wedding dress before you can whistle 'The Eyes of Texas are Upon You.'"

"Watch and learn, little brother," Brodie said with half a smile and then wondered how he or either of his brothers could find a bit of humor in their hearts.

"You can bet I *will* be watching, but I'll be the one picking out the women for my own dates." Knox had always been able to lighten the mood—evidently even in the aftermath of a tornado. He was the outgoing twin, the life of the party, and ready for a good laugh. Tripp was the introvert, happy to be left alone to do his leather work or even help out in the orchards and strawberry, watermelon, and cantaloupe fields.

"Don't worry," Brodie sighed. "Aunt Bernie seems fixated on finding a woman for me, and if history is repeating itself, Tripp will be next. So, you've got a little while to bask in your self-proclaimed bachelorhood."

"Did I hear Aunt Bernie's name?" Ursula asked.

"Where is she? I've seen everyone here but her." Knox asked.

"She's watching my baby take his afternoon nap," Ursula answered and then lowered her voice. "Don't try to live in a travel trailer stacked up like sardines or go to a hotel. The Paradise has lots of empty rooms, and the folks have been lonely in that big house, so let them help you."

"Are you sure?" Brodie asked. "We don't want to impose."

Ursula laid a hand on his shoulder. "You would probably offend them if you didn't take them up on the offer."

"Okay, then," Brodie agreed. "We'll go for a couple of days until we can make up our minds what to do, but before that, we need to make a run to Nocona and get a few things. Everything we had was blown away."

"I understand," Ursula said. "But don't be late for supper. Tertia is bringing over food from the restaurant. They had to close down early because of the storm, and there were lots of leftovers."

"Yes, ma'am," Brodie replied with a nod.

About the Author

Carolyn Brown is a *New York Times*, *USA Today*, *Wall Street Journal*, *Publishers Weekly*, and #1 Amazon and #1 *Washington Post* bestselling author. She is the author of more than one hundred novels and several novellas. She's a recipient of the Bookseller's Best Award and the Montlake Romance's prestigious Montlake Diamond Award, a three-time recipient of the National Readers' Choice Award, and a three-time winner of the Central Regional Oklahoma Writers' Award. Brown has been published for more than twenty-five years. Her books have been translated into twenty-one languages.

When she's not writing, she likes to take road trips with her family, and she plots out new stories as they travel.

Website: carolynbrownbooks.com
Facebook: CarolynBrownBooks
Instagram: @carolynbrownbooks